Storm Chasers of Wentworth Hall

Majestic Estates Series

IreAnne Chambers

Published by Purple Storm Publishing, 2019.

STORM CHASERS OF WENTWORTH HALL

First edition. April 18, 2019.

ISBN: 978-0996414630

Written by IreAnne Chambers.

Table of Contents

DEDICATION

To the family I love and best friends of forever.

A STORM IS BREWING

When wild hearts collide in the eye of a storm, anything is possible...

A storm is brewing in Regency England and the first storm chasers are born. Lady Ariana Wentworth devises a storm of her own to avoid an arranged marriage, but when her life is threatened one man comes to the rescue.

Lady Ariana Wentworth doesn't care that the future Earl of Warwick would be a suitable match for her. She has no interest in marrying him or anyone else. Unfortunately, her father has other plans—and to her consternation, the deal has already been brokered, the marriage arranged. The only thing she can do now is refuse to meet her intended until the day of their wedding and hope she'll be able to devise a way out of this fiasco before she's forced to walk down the aisle.

Or, perhaps the enigmatic and entirely too intriguing storm chaser she just met is the answer to all her prayers ...

But before Ariana can even begin to reclaim her independence, she must contend with scandal, attempted murder, and more family drama than she ever thought possible. Who knew the road to happily ever after could be so tempestuous?

AUTHOR'S NOTE

The inspiration for Wentworth Hall is patterned after Wentworth Woodhouse although some artistic license is used to fictionalize the setting and create Wentworth Hall. Any discrepancies between fact and fiction with regard to the majestic home of Wentworth Woodhouse is intentional and used strictly for this work of fiction and for the enjoyment of my readers. Artistic license is also used to fictionalize the settings to create Harlaxton House and Toddington Peaks using other majestic homes of England.

The characters and events portrayed in this book are fictitious or are used fictitiously. Any similarity to real persons, living or dead, is purely coincidental and not intended by the author. Pivotal dates in history, places, and relevant historical figures may be mentioned or make cameo appearances, but the details associated with these dates, places, and people as they pertain to the story are a work of fiction for the enjoyment of my readers and not intended to portray actual events in history.

Care has been taken to avoid dialogue/narrative that may be considered offensive to some readers in modern times. However, please know the words and thoughts in this book are portrayed by characters in the time of 1798. Any use or perceived use of any such offensive dialogue/narrative does not reflect specific viewpoints of the author, but may be used very minimally to create historically accurate content. It is not the intention of the author to promote or condone anything that may be considered offensive in modern times.

CHAPTER ONE

Wentworth Hall – Spring, 1798

He is heading straight for her. Now what? The heavy echo of her breath drones in her chest. Silver stained skies frame the parklands edging Wentworth Hall. Lady Ariana Wentworth is alone on the grounds of the estate, her lady's maid left at Wentworth Hall. Tempests are not enjoyed by all in her household. His hand waves in her direction. Ariana pretends not to notice.

The air is crisp. The rap of the wind sweeping across the land fills her with anticipation. It plays with the trees, sways them, strains to bend her, calling out 'I am coming.'

He is still coming, too.

The soft smell of wet grass is adrift in the air. Her eyes are closed and her head is upturned while the wind swirls around her face. It pleases her. Stray ringlets stick to the clammy moisture on her cheeks. Holly blue butterflies dance above her favorite patch of lavender unaware of what is coming. Each one hovers, dips as if to a song conceived in flight.

Ariana heaves a shallow breath. This should be her time. Her freedom. Her release. To meet a stranger for the first time is more fearful than the thought of meeting the storm head on. To run for the house plays in her thoughts. What is he doing here, what does he want? Deep breaths of momentum surge with each step, closer, heavier, louder.

No way to avoid it. He calls to her now. “Hello there!” The dead in her stomach moves to her throat and swells. The closer he comes, her breath, more constricted.

He looks the part of a gentleman, sporting a dark green waistcoat and tailcoat, buckskin breeches, and black hessians. The sight of him nearly depletes her vocabulary. He waves again. “I say, I seem to have lost my way. I daresay I am quite turned about.”

Another sigh whiffs through her teeth, but the swell remains. She smooths her hands against her pale green muslin undress. Her gloves. She isn’t wearing any gloves! She swallows, chin high in the air. More than one governess instructed her so. Her voice must not fail her. Haughty and low, she tries to speak. “Well, sir, ye are currently on the grounds of Wentworth Hall.”

“Wentworth Hall, you say? How in the dickens have I made such a blunder?” His voice is mild and cultured. The fear and unease she first anticipated is quelled.

He perches his hand above his brow line to search in one direction and then the opposite. “I was out walking, exploring the grounds of Harlaxton House, observing that cloud formation over there.” He points to the same silver canvas that attracted her attention. “I must admit my sense of direction seems to escape me once I have my sights set on my quarry.”

His quarry? Harlaxton House? “I find that to be true of many, I’m afraid. I must own, however, I donna suffer such failings when it comes to my sense of direction. Once I know where North is, I am quite adept at finding my way.”

“Would that I could be the same.”

He finally stops pivoting and turns to face her. The calm set of his jaw and loftiness of his gaze focuses on her. He must have a place in good society. This realization relieves the swell in her throat, somewhat. Her courage to speak returns.

Suspicion replaces the swell. Unanswered questions fill the rift. Ariana studies his face. His stance shifts from right to left and left to right. What is his quarry? The grounds of Harlaxton House are extensive. It's hard to believe someone can stray so far from the main house no matter how lacking in the art of direction.

Earlier this week, Ariana called at Harlaxton to visit with Lady Salisbury and her daughter Victoria. Lady Salisbury informed her they would be taking a small party to Bath. So, who is this 'guest,' and who is he staying with? Observing cloud formations? Odd.

"Ye're staying at Harlaxton House? I was unaware anyone was there at present. I called on Lady Salisbury only recently and was under the impression the family was away to Bath."

They turn to walk in the direction of Wentworth Hall. His quiet perusal dismisses her concern. Was her accusation too forward? Too subtle? "Ah, yes, rightly so." He circles his hand in the air before linking it with the other behind his back. "I was informed of Lord Salisbury's impending departure when I wrote to advise him of my arrival. He assured me I may stay at the family estate while I conduct my business, regardless of the family's absence." No further response. No further explanation. Nothing. Very strange they've never met before. Rare, indeed, for anyone of either house to be unknown by the other given the amount of time spent together over the years.

His eyes remind her of the holly blue butterfly. Miss Cromwell would certainly scold her if she knew what's going through her mind, that is, if she were still her governess. In fact, her current contemplation of this gentleman would certainly earn her at least one round of practicing her letters. His muscular torso— hot flushes burn her cheeks. She imagined him shirtless! Uneasiness starts to build again. This reaction to a man is unfamiliar, but despite her misgivings, Ariana wants to know more about this man. Something must straighten her thoughts, put her back to clear thinking. What is that book he's carrying? She leans forward a bit trying to make out the title. It doesn't have one.

He stops and looks her straight in the eyes. He's amused. Does he know what she's thinking? "Shall I make your acquaintance before we proceed any further? I am Raby. Baron Neville Raby."

He bows in front of her. His brown hair is loose from the wind. Why can't she stop looking at his form? Of course, this doesn't help the mound permanently lodged in her throat. She follows his lead with an informal curtsy. "And, I am Lady Ariana Wentworth."

He must be as uncomfortable as she. He dips forward, drops his book, picks it back up and deposits it in his left breast pocket. She still can't read a title.

"Pleased to meet you, my lady. And, your father is Lord Stratford?"

"Yes, William Wentworth, the Earl of Stratford."

A low rumble thunders in the distance. They will need to find shelter. "The storm is going to overcome us. We must make haste to the house before we are drenched! Join me for tea for ye will never make it back to Harlaxton before the downpour."

"I should be delighted although I would not mind being trapped in the downpour with such lovely company as you." The blue of his eyes deepen as the rumble becomes a roar.

"My laird, I dunno if I should thank ye for the compliment or be appalled at the insinuation."

Their eyes lock. Splashes of heat pinch her cheeks, also not something she is accustomed to. He offers his arm. It flinches when she touches it. His closeness warms her, beckons her. Is he leaning closer? Ariana averts her eyes to the side. Silence falls between them. They pick up their pace. Grass crackles beneath their feet. An odd silence surrounds them. The ambiance right before it rains is always so invigorating, a power moving them forward to unknown destinations. This is the first time she has shared this experience with anyone. Anticipation energizes. In unison they peer behind at the path they left. Rolling clouds lay creases of sound and force. The storm is still coming.

THE EVANESCENT BLUSH does not escape Lord Raby's notice. A dark, auburn ringlet clings to her rosy cheek, and she tugs to put it in place. He is not unaware of what a young lady's blush implies. This lady intrigues him with her slight Scottish accent. Her bright, almond-shaped eyes are the color of emeralds, a shade he's never encountered although he has chanced upon many delightful gems throughout his eight and twenty years. Lady Ariana's, however, are more than delightful. A rich, deep hue that compels him... draws him... enchants him. Is she a woman he can be happy with? Fall in love with?

The two proceed across the meadow through to the splendid knot gardens of Wentworth Hall. He scans the sky. It will not be long, but they need to continue forward at their current pace.

Lord Raby is impressed at the beauty yet simplicity of the gardens. Intense colors of purple, red, and yellow dotted with flecks of white splash the landscape between neatly pruned pyramids of evergreens in deep shades of green and lime.

Awkward silence continues between them. He fills it. "The gardens of Wentworth Hall are quite eloquent in their placement about the grounds with the small fountains and statuettes intermingled. Have they always been so?"

"The gardens themselves have been here since the sixteen hundreds, but my mother..." This woman before him stops and raises her hand to her chest. She coughs to clear her throat. "...She took a great interest in the estate gardens and developing them to what ye see today." The lids of her eyes droop. Her voice tapers to a whisper.

He bends forward slightly to look up into her eyes. "And, you do not share in her interest?"

Round, wide eyes face him. "Oh, no! Quite the opposite. In fact, over there is the lavender patch. It's my favorite spot in the garden. Sometimes, I feel as though she is with me. I love the smell of lavender. Can ye smell it? There is usually a strong scent in the air before it rains."

"Is that so? I own I have not had occasion to notice." They pause to take in the fragrance. What an odd feeling to be standing here with her in search of the lavender in the air. The effort is not entirely without benefits. She is quite lovely and pleasant to look at.

"Of course not. I suppose gentlemen such as yerself donna make a habit of knowing such things." A quirky smile that lifts her cheeks appears when she closes her eyes to breathe in the lavender scent. Strange just standing here. Quite a different type of observation than he is accustomed to. She is right, though. He does not pay attention to the fragrance of flowers. He is more in tune with the fragrance of ladies. Her observation that the fragrance is more intense before it rains compels him to test her theory.

Lord Raby closes his eyes as well. Instead of focusing on the lavender, he cannot keep from peeking over at her from one eye. The softness of her profile beckons him closer. He reaches out to touch a wisp of hair blowing in the wind just as her lids flutter open. His movement is too sudden, and his hand clutches at nothing before it drops empty to his side. He must divert her attention back to conversation. "Shall I have the pleasure of making your mother's acquaintance once we arrive?"

The sadness is there again. "No. My mother passed quite some time ago when I was but a young girl." She reaches down and plucks a bit of a green plant from the ground, rubs it between her fingers, smells it, and puts a pinch in her mouth. She hands a few leaves to him. "Here, try this."

"What is it?" He studies it and looks at her.

"Just try it." He puts some in his mouth.

"It tastes like mint."

"It is. Isn't it lovely? It's what they make comfits from."

"You know, these gardens are a beautiful tribute to her. Have you continued in her tradition then?"

"Yes, I suppose I have. It's been only papa and I for many years so I have quite taken over I'm afraid." There it is again, that slit of a smile that lifts her cheeks.

"Well, from what little I have seen so far, I find the grounds very grand indeed. I wonder how it is we have never met in all the years we've been mutually acquainted with Salisbury."

"I was wondering the same myself, although I suppose it cannot be entirely unexpected since papa never remarried I have been quite busy with my duties here at Wentworth Hall. I'm a bit independent, ye see."

"Is that so?" She is so easy to tease. There is a spark in her eyes.

"Are ye being sarcastic, my laird?"

"I assure you, my lady, I do not do sarcasm. It's quite apparent you are a 'bit independent' since you are so far out and about without anyone with you."

Ariana clears her throat. "Perhaps ye are right on that account. And, maybe a bit 'too vocal' at times. But I cannot abide having someone attached to me at all times especially on the grounds of my own home. And, well, I must admit, I've a penchant for being out before the storms."

"Is that so?" *Crack!* The blue green light whips across the sky. "Drat! I am sorry, my lady. I was not paying attention. The storm is almost upon us."

"It appears we may need to make a run for it! The rain is here." Excitement starts to build between them. Another rumble quickly follows. Ariana's eyes shimmer. Fear or anticipation?

"I'm afraid we shall not make it, my laird. Follow me. We can take cover in the aviary. The rain usually doesn't last long."

Then he hears it. The sag of the trees, the thrashing of the wind against the leaves, the sound he's waiting for. He turns to Ariana, her somber gaze at the onslaught of wind and rain coming their way surprises him. This storm looks to bring more than just rain, but he cannot be certain. To stay and observe it, that is what he wants. Ariana stands motionless staring. The gray mass bowls in their direction. Another *Crack!* snaps his attention back to the needed shelter. He needs to get Ariana to safety. "Aviary?"

"Yes! Quickly, my laird, here it comes!" She squeals, grabs his hand and drags him while pointing in the direction of an overhang.

His pulse races, the touch of her bare hand now in his scorches his insides, or is it the impending storm? Not sure. Either way, energy rushes through his veins. They run. A few drops overtake them before they reach the outer shelter surrounding the aviary.

Breathless from their trek across the lawn or possibly something more, Ariana inhales a deep breath and places her hands on her hips. "The house is just past that line of spruce. I'm sure it willnae be long before it stops."

He looks around. The enclosure appears to be a large cage. Black and gold iron rods shape the sides and curl to a point at the top. "So, what does one do with an aviary?"

She laughs. It sounds indelicate to say the least. It reminds him of a dog he had as a boy. "Papa asked me the same question when I first proposed the idea. I find it to be verra accommodating. It houses many exotic birds. I like to use their feathers in my feather-works ye see. Plenty of peacocks, pheasants and swans roam about the estate, but I find the colors in the exotic species more to my liking."

"Well, since we're here, let us go in and see these 'exotic species' of yours."

"How improper!"

Is she toying with him? "Certainly, a lady of your *independence* is not worried about a short walk through an aviary!"

"Certainly not." Ariana's eyes gleam excitement as they enter the enclosure.

The aviary is quite impressive. Not at all what he expects. The entire area is ornate with wrought iron scroll designs from floor to ceiling and flower and leaf accents painted in gold.

"Come, my laird. I will show ye my favorite." He follows her through another gate. She pulls him immediately toward the back. "Here, see there?" He stands behind her while she points to a group of birds perched on a low hanging branch. She turns and continues around the back section once again pulling him along pointing out the different species. She does not release his hand. Content in its current position, he has no desire to remove it.

"Those are the parrots, parakeets, and there, those are my pink cockatoos. Lovely, yes?"

"Yes, I quite think they are. Why is that one acting like that— you know, with its head and all, bobbing up and down?"

"I know, isn't it silly?" She giggles. This time, less indelicate.

"This is Max." She holds out her hand and whistles. Max pushes off his perch and flies to his new perch, her hand.

"Max?" Raby's brows raise.

"Yes, he's my favorite. I'm teaching him to talk." She bends her head to the bird's crown. Bright pink feathers fan out front to back, crowning his head. "They are such a lark." Max whistles and dances. He steps off her hand to the banister in front, his crown of feathers still spanning the length of his head. He spreads his wings to show the expanse. She tickles his tummy. Max squawks and pushes off to another perch above.

Raby now lowers his head closer to hers and whispers, "What are you teaching him to say?"

Her enchanting green eyes turn and capture him. They stand frozen for a moment as if communicating the answer silently between them. Their gaze does not falter, her response a whisper. "I think the rain stopped. We should get to the house before someone is sent to find me."

"Quite right, let us be going then." He moves closer to her. She doesn't move. He can't ignore the urge. What man in his position can resist such loveliness only inches away giving him unspoken permission? This unexpected encounter with *this* lady captivates him. He wants to know her.

He bends his head to partake the fullness of her lips. "Ugh! Egad! This cannot be!" He growls, wipes the slime from below his right cheek, looks briefly at the grayish white substance before he swats his hand toward the ground. His gloves are ruined. Ariana lets out a roar of seized laughter and stifles a snort. Who would have thought a young lady can sound so *un*ladylike?

"How can you be laughing?" He slaps his handkerchief from his pocket to clean the mess from his face and hand.

"How canna not? Ye cannot possibly think I didn't know ye were going to kiss me and just before the anticipated event—" She covers her mouth and starts again.

"Kiss you? Absurd! Anticipated event?" He teases her with his sarcasm.

"Oh, come now." She sobers and lowers her voice. "I thought ye didn't do sarcasm. Ye know you were and I was going to let you."

"*Let* me, were you?" The hilarity of it makes him smile. It's true. Kiss her is exactly what he was going to do. The thought she was going to let him alleviates his distress.

"Yes. Let you. I must say, though, papa would most definitely be pleased with my Max now if he knew how he stopped me from being kissed by a gentleman I only just met." Mischief glints in her eyes.

"Oh, all right. I concede I was going to kiss you— and might yet." He cannot help but play with her. She is delightful standing there teasing him back. He reaches out to pull at her waist. "But, I promise you never to own to this particular event in public." She pulls away and pushes him back.

"In public?" Her back faces him now as she starts to walk in the direction they came from. "Who would believe it? They would certainly say we made it up. I am known for my '*vocalizations*' ye know." She twirls around and walks backwards. He starts to follow.

"Which is what I will say if you ever tell."

"Rest assured your secret is safe with me. It is in both our interests ye know. Now, we must leave before someone is sent to look for me." He reaches out again to tug at her waist. "But, I promise ye. I willnae admit to it in public." She quickens her step and he misses.

THE WALK TO THE HOUSE is now quiet and peaceful. The storm is gone but still visible in the distance. Lord Raby surveys the area. It is calm and the air is heavy. The "chastisement" at the aviary, or rather events prior are still fresh in his mind. Ariana breaks the silence this time. "How long do ye intend to maintain residence at Harlaxton?"

"I had intended to only stay a few days. I see now I may be delayed from returning due to...um, *business* I have only recently become aware of."

A moment passes. A calm and tender voice responds. "Well, my laird, I am glad your recent *business awareness* delays ye from your return. I find I quite enjoy your company."

Was it that obvious? Did she interpret the meaning of his 'business' as having something to do with her?

"I'm sure my father would welcome the opportunity to add another gentleman to his hunting party. There are so few hunters in this county to choose from. He is well known for his hunting dogs. They say he has the best in the area."

Lord Raby nods in acknowledgment as they reach the outer veranda of Wentworth Hall. The immensity of the mansion before him demands respect. A great Hall indeed, three stories high including the lower level. Massive stone pillars at the entrance of the mansion hold up the stone engraved pediment. The front steps leading up to the main entrance invites a moment to take in the grandeur of the stone ornaments lining the top of the great house. The inscription on the pediment reads "*mea gloria fides.*" Faith is my glory. Latin from his days at Eton still proves useful.

"I am always game for a good hunt— but remember, no telling of our adventures in the aviary."

"Of course, but I must think of something for ye to provide me in return for my silence." She is teasing him now. She swirls around to ascend the stairs.

"So, I am to be blackmailed now?"

"Blackmail? No, I am to be compensated. It is a business arrangement, ye see." She moves inside with all the grace and ease of home.

He lingers just for a moment outside before following her in. The deer graze in the distance under the trees that line the front gardens. The mist left over from the rain hovers over the grass like a low lying cloud. Lady Ariana enthralls him. There is no doubt of her Scottish heritage although her accent is slight and sometimes non-existent. This lady is one he most definitely wishes to further his acquaintance.

Ariana gives instructions to the butler for tea and they make their way in towards the parlor. A stone engraved mantel piece is installed above the fireplace. The great mahogany staircase leads up to the parlor. It curves in half circles on both sides. The parlor is filled with great wall paintings and tapestries hanging upon crimson walls with moldings trimmed in gilt.

The view from the window reveals the knot gardens they just came through. The symmetry of the herbs and evergreens enhances the colors of the roses glistening like diamonds from the drops of rain remaining on their petals. The hedges are so exquisitely preened to produce the desired effect of a maze.

From a young age he appreciated the beauty in creation and the awe-inspiring talents of the designer. One creation he particularly finds interest in, albeit quirky smiles, and awkward laughter requires the immediate return of his attention to her 'symmetry' until such time as a dark presence appears in the room.

"What is going on here?" This man turns from one to the other. The bellow that ensues shakes the rafters. "Ariana? Who is this gentleman with whom I have not had the benefit of an acquaintance?"

Maybe hunting is not a good idea.

CHAPTER TWO

Toddington Peaks – Spring, 1798

"You must marry a woman of good birth and fortune. You are a Warwick. The Earls of Warwick have always made profitable matches and you will not dishonor this family by doing otherwise."

Nicholas, Earl of Warwick, recently returned from a London meeting of Parliament, is now addressing his son, Alexander, on the subject most predominant of late.

The viscount slouches in the leather armchair of his father's study. He listens to the same discourse he has heard for the better part of his twenty-eight years. The words form and are lost in the air. The crackle of the fire absorbs his focus. His father paces. He understands his father's concerns, and he understands them every time his father tells them. Until now, the inevitable has been dissuaded. The pacing continues. Back and forth...on and on...will it ever end? Hues of blue, orange, and red flames flicker. Hot stars sparkle up the chimney, mesmerizing.

"Well now! What have you to say?" Lord Warwick's voice resonates off the walls. Alexander jumps in his seat.

He summons a voice somewhat milder to respond. "Father, I should like to marry a woman who is not specifically interested in my purse strings, someone interested in more than the latest scandal or fashion. Someone with whom I can have a lively conversation. Someone who understands my passions."

His father pauses in front of the leather arm chair. His eyes dart like arrows to its prey. "Pah!" the earl barks. "Your passions?

You mean your dilly-dallying about the estate and who knows what else watching the clouds and looking for tempests? *Pfft.* Such nonsense."

"Father, it is not just the clouds, and there is more to it than tempests I am sure. As I have told you there is a connection and a science I intend—"

"Science indeed. It matters little. In any event, I am sure the lady will not care whether you cloud watch or not. She may even find it romantical or some such drivel."

"Father, try to understand—"

"Your mother and I had an arranged marriage and we have managed fine. While I'll own she is quite enthralled with the latest what-have-yous, and can be quite extravagant in her collection of trinkets, we have been quite happy. You will have plenty of time to fall in love in the years to come, and you would not be the first to take another under his protection if you were so inclined."

The earl clears his throat. The pacing begins once again, this time his hands fold behind his back while looking at the floor. "What I *mean* to say is, while *I* was not inclined to do so, because your mother is as fine a woman as I could ask for, it is not unheard of for a man of quality to look elsewhere for his pleasures while fulfilling his duty to his family."

The viscount's head bobs once more from one side of the room to the other watching his parent glide to and fro. The supplications are relentless. His thoughts scurry elsewhere amidst the calming effects of the flames. Marry a female he does not love? No. Nor will he marry one who is unsure of her own feelings toward him. Mutual equanimity, mutual respect for one another. That is what is important in marriage. Bluestockings, well, not so much. However, a wife with whom he can have a civil conversation, most agreeable. Understanding. Also, most desirable. His wife must understand his obsession with the weather and not fear it, would not go into a faint at the thought of him approaching it. She must understand the value of his research to society, to life and to the King, the King's Navy even, to be able to predict inclement conditions. Yes. This is the woman he will marry. Is there a female such as this?

Duty. The dreadful *duty* to 'marry well.' What about duty to himself? Marriage to a woman of substance, not someone hanging on every word, meddlesome to the point of irritation. That is a marriageable woman, indeed. How *does* one go about finding this person?

The wood on the fire collapses and a log rolls out onto the hearthstone in front of the fireplace. Alexander shoots forward to restore it to its place in the pit.

Lord Warwick finally stops to take a breath. "We have servants for that."

"Yes, but shall we wait for the house to catch fire?"

"It certainly is not all that impressive that it could not wait, I am sure."

To Alexander's relief, his mother, Lady Anne Isabella, enters the parlor and rings for tea.

"My love, what *is* it you go on about? I can hear you all the way through the house. Don't you see our son is on about something else? He will marry when it suits him. He is descended from *you*, after all. *You* would not do what your heart told you not to, is that not so, my love?"

The earl glares direct, mouth open as the Countess glides in front of him. He appears to be contemplating his response.

Censure her? Or acquiesce to the compliment. Apparently, the latter is decided.

She daintily places herself on the settee between the two men, the leather arm chair on her left and the earl still standing on her right, establishing a truce of sorts.

Alexander views his parents with warm affection. His father looks as though he regained his senses and joins his mother on the settee. They begin to speak quietly about their plans for the Season. Although his mother comes from a great family, their marriage is clearly based on more than duty. This is the kind of woman Alexander wishes to procure. One that will compliment his strengths and help him to temper his weaknesses. Why can't his father understand this?

"My dear," Lady Warwick coos, "I recently received a letter from my dear friend Lady Salisbury who has so kindly invited us all to join her family at their townhouse in Bath. I would so love to take in the waters. You know how good it is for my *entire constitution*." she drawls. "Please, my lord, we simply must accept. We must."

The earl lifts his lady's hand to his lips then states as a matter of fact, "Of course we must go. I surely would not do anything to hinder *your* constitution."

Improving *his* constitution is not something of great importance to Alexander. His previous arrangements to meet with colleagues on the matter of wind measurements have already been made and the season for storms is upon them. Storms are coming this way and he refuses to miss them. "Mother, I must decline the offer for I have previous engagements in London, which I most certainly cannot change."

"Alexander darling, you *must* join us. Lady Salisbury has not seen you in years and you and Lord Edmund get on so well. Growing up, you were the best of friends." Lady Warwick claps her hands together. "Oh, the trouble you boys got into! You remember the summer Edmund spent here at Toddington Peaks, while his parents visited the continent? I will never forget when you and Edmund got into the washroom, got a hold of Grandmama's unmentionables and removed the busk, gallivanting all over the house pretending to be the Duke of Cumberland at the Battle of Culloden. Your swordplay went on until Grandmamma recognized the whalebone and proceeded to scold you both profusely. Why, I believe she may have even threatened to throw you in the dungeon."

Meecham appears with the tea. Lady Warwick pauses, great amusement lingers in her eyes. "After you and Edmund were removed to the school room, grandmamma and I enjoyed a hearty laugh." Lady Warwick pours a cup of tea for each of them and offers the first to Lord Warwick. "You must join us for this happy reunion. You must. I would so enjoy the opportunity to see you and Edmund up to your old tricks." She offers a second cup to her son. "Surely you are not meeting with those weather predictors again?" A third cup for herself. "As if the weather can be predicted."

It does not please him to go against his mother's wishes. Alexander sips his tea. "It is true I would enjoy catching up with Edmund. And, yes, I do have plans to meet with the weather predictors as you put it. We hope to be able to come up with a way to determine the weather by observing the clouds and measuring the wind. We hope to find an actual storm with winds strong enough to test our theories."

"The clouds? And wind? What could possibly be learned by observing clouds? Surely, you will not stand in the midst of one. You will catch your death."

He dismisses the naiveté of her comment, sips more tea, then sips again. His mother will never comprehend the correlation between clouds and weather. He does intend to stand in the midst of one, as close as he possibly can. If he can find a whirlwind, it will be even better, for there have only been a few recordings of such a sight. Still, there is no need to alarm his mother further. "How about this? If I may be permitted to join you for a few nights at Harlaxton House before your departure with Salisbury for Bath, and if I may trespass upon the family's hospitality during their absence at Bath while I conduct some of my observations from there, then I should be delighted to change my plans and accompany you to Harlaxton for a few days."

Lady Warwick's face plummets. The silence grows stifling. She places her tea, halfway to her lips, back on the tray. Her fan slaps open, a slight flutter ensues. She turns to look out the parlor windows. "You mean to observe clouds? At Harlaxton?" Another moment passes. Lord Warwick sips his tea. She turns back to Alexander, slaps her fan closed on her lap, a half smile appears, almost genuine. She refreshes her tea and sips. "If that is the only way we are to tempt you to join us then so it must be."

Lord Warwick sits curiously silent on the subject. He holds his tea in one hand and absently plays with a stray hair of his wife's coiffure. He stares at the fire. Shadows of flames dance on his face. Why is it he is silent now?

"I assure you, mother, there is much to be learned from these observations. Would it not be an accomplishment to be able to predict the damage caused by that whirlwind in Nottinghamshire back in 1785? And what about the possibility of predicting storms at sea? Surely, the King would be interested in such predictions. Think of the lives that could be saved. The bounty saved from the sea if course could be altered to adjust for inclement conditions? I tell you it is an important occupation to say the least."

Lady Warwick replaces her teacup on the tray and rises for a turnabout the room. The earl's hand drops to the cushion of the settee. Lady Warwick responds, "Whirlwind, indeed. I know not how such things could be predicted. And, how, pray tell, do you know it from clouds?"

"Precisely. How do we know if we do not observe to start with?"

Lord Warwick unsilences himself. "My dear, do not distress yourself. This is one of the reasons Alexander must marry. He will settle as all young men do once they are married and setting up their nursery."

Alexander rolls his eyes at the ceiling, finishes his tea and sets it on the tray. Lady Warwick crosses in front and circles back to leave the room. "Oh, I declare, if that is all you can do then, fine. All this talk of clouds is quite exhausting. I shall leave you to your own devices, for I must write to Lady Salisbury directly regarding the arrangements."

"NOW THAT YOUR MOTHER has left us, I'll not have you allow her to run interference. You well know it is high time you take a wife and I have arranged the matter for you."

Alexander stands up and faces his father. "I'll not do it, I say. I will marry, but I will marry a lady whom I choose."

The earl matches his height and bellows, "Then you will *choose* the lady I have selected for you."

Alexander pauses a moment. Concern replaces his anger. "What is this father? What is really going on here?"

"I'm sure I don't know what you are talking about." The earl turns and takes a seat behind his desk.

Alexander follows and stands before him. He leans forward and places both hands on the front of the large mahogany desk. He sees his own arrow-like stare reflect back from his father's face. Amber eyes match pale blue. "We have had our differences over the years but not like this."

The intensity of their glares lessen. "You mean, you have always been able to persuade me to your way of thinking."

Alexander pushes himself back from the desk and slams down in the chair in front, arms raised to the ceiling. "Certainly not! For you well know once you have set your mind to an event there is no changing it."

"No changing it? Why should I change that which is decided?" The earl sits back in his seat.

"You *are* intolerable. You know exactly my meaning." He slouches and folds his hands in front of him, elbows on the armrests.

The earl bends forward, leans on his desk and steeples his fingers. "Alexander, you must accept what is done unless you have designs of striking out on your own without the financial support to which you have grown accustomed."

"What do you mean? If I do not accept this arrangement you will actually withdraw your support?"

"That is exactly what I mean." There is no expression on his face. No crinkle, no twitch, no remorse. Just the father he has known all his life. A father always there for him. A father never once forcing an issue of marriage on him. A father he always respects regardless of differences of opinion. But this time it's different. Alexander rises again from his chair with renewed resolve.

"You cannot possibly be serious. It is not done. The law will not allow it. Property goes with the title. You know this. Who will be your heir?"

"I am serious and I will find another heir. I can name my brother's son."

"Your brother's son is a dandy and a nitwit. One cannot even understand his stutter when he speaks. I cannot believe you even consider it."

"Even so. I shall and I will. I mean it. I will find a way Alexander. Maybe I'll live forever." Alexander studies his father. He bites hard on his teeth. He cannot give in. Even if it means losing his father's support until he inherits the title.

"Well, then, withdraw your support because I refuse to marry any woman I do not choose."

"Alexander, I am sure you don't mean that."

Alexander leans forward again, placing his palms flat on the desk. He narrows his eyes straight into his father's. A thought picks its way through his mind. "What is driving this, really? Why is *this* lady so important? Are there not plenty for me to choose from?"

The same expressionless face stares back. "It is important because it will ensure the continued growth of Toddington Peaks and further build the wealth of this great estate."

Alexander steps back with raised brows. "You mean you have debts?"

"I mean no such thing. That is, of course we have debts. What great estate does not? I simply mean I have made an arrangement with Sir Andrew Watson. He offered me a sum and a proposition I could not refuse."

"A sum? A proposition? I am to be married to a lady I have never met for a sum you could not refuse? You have always allowed I would choose my wife and now you are insisting the opposite. How much is this sum and what is this proposition?"

Boyish excitement and a sparkle replaces the blankness in his father's amber colored eyes. The earl eagerly rises and steps to the window looking out over the boxwood mazes of Toddington Peaks, arms folded behind his back. He slaps one hand into the other and peers into the vastness of the grounds. "It is quite significant, I assure you." The earl stands motionless. Thoughts crinkle his brow. "In addition, Toddington Peaks will enjoy much more influence over this region of England."

Alexander joins his father at the window. He places his arm on his father's shoulder to turn him to face him. "Do you hear what you are saying? How much more must we have? Who is this Andrew Watson? This sounds mad. Such a plan sounds like treason."

The earl whirls around full force. "Do not say such things. Treason? How can you speak such a word?" His voice rises with each syllable. "I had my solicitor look into this and it is all quite legal." The plan is to form an alliance and gain more oversight of this area. It will allow us better control over what happens here. One can never have enough leverage."

"I'm sure once Prinny hears of it, he will have something to say about it." Alexander goes to the cabinet, pours whisky into two glasses, hands one to his father and takes a swig of the other. "You must be at sixes and sevens to be thinking such nonsense. May I remind you, it was not so long ago that the Jacobite's intended to change England's government. We all know what happened to them. Treason."

"Change England's government? Are you daft? I am not trying to change England's government! Watson made his proposal and I see it as a most advantageous position for Toddington Peaks." He swishes the drink in its glass, sets it down and returns to his seat in front of the fire. "Leverage. I'm talking about leverage."

Alexander joins him and crosses his feet on the footstool. "Tell me more about this man. I have never heard of him. Is he the father of this lady you wish me to marry?"

"No. He is a baronet over in South Yorkshire, I believe. He's taken up residence at Wentworth Abbey. I've heard some such dribble about the Abbey and another estate being joined together. I don't know how they propose to accomplish that."

"Sounds a Banbury tale to me." Alexander takes another swig.

"Banbury tale! It certainly is not. I have told you, I had my solicitor research the matter. It might be inherited by a cousin, I believe. Of course, this does not pertain to my particular interests in the alliance and Watson's plans for which I wholeheartedly support, as will you." He downs his drink.

CHAPTER THREE

Harlaxton House – Spring, 1798

Lady Catherine, the Marchioness of Salisbury, is breakfasting in her room at Harlaxton House when she receives a letter from her good friend Lady Warwick. *Of course, he may remain here. I would not have it any other way.* She sips her tea.

"I must write to Lady Warwick immediately to put her mind at ease. It will give us no greater pleasure than to have Alexander stay as long as he likes before returning to Toddington Peaks," she comments out loud to no one in particular.

She swallows the last of her tea and calls for her lady's maid. "Moira! Make haste! I must be dressed at once."

Excitement sends her flying in preparation for their arrival. But first, a refreshing application of Olympian Dew. There is much to be done. Edmund Philip, the Earl of Dorset, must be informed of Alexander's arrival. Lord Salisbury must be advised on the arrangements for Alexander to remain after their departure. "And, of course, I must write Aunt Cecily to immediately send Victoria home for the viscount would make a most agreeable match," once again to no one in particular. Lady Salisbury stands up, swallows the last of her crumpet and downs her tea, but the cup is empty. No matter. She places it upside down on its saucer.

"Moira, hurry for I must not be late. I should like to wear the spotted muslin undress bordered with cerulean blue."

"Right away, my lady. And will ya be needin' the head-dress to go with it then?"

"A simple coiffure will do for today, Moira."

"Yes, m'lady."

Sometime later, but no sooner than normal, Lady Salisbury makes her way downstairs where John Spencer, the Marquess of Salisbury, finishes his breakfast on the east veranda where she joins him. The day is brisk and full of color. She stands back for a moment to enjoy the view. This Corinthian, *her* Corinthian, still most agreeable. Victoria must find such a match. Lady Salisbury tiptoes silently behind him but stops for a brief moment. What might she do to overtake him by surprise? There is no way he can know she is here.

Without warning, he spins around, grabs her waist, and pulls her down positioning her tightly upon his lap.

"John!" she squeals and pulls his arms apart to separate them from the clasp. His grasp is tight.

"You should know you cannot best me, even after all these years." His whispers tickle when he nuzzles his face against her cheek. "But, you must keep trying. It's good to keep your skills honed."

His breath is warm and his skin soft. He must have just had a shave. Orange and spice invade her senses.

"How do you always know?"

"Ah, that is the question. You know, my dear, I could never tell you lest I give you an advantage I am not yet ready to relinquish." He tightens his grip. "You must use your powers of detection. Train your mind and your senses." No training her senses now. They're on overload.

"Come, now, after so long can you not give me a clue?" She finally manages to thread her fingers through his, but still he holds her close.

"Hmm. A clue...let me think on it, and I will let you know what I decide."

"Indeed, you always did love a puzzle. Perhaps you can puzzle out my news. I have received word from my good friend Bella." Lady Salisbury's legs hang and waggle like a school girl on a swing. "They have agreed to join us to take in the waters at Bath, but dear Alexander will not be able to join us there and, instead, wishes to stay on here for a bit before making his journey to London. I told her, of course, there would be no problem."

"Of course... mmm..." Her Corinthian's mumbles tickle her skin. He skims her cheek with his face and kisses her right lobe.

"John! You're tickling me, and I am trying to prepare for our guests." Her giggles morph into a yelp. He releases her hand and the tight hold, but then moves his hand gently across her midsection.

"Yes, dear, but you know how I love the scent you are wearing, what is it? Roses?"

Her lips curve up. Satisfaction prevails. "You know full well it is as I have worn it all these years only for you, my love."

He murmurs into her left lobe. "And, you know how I adore you for it."

"John, please." She squirms some more. "I must get back to the task at hand."

"Surely, it can wait a little longer, for you have not even sent word yet?" He nuzzles closer, kissing the corner of her mouth, soft and gentle.

"I suppose..."

Sometime later she adjusts her muslin and he straightens his cravat. She reminds him of his earlier words. "So, have you decided to give me that clue?"

"Clue? My dear, weren't you paying attention? I have already given you the clue you were looking for."

"I can assure you I was most attentive to your efforts this fine morning and you certainly did not for I clearly recall when the conversation moved in a different direction." She turns him to face her and proceeds to adjust the fold of his cravat near the pin she gave him for their most recent wedding anniversary.

"Were you now?" He places his hands on each of her hips. His sparkling eyes do not look away from her face.

"Stop, you are playing and I will not be gulled." She pokes him with her finger then places her hands firmly on his chest and begins to play with the folds of the fabric once again. "It is no matter now for I will figure it out."

"I know you will, my dear. Remember what I said about powers of detection. Use all your senses. And, by the way, I should tell you to plan for Raby to join us prior to our departure to Bath. We have some directives from the King to discuss. He, too, may be joining us in Bath a few days, but he will need to take care of business here first. It seems, my dear lady, Harlaxton House will be entertaining without us." His grin widens. She straightens her fichu.

"I've no doubt the 'House' will give quite a performance, as we all know."

"No matter, Lord Raby and the viscount should get along splendid. They will have much in common don't you agree?"

"Well, let us hope. I've no reason to believe otherwise." They sit silent as they enjoy their breakfast. The Marquess finishes first.

"Now, my dear, I must leave to attend a meeting with my man of business. I've no doubt you will take care to arrange all that is needed for a successful event." The Marquess leans in to give his lady a light peck on the cheek and makes his way to the door. He hesitates and looks back. The concerned draw of his brow fades when he turns to walk away.

Lady Salisbury settles at her desk to write to Lady Warwick of the arrangements.

My dearest Bella,

How pleased I am to hear of your acceptance to join us in Bath. I anxiously await seeing you, for it has been far too long. I own I am sad to hear that Alexander will be unable to attend but look forward to his joining us, however briefly, at Harlaxton House before our journey on to Bath. Of course, Alexander is most welcome to stay on at Harlaxton House for however long he may require. He will not be alone, for we are to have another gentleman joining us for a short time as well, Baron Neville Raby. He will be here on a business matter with the marquess and then will be joining us later in Bath. I am sure the two will be great company.

My dear Bella, I so look forward to seeing you and your wonderful family again. Give our regards to yours,

Cathy

Since Lord Raby will also be joining them, Lady Victoria must return from Brighton. This will be Victoria's second season out. Her daughter's visit with Aunt Cecily must come to a close. There will be two possibilities for her. Every opportunity must be afforded to her. Yes, a letter to Aunt Cecily is next.

Lord Raby is of lower rank than she prefers, although he is still a fair prospect for Victoria. The marquess may need some inducement. Victoria is not going to be a diamond of the first water. However, she is quite pretty. Lovely, in fact. Her burgundy hair and hazel eyes are the envy of many ladies. Her accomplishments are known by all. She will make a suitable match this season.

Her daughter with the viscount. This thought is quite pleasing. He most certainly is the better catch. Victoria and Alexander have known each other since childhood. Although Victoria had on prior occasions made it clear she felt they would not suit, it is no matter. What is important is how it is now. Victoria may find she and the viscount suit after all and if not, well, a little competition with Lord Raby will not hurt. Lord Raby is quite handsome and very attentive to the ladies.

Chadwick will post the letters as soon as may be. The ink and quill are returned to their place in her desk. Done.

Lady Salisbury stands up and twirls to the music singing in her head. Victoria's possibilities are pleasing. A loud slam down the hall startles her out of her musings. She peeks out of the room. Which servant is overcompensating this time? No one appears afoot. Flumakin. She returns to her room to make a note to speak with the housekeeper. Apparently, it's again time to remind the servants to take care in their work. The portrait hanging over the fireplace is, once again, upside down. When will they ever learn?

THE WARWICK PARTY DEPARTS from Toddington Peaks to their destination at Harlaxton House

"My lord, please ask the postilions to be more cautious on these roads for I cannot bear to be tousled to and fro. My coiffure will be an absolute monstrosity by the time we get there. Do tell them to slow us down."

"My lord, these squabs simply must be worn out. Please make arrangements for their replacement before our return. I simply cannot abide worn out squabs in our post chaise, you know. I daresay, I won't be able to sit for a week after we arrive."

"My dear Nicholas, *please* ask for more blankets for I am sure to catch a chill. It is only the *beginning* of spring and the cool air has not yet dissipated."

"My dear, please ask the wheel-boy..."

Alexander begins to doze. His mind drifts to tune out his parents' prattle. He leans his head back so his beaver hat hangs over his eyes. He smiles. Familiar recognition. His mother's usual repartee during their trips followed by his father's calm, accommodating demeanor. It lulls him.

Alexander listens. How does he do it? His father calmly administers to his lady as if they are just married, constantly striving to please her. She, in turn, is quite settled by his attentions.

After what seems only a few moments in time, the earl pipes up. "We will not be far from Wentworth Hall, you know. I do believe it to be an adjoining estate to Harlaxton House. Alexander? Alexander? You cannot be asleep I am sure. Did you hear what I said, my boy?"

Alexander sits up and pushes his hat back. His father is, in fact, addressing him. "I'm sorry, I was not entirely asleep, but I own you caught me woolgathering. What is it you said?"

"Cloud watching more like it. I said, Wentworth Hall is a great estate and I am very pleased at this arrangement between you and Lady Ariana. It may prove to be the perfect opportunity for the two of you to meet."

Alexander shoots up. "Lady Ariana? What do you mean, Lady Ariana and I?" His words stick in his throat.

"Yes, you and Lady Ariana Wentworth."

"Father, I thought we discussed this? I will not be marrying someone I do not know. I will not marry someone I do not *love*, for that matter!" Alexander swallows hard to get more words out. "How is it you speak of this as if it is done?" Every thought pressing to come out, does. "I have made my intentions quite clear. I have not even met the lady, only now have you told me her name. I cannot believe she would be agreeable to an arrangement such as this. I certainly have not entertained the idea since last we spoke and I request again you dismiss this notion of yours for I will not marry her!" Alexander folds his arms in front of his chest and further punctuates his point with the scraping sound of his boots when he crosses his ankles in front of his seat.

"Dismiss it? Why ever would I do that?" the earl howls. "I told you it was arranged!"

Alexander doesn't budge. His father can roar louder than a lion and he won't change his mind.

"The subject is closed."

Not by an inch.

"It does not matter whether she agrees or not. Why should it? Watson and I have an agreement. Lord Stratford and I have shaken hands on the subject. There is no going back on my word! You *will* marry Lady Ariana!" Lord Warwick also folds his arms in front of his chest and continues his rant less momentous, still determined. "It is a great prospect. This alliance will do great things for England and I cannot believe you do not welcome it!"

"Welcome it?" Incredible. "I have allowed you to control a great many aspects of my life, but I assure you I will not allow you this." Alexander's heart races. A heavy breath escapes from his mouth.

"Control you? Alexander, it is my duty, and yours, too, I might add!"

Lady Warwick sits up straight from her reclining position to intervene once again.

"My dears, please. Must we have this conversation now?" She flips her fan open. "Certainly it can wait until after the two have met?" Lady Warwick's quick oscillating movements draws the attention of both gentlemen. "Alexander, I implore you not to be so stubborn with your fortune, for you well know your father will pull his support and you may even like Lady Ariana and all of this fuss will be for naught."

Alexander focuses on his mother's eyes rather than the quick movements of her fan. "Forgive me, mother, but I do not intend to marry a woman I do not love! I shall not."

"But that is my point, my dear. You do not know you will not fall in love with her."

Alexander opens his mouth to respond, but the earl interrupts before he can speak. "There will not be any room for stubbornness, my dear, it is done! I'll not have my son in the almshouse over his own stupidity. The boy will marry Lady Ariana. I gave my word to her father."

The two men turn their heads in opposite directions. One fan slaps shut. A wall of silence smothers them all until the illustrious towers of Harlaxton House come into view.

The magnificent domed towers and the clock on the front of the belfry elicit nothing but awe. The road leading to the front entrance is lined with tall, silver birch trees on either side of the road.

Lady Salisbury's open arms greet them as soon as their carriage reaches the door. "My good friends, welcome!" Lady Salisbury hugs her friend with great joy and immediately changes to her more intimate mode of address. "My dear Bella, how was your trip?"

Excitement radiates everywhere and Lady Salisbury does not wait for a response. She turns to the earl next and offers her hand. "My lord, welcome to Harlaxton House." The earl bows in response and takes her hand to his lips.

Lady Salisbury ends at the younger of the two gentlemen in the party.

"Alexander! how handsome you have become. I swear I cannot recall when I have seen you last! You remember Victoria?" She pulls her daughter from behind and establishes Victoria by her side to reacquaint them.

"Of course, Lady Victoria. It has been too long. You have become quite a lovely young lady. How have you been? I cannot wait to hear your news and become reacquainted." He winks. Her response? Not what he expects.

Victoria's cheeks color pink, but before she can reply, Lady Salisbury ushers the party inside and informs the group, "Edmund, of course, has not yet returned from the estate grounds with Lord Salisbury, but they are expected soon. Let us get you all situated into your rooms to rest and dress before dinner. I expect we will dine at six."

The ceilings of Harlaxton draw attention up. The medieval crosses, squares and florals are of shapes that appear foreign. They protrude downward and are defined with gold reminiscent of Solomon's temple. When they enter the great hall, a crystal chandelier takes up the expanse of the ceiling with crisscross spirals that end where the cedar staircase begins. Lady Salisbury gives instructions to Chadwick, her butler, to have their guests shown to their rooms. Above the staircase, the most brilliant mural of clouds are painted on the ceiling. It's hard to focus on anything else.

"Do watch your step, sir..." Chadwick's voice snaps Alexander's attention back to their ascent.

"Yes, thank you. It is a most intriguing mural to be sure."

"Yes, and more guests than I would like to count have been drawn in by it and lost their step."

"Yes, well, thank you."

Alexander reaches his room. Much needed rest before dinner is welcome. Thank God the customary introductions are over. His room overlooks the garden with a view to the stables off to the right. The decor of the room suits his mood, being in hues of blue trimmed with gilt, as is a matching counterpane. The fire prepared by the servants prior to his arrival provides enticing warmth. He collapses into a large brocade armchair near it. The watercolor painting above the fireplace appears to be a replica of Harlaxton although the clock is missing on the belfry. The artist at least aspires to be accomplished. The colors are vibrant. The sky is overcast in the backdrop. It soothes him, relaxes him. His mind is drawn back. Once again, he succumbs to his father's onslaught of confabulation that he must marry. At least now he knows the chit's name is Ariana Wentworth. Heavy eyelids weigh on him. How in God's name will he get out of this? It's not like he can't have his pick of the many ladies out in the Marriage Mart. But, that is the problem. How is he going to know if she loves him for who he is or if she loves his title? Confound his father for trying to control his life! He is a man of eight and twenty. One would think he has earned the privilege of choice.

Lady Salisbury. She may have designs of her own from the way she presented Victoria before him upon their arrival. Although a few years have passed since he and Victoria have seen each other, he is quite confident the two of them do not suit. Victoria made that clear on many occasions in the past when he *had* tried his hand at enticing the young lady. She will not have it.

How can we? I feel for you as I do my own brother. Those words still ring in his ears. She is no doubt right, but for a young man at the time, it did not do much for his own self-esteem to have her refuse his advances— however awkward they may have been. Alexander opens his eyes. The watercolor is still there, and he allows himself to drift back to his thoughts.

Victoria is a beautiful young woman now. She definitely blossomed over the past few years. Plump curves in perfect places. Can he see himself attached to her? Can he be so bold as to attempt to entice her again? That will send a firm message to his father about his thoughts on this arranged marriage. Alexander opens his eyes and stands up to look out the window. He feels the same void inside, open and empty, like the expanse of the lawn. The waves in his stomach sicken him. Arranged marriages happen all over England and abroad. Yet it has never been so for Warwick, until now. He always accepted he will choose for himself. Alexander streams his fingers through his hair and heads for a liquor cabinet in the room. A drink is what he needs. He sinks down once again in the armchair, putting his feet up. Not long after he finally falls asleep, he is awakened to dress for dinner. He pulls on his waist coat and turns to leave. He lingers for a moment to peer at the watercolor painting he admired earlier. Why has no one noticed it's upside down? Had it been so earlier?

THE TABLE FOR THE EVENING is most extravagant with a beautifully crafted triangular centerpiece at each end of the table. Lady Salisbury boasts the exquisite flowers, purple orchids and lilies, come from her own hot house and gardens. Alexander is seated on the left of Raby, a gentleman Alexander just met this evening. Lady Victoria is seated to the right of this gentleman and clearly intent to focus her attention on him. The last time he actually saw Victoria was before Edmund left for the continent. She is quite an agreeable sight still, with her hazel eyes and maroon hair, a unique color she is known for. Maybe they will suit. These thoughts mull around in his brain. That will show his father he means what he says.

Ladies with green eyes. What is it about green that appeal to him? If there will be any further designs on Victoria, it will depend on her. No doubt Lady Salisbury will welcome his attentions to her daughter. However, it is clear she is not opposed to matching Lord Raby with Victoria either.

Lord Raby proves to be pleasant company. Any interest Alexander may entertain for Victoria is soon forgotten. Lord Raby's views on the French Republic's abolishment of slavery and the arrest of Vicomte de Beauharnais and his wife Josephine are similar to his. More important, Raby does not hide his enthusiasm on Alexander's insights into the observation of clouds and tempests and the use of this data to predict weather patterns. They discuss his most recent data compilations and his last adventure running down a storm.

"I may have to begin taking notes myself the next time I am out. I find this most enlightening." Raby wipes his mouth and places the cloth by the side of his plate.

"Yes, indeed. And, when you spy a storm, take note of the formation of the clouds for you may be able to ascertain the strength of what is to come."

"Certainly, we all know a dark storm cloud brings rain." Raby signals to have his wine refreshed.

"Yes, yes, but the shape and the rotation, I believe, can tell us how severe it may be."

"Fascinating! You must introduce me to your colleagues." Raby raises his glass and takes a sip.

"My pleasure. I think you will find the most compelling data can be acquired when actually trailing the storm itself. There is no greater exuberance."

"I believe I shall look forward to the next encounter."

Victoria rolls her eyes and pouts profusely. Typical reaction to the topic. Lady Victoria continues to persuade Lord Raby to turn his attention toward his right as opposed to his left. Her one final effort to acquire his notice fails miserably. "I find Mary Wollstonecraft's *A Vindication of the Rights of Women* to be quite an excellent insight into the challenges facing the education of ladies in today's society. Have you heard of it?" The hollow sound of silver clanging against the china and open-mouthed expressions are the least of Victoria's worries.

"Victoria!" Her mother barks from across the table.

Amusement at his young friend's attempt to gain the attention of her dinner companion is hard to control. He should not have ignored her. It seems she has not yet outgrown the impulsive behavior of her youth. He glances over to his mother who looks the other way while placing a bite in her mouth. Of course. Now, when he can use her skills as mediator, she remains silent. Probably best.

"I only meant..."

"You only meant to imply such views are to be left for those who are qualified to make them."

"Yes, father, of course."

The glare from Lady Salisbury shoots bullets. "Ladies, I believe now would be appropriate for us to retire to the drawing room. Shall we?"

Poor girl, though Victoria will recover. She probably did it on purpose to move the party out. He smiles. The servants pass the cigars. Lord Warwick begins to discuss his plans for Toddington Peaks. "You know Salisbury, I should like to introduce you to a friend of mine. Very intelligent man. Let me tell you about his newest venture.

CHAPTER FOUR

Wentworth Hall – Spring, 1798

William Wentworth, the Earl of Stratford, reaches Wentworth Hall. His trip to London has been a success. Wentworth Hall will be safe with the Warwicks at the helm when the time comes. No doubt Ariana will be engrossed in a novel in front of the fireplace. He enters the parlor. Ariana isn't engrossed in a novel at all. She's engrossed in conversation. In conversation with a most elegantly dressed gentleman.

"What is happening here?" His voice barrels through the room. A bit too harsh. No matter. He turns from one to the other. They jump to attention in unison. "Ariana? Who is this gentleman with whom I have not had the benefit of an acquaintance?"

Ariana begins to make the proper introductions. She walks in his direction and reaches out her arms to bring him closer, "Papa, may I present to ye Baron Neville Raby."

She turns to face her father, "The Earl of Stratford."

"I came upon Laird Raby earlier today during my walk into the parklands. He's staying at Harlaxton and lost his way, so I invited him to take tea with us."

The gentlemen bow and the earl then makes his way, tall and stiff, across the room to the sofa, his eyes glued on Lord Raby. Ariana offers him tea. He takes his seat, eyes still focused. "Hmpf." Splendid. The full aroma of the tea reaches his nostrils. He takes a sip. His nerves calm. "Well, now that we have that out of the way. Harlaxton, you say? We have kept company with Salisbury for years. How is it you know them?"

"Well, sir, it happens that Lady Salisbury... that is to say, I came to discuss some business with the marquess and so decided to stay on to see it through."

"I see." Something's off. "And, what pray tell, is the marquess up to these days? Eh?" The chair across from Raby is closer to the fire. Stratford moves there and takes a deep slurp from his drink. "I must say it has been some time since we have shared a hunt." Best way to get to know a man. "It was not so long ago when our two houses hosted hunting parties on quite a regular basis. Between our adjoining estates we have some of the best fowl, elk, and reindeer in the region. Do you hunt?" Let's see what this Raby is about.

"Yes, sir. I do enjoy a good hunt and I could not help but notice the deer earlier."

"Reindeer, my boy, *rein*deer." Can't anyone keep them straight? "They are much desired around here my good chap. I've taken great pains to ensure their survival. Had them imported. They do quite nicely here. Beautiful creatures. The stags in their full growth in the winter are a thrill to see. What say we make plans for a good jaunt about before you leave?" Suspicion grinds each second away. Why is Raby taking so long to answer? "I know the best hunt is in the fall, but we'll remain on the grounds so it shouldn't be a problem."

"I would be delighted!"

"Splendid! I'll have my man send for you at Harlaxton by week's end and no doubt you'll pick off a fair amount of sport before you leave I am sure." Manton's double barreled shot-gun will do nicely.

Ariana rises and leaves the room. The tip, tap of her shoes is lost to the men's conversation.

IT COULD HAVE BEEN worse. What if he found them in the aviary? Her father would have had an apoplexy. It's best she remain in her sitting room with her needlework. Let them discuss their hunting and other things that interest men. She'll learn more of him later.

Ariana looks up from her work. Her father is staring at her from the doorway. "What is it papa? Do ye not find Laird Raby agreeable?"

Lord Stratford enters and takes a seat opposite her. "Do not be concerned on that account, but I do not approve of you keeping company with gentlemen in my absence. It is not proper."

Here it comes. "I know, but Becky was stationed outside the door." Lord Stratford stares at the lace being worked in her lap. He scratches and rubs his jaw, then circles around to his upper lip. Nerves begin to erupt right below Ariana's ribcage. She knows her father's expression.

"Yes, well, I can't say I understand what possessed him to walk all the way over here." Does he know about the aviary? Ariana swallows and clenches her teeth. "There is something of great importance, though, I need to speak with you about and I don't know quite how to start."

Ariana puts aside the embroidery careful to not lose her place and directs her full attention to him. Focus eases her wrecked nerves where her father is concerned. Usually. "What is it? Whatever it is I can handle it." She's not sure if that is entirely true, but he must tell her. It's best to make it as easy as possible for him and get it over with. She moves to sit next to her father and reaches out to take his hands.

He covers her hands with his own. He starts slow. His words quiver. "Ariana, I know I have always encouraged you to be your own person. I allowed you to indulge in your own pursuits thinking you a girl with unique talents. I always loved your independent nature. It reminds me so much of your dear departed mama."

Where is this line of conversation going? His eyes are murky. She hates to see him like this. Focus isn't helping.

He pauses and takes her hands between his. "My girl, I feel very strongly you should think seriously about marriage."

"Marriage!" Ariana pulls her hands away. Nerves overpower focus. What is this her father is on about? She manages the estate as well as any son. She is content. She thought he was content. Life can continue as always.

"Papa! Why? We have always got on so well as we are! Ye know how I feel about leaving ye, about leaving Wentworth Hall. Ye never encouraged that which I would not choose for myself. Are we not content just as we are? Surely ye have no complaints about the estate?" Her hands cover her mouth. She shakes her head. "Oh, no! Are ye ill?" Fear swallows her nerves creating an empty hollow.

"No, no, my goodness *No!* I am not *ill*, child!" He grabs her hands back into his" "Such imaginings! Calm yourself."

If only she could say the word and be calm. "Then, why? Why should I think of marriage? I have everything I want here. Surely there are no complaints over my duties around the estate, and I still keep busy with many activities for self-improvement and perfecting my accomplishments." Anything but marriage.

"No, of course not! You get on splendidly with the estate—better than any man I have had in my employ." He pats the top of her fingers. "And, of course you play the harp quite exquisitely. Whenever you sing, you captivate those in attendance with your most angelic voice. Not to mention the brilliant talent you show with your watercolors and feather-work."

"See? I donna need to marry for I've all I could ever want, here with ye. I'm certain ye donna want your only daughter to marry someone she doesn't love? Someone only after a fortune? Someone she cannot be a true equal partner with, like mama was to ye?" Will he listen?

Her father never insisted she marry before. It is her duty to make a good match— at least that is what Miss Cromwell always told her. He's never once forced her to accept an offer. What's changed his views?

LORD STRATFORD STUDIES his daughter's steadfast reasoning.

"Ye know how much I prefer my life as it is now." Her puffed eyes plead with him. "How can ye ask me to marry a man I donna love, who may never love me, who would be intent on controlling my every move?"

Ariana's efforts to change his mind are hard to hear. His heart twinges for her. Everything she says is true. He puts his arm around her shoulders and pats. "Now, dear, it doesn't have to be so. You and your husband will work things out together."

All her reflections on the subject are familiar. Many past conversations perform their way through his memory. It is difficult to truly know a person in today's society. Her hoydenish ways and independent spirit are well known. The wheels on his curricle scarcely survived her races down the long drive leading to Wentworth Hall whenever he would allow her to handle the ribbons. She barely missed the gatehouse. She certainly knows how to manage the horses. He may have indulged her a little too much.

"What are ye smiling about? Do ye think it amusing to torment me this way?"

"Of course not, my dear." Laughter weaves between his words. "I was simply reminded of the time you just missed the gatehouse."

"Now is when ye choose to recall that? How cruel can ye be?"

"Calm yourself, dear. It does warrant the discussion, you know." Stratford offers his handkerchief. She takes it and dabs the teardrops clustering each corner of her eyes then crumples the cloth in her hands.

"How so?" She sniffs. "Do tell me for I cannot imagine how." Ariana dabs some more.

His heart is heavy. The only reminder of his lovely wife Arabella is being forced into something she feels so strongly will make her unhappy. A sight he rarely can endure and one he often avoids. Not this time. She resembles her mother in many ways. Even when she lilts back into the slight Scottish brogue learned from the few years she had with her mother. And the bright green of his lady's eyes. A remarkable characteristic, one which Ariana inherited. Now, the sight of those beautiful green eyes—

eyes that always get her what she asks for— will not be enough to change his mind. Not today. Today, he must break his daughter's heart.

"Well, are ye going to tell me or what?"

He sits silent a moment longer. "I was only remembering that time racing down the drive and it reminded me of how strong you are. How it would be a rare man, indeed, who would be able to control your every move."

A smile peeks through between her sobs. "Ye're just trying to soften me. I willnae have it. Ye must tell me why it's so important that I marry now."

Stratford takes a deep breath. This will be an exhausting discussion. Wentworth Hall is in dun territory. "Ariana, you must know that being a female you cannot inherit." Ariana starts to respond, but he raises his hand up to silence her before words become sound. "I assure you. The law is very clear on the subject. Nothing can be done to change it and I need to make sure you are cared for properly."

"Papa, ye *are* ill!"

"No, no. Dash it! I am not ill. I simply want to be assured you are taken care of in the future. You must know all fathers look to ensure the continued protection of their daughters. Er, all fathers with a wit about them." Keeping the true financial situation from her? More like wits to let. Stratford wipes his forehead. Beads of sweat coat his fingers. "I cannot fathom the thought of you in the almshouse for any reason. How would you live? Your mama would think me wretched indeed were she alive had I not taken care to provide for you properly."

She stares directly into his eyes. He tries not to blink. "Ye're sure ye aren't ill? For I cannae understand why this must be done now. What has changed?"

"Ariana, there is no avoiding it. You simply *must* marry to ensure a lady of your station is able to maintain the quality of life you are accustomed to."

"But, I donna understand why now? Can we wait a little longer? Maybe the law will change?"

"The law change? Ariana! The things you think of. The law will never change. Why do you think those ruffians in the new world fought so hard to separate themselves from England?"

"*Shh*! Ye shouldn't speak so. Someone may hear ye and think ye're a sympathizer."

"You know I only talk. I want you to know this is the way it is. You must know the importance of keeping our family established here at Wentworth Hall. The other side of the family inherited Wentworth Abbey and I intend for my side to keep Wentworth Hall. If only you would have set your cap for some respectable chap, then we could have avoided doing all this arranged marriage business."

"Arranged marriage? What do ye mean? Ye've already had it arranged?"

Here it is. He must brace himself for what will come next. "I had hoped a London season would help to expand your prospects, but such was not the case." He is only delaying the inevitable.

"Papa, ye know I did my best."

"Yes, I know which is why I decided to help you out."

"What do ye mean?"

He swallows hard. He cannot not help himself. It's as if his dear Arabella questions him. If only they could have borne a son to go with their daughter. All of this could be avoided. Ariana's swollen eyes stall his heart beating in his chest. She is the son he never had the chance to father and the daughter who keeps his heart from breaking each day. He is about to break hers. He swallows hard again.

"My dear girl, I know this may be a surprise and you may at first be very angry. But, it is all arranged. I have spoken with Lord Warwick and we have come to an agreement."

ARIANA SITS MOTIONLESS. Her father is not wavering. Her stomach churns. Marriage. Duty. Fear. What if she marries and then meets *him*? The *one*. The one she's waiting for. The one she can truly be equal partners with, the one she truly loves, the one to spend the rest of her life with. This man is the reason she cannot agree to any of the offers. Yet.

"What do ye mean ye've come to an agreement?"

"Ariana, listen. It's not as bad as you may think. Arranged marriages happen all over England. It is the way it is done. You know this. Love comes in time. You will see you can be very happy. I've no doubt the viscount is amiable and a most sought after alliance by many young ladies."

"So, he's a viscount. Which viscount?"

Ariana stands up and walks over to the window. "I cannae believe ye're doing this. Ye know I willnae be settled with mere contentment. I know ye want for me what ye shared with mama! What's changed? Why do ye all of sudden come at me with an arranged marriage?" She twists the cloth in her hands into a tight swirl and dabs at her nose. "Papa I cannot! I willnae!" The churning in her stomach feels like it's whipped.

The earl follows her to the window. He gently pulls her close. His words are softer now, less hesitant, less harsh. "Ariana, Alexander will be the Earl of Warwick and it is most advantageous for you and for Wentworth Hall to ally ourselves with him. I know you have caught wind of the difficulties I have with Wentworth Abbey. That side of the family always maintained Wentworth Hall should have been included in their inheritance and we simply must keep from establishing any alliance, or *no* alliance for that matter, that affords them any advantage over Wentworth Hall."

"So this is about Wentworth Hall?"

"Yes, and no."

"Which is it?"

Lord Stratford places his hands on either arm to turn her to face him. "My dear, try to understand. You know Sir Lewis Rockingham?"

"Of course, he is our cousin, is he not?"

"Yes, that's right. His father and my father fought side by side during the Jacobite rebellion of 1745, but that is neither here nor there. The investments we made together were not as profitable as originally expected— not to mention the current state of the economy since the rebellion."

Her hands twist the cloth once again. "So what ye're telling me is we're financially ruined." The rock in her stomach must be butter.

"Sir Lewis informed me recently Wentworth Hall is in danger of being liquidated and, well my dear, can you not find it in yourself to see the wisdom of a good match? Wentworth

Hall must survive. It has been the family seat since the sixteen hundreds."

Her father stands in front of her, brows raised, waiting. Ariana cannot think. Dark circles underscore his eyes. Life away from Wentworth Hall is unimaginable. No more churning in her stomach. It's just plain sour. Anger adds to the mix. How can life be so cruel? She refuses to speak another word— to anyone. She storms out and up the stairs to her room. Tears fall despite her attempt to stifle them. She throws her father's twisted handkerchief across the room and soars face down on her bed. Her face flattens the pillow. Thoughts of her mother flit about her head. What would she say if she were here right now? She would never condone an arranged marriage. How can her father allow their home to come to such distress? Alliance indeed! Why does there have to be such absurd notions as if her actions can avert this silly feud through marriage with Warwick!

Ariana sprawls herself across the great featherbed, uncontrollable sobs mewl through the evening. Overcome by exhaustion, her last thought, "Who is this *Viscount and future Earl of Warwick* anyway!"

CHAPTER FIVE

Wentworth Hall – Spring, 1798

The morning finds Ariana far from her usual high-spirited self. She's still sluggish from the night's restlessness. A long ride on the grounds fuels her waking hours. She needs to feel unrestricted. The only way she knows to accomplish this is atop her favorite thoroughbred.

To marry this man her father arranged for her is beyond her feelings of sensibleness even though it is expected. She's cried to the point of numbness. There are no tears left, no fight left.

Vanora belonged to Ariana from the day her father brought her home from Tattersall's. Vanora's white coat and touches of gray above her hooves, gray tail, and mane remind her of Pegasus. No sidesaddle today. Ariana intends to fly in true Pegasus form. She can't remember the last time she actually did ride in a proper saddle for a lady. How will her new suitor feel about that? More distress fills her heart.

Vanora and Ariana sail across the parklands. The edges of the vast field framing the inner grounds of Wentworth Hall calls out to her. She reaches it and breaks into a canter then a gallop. Nothing compares to the release of the wide openness of the ride. She's going to ride far out across the countryside and not look back. Ariana passes the aviary and recollection sparks. She is free and alive. No one to pressure her. She rides. She contemplates. Defiance fills her. Can she do it? Defy her father without bringing him shame?

Duty. She must honor her father's wishes. He's forcing her into this so she will make everyone aware she is not happy about it. She will refuse to meet the man. He wants an arranged marriage— fine. She kicks Vanora to urge her faster.

The future Earl of Warwick can wait. He can wait until the wedding day for his bride-to-be. Or maybe she'll make this viscount refuse to marry her. Is that the way out?

If *he* cries off, she'll not be in defiance. She'll secure society's sympathy. Maybe. In this frame of mind her day at Wentworth Hall will be tolerable. A renewed spirit and plans to make rejuvenate her. The first step? Write to Victoria.

Ariana reaches the stables, slides off and pulls the reins over Vanora's head to guide her in. The horse's mane deserves a pat before she hands her off to the stable boy. Ariana makes a beeline straight to her father's study to discuss the possibility of going to Bath. He'll not deny this request. Not after asking her to do what she clearly is not agreeable to. He is sure to indulge her this one last time. She finds him in his usual place. The study, feet up and in front of a robust fire.

"Ariana, how are you this morning?" He puts his feet down and turns to face her. "I was most concerned about you last evening. I don't think I slept most of the night. What in the name of God are you wearing?" His question quickly becomes a snarl.

"Papa, let us not discuss that matter for now." She sits across from him to enjoy the fire. "I came to ask ye if it would be possible for us to take a trip to Bath for a short while. I feel I would like the opportunity to spend some time with Victoria. As ye know Salisbury is already in Bath." She reaches for a cake on the tray next to the chair.

Lord Stratford is quick to address her request. She knew he would. She watches the expressions on her father's face merge from alarm to contemplation to resolution. "Capital idea! I shall task my steward to procure a townhouse for us in Bath as well as admission to the Bath Assembly Rooms. I could well do with a soak in the waters, hey my dear? Surely your pending nuptials to Warwick will be credible enough to secure us the best locations."

Not the best result. Being any more beholden to him is not the plan.

"And, by the way, I must insist you leave your current attire to the servants. I do not wish to see you dressed so again."

Almost perfect. At least she's on her way to a *predicament* to cause the viscount to cry off.

Ariana kisses her father's cheek, determined to ignore his less than subtle attempt to express his displeasure in her "riding habit." "Yes, it would do us both a bit of good, I believe. I must go at once to get a letter off to Victoria."

"And change that dreadful outfit you're wearing! The viscount certainly will not put up with his lady venturing out and about wearing men's breeches!" His voice trails her all the way out the door.

Ariana calls over her shoulder while snapping the tip of her riding boots with her crop. "I donna why ye go on so. Ye know I wear them when I ride,"

"Yes, yes, but you always know of my distaste for it..."

Distaste, indeed. What about her distastes? She is being disrespectful. She doesn't care. She may wear them all day.

Ariana pens the letter to Victoria and rings for Hawthorne to post it. Not long after, she is notified Lord Raby is waiting on her in the drawing room. Now she must change. She chooses a dark green muslin bordered with ivory lace, lime and peach ribbon. Becky can probably come up to help if she rings for her. *Pish!* Doing it herself is faster. *Visitors waiting too long cannot be tolerated.* Once more, Miss Cromwell's voice sings soft in her head. Ariana tidies her hair and makes for the parlor, but then quickly returns to grab her gloves. Their time spent in the aviary flash in her head.

She pinches a bit of color into each of her cheeks and descends the staircase. Chin up, casual, confident. Her insides are shaking. Anticipation builds with each step. She passes by the settee to acquire a seat opposite him, but the heel of her slipper catches the lace of her petticoat, and she topples face down into the room at his feet, as graceful as a goose protecting her chicks.

ALMOST AT THE SAME time, Lord Raby anticipates the event, but not soon enough. He immediately stands and attends to the task of helping her to her feet. He doesn't want to add to her embarrassment. He tries *somewhat* successfully to contain the mirth bursting to come out. Her sprawled out form reminds him of a newborn foal trying to gain footing. The small dimple over her left shoulder does not escape his notice. How endearing. He focuses there to maintain control. Her tactful adjustment of her fichu draws his attention next. He desperately attempts to monitor his expressions.

He offers his hand and she rises to address the cloddish spectacle. His eyes greet hers and she breaks out laughing. A scene, he knows, can only end with a snort. The last time her infectious giggle caught him was in the aviary. At his expense. Good to know she can laugh at her own mishaps.

"So, now that I have deposited my impression indelibly in your mind, to what do I owe the pleasure of your visit?"

Her impression is already unforgettable. He has been hard-pressed for a return visit. Their last meeting in the parklands a few days before consumes his thoughts. He keeps that bit of information to himself.

"My dear lady, I so enjoyed our conversation last evening I thought I might seek the pleasure of your company, yet again, for a ride in my carriage if you would be so inclined."

"Unfortunately, I must decline. We're in the process of preparations to away to Bath."

"I see." She motions for him to sit. "You know, I wouldn't mind a trip to Bath now that I have been delayed. I've just had word my family is also in Bath." Will she see through his attempt to spend more time with her?

"Oh?" Ariana takes a seat opposite.

"Might I be so bold as to impose my presence upon you in asking for the privilege of joining you on your trip?"

"I donna see why not. I'm sure my father would welcome the company of a gentleman during the excursion." Ariana calls for Hawthorne stationed outside the door. "Please ask Lord Stratford to join us in the parlor directly."

The dreaded silence looms around them once again. Ariana fidgets with the ribbon weaved into her hair loosening it. Her inelegance is refreshing. Wispy loops frame her face. Lord Raby crosses his legs and swipes his arm to remove a piece of lint—or was that a feather? He could not be sure. He must not be seen to admire her too much. One can definitely fall in love with a young woman of Lady Ariana's innocent beauty, but will she be the sort of lady that reciprocates his passions? Or will she see only what most ladies see. A title and fortune?

Lord Stratford enters the room in familiar robust pomp, annoyed with the interruption. Upon seeing Lord Raby pomp becomes plain, annoyance comes calm.

"Lord Raby, how are you? Did you come to take me up on my offer so soon?"

"Actually, I came with the intention of taking a ride with Lady Ariana, but she informs me of your intention to leave rather soon to Bath. I had thought to ask if I may trespass upon your generosity and join you for I, too, have a party which awaits me there."

"Of course, my boy! Think nothing of it. We shall leave as soon as may be reasonably accomplished. I should look forward to a livelier conversation. No offense, my dear girl."

Ariana touches her father's arm. "None taken, papa. Of course, I will now need to endure the conversation of male camaraderie, but I think I may be up to the task."

"I'm sure you are, my dear. I know none too well of your upbringing." Ariana's father pats her hand with his. "You shall not want for enjoyable conversation. Now, I beg your pardon, I must get back to my study. I have unfinished business to attend to, you know."

Ariana lingers with him in the drawing room staring at the fire. Embers begin to spark. Emeralds of her eyes are alight. What thoughts can she be puzzling? Something is brewing and he must find out.

CHAPTER SIX

Bath, England – Spring, 1798

The trip to Bath is cumbersome, somewhat. Ariana nods her attention back and forth between her father and Lord Raby. The latest sale at Tattersall's, Lord Stratford's hunting dogs, news of the war, and state of the economy fill the gaps.

Constant interjections of opinion interrupt Ariana's busy attempt to contrive her own schemes. Determination. This viscount shall not be pleased with his bride-to-be. How to create a scandal without too much emphasis on *scandal* are first and foremost. The men and their constant effort to include her in their discussions are not to her liking. She will have none of it. Her plans with Victoria are more to her taste.

Ariana puts her head back and closes her eyes. Maybe this will persuade them she is tired. She needs time. The spider knits its web, her web.

A porcelain factory appears through the carriage window. Lord Raby's voice pulls her back to their presence. "We're coming upon the Inn at Birdlip. Might it be prudent to overnight here before continuing on?"

"I say, I must agree. Ariana, I'm sure, could not brook any disagreement. Is that not so my dear? Ariana? Do you hear me?"

"Yes, papa. I agree I am feeling the fatigue of the trip. A delicious meal and a good night's rest sounds just the thing."

"Excellent!" Lord Stratford knocks at the door and apprises Coachman of their plans for the evening.

The innkeeper's wife greets them and offers their best accommodations. "Welcome to the Inn at Birdlip. I've a private parlor open if'n you be needin' one."

"Yes, most assuredly and we will require three private rooms."

Ariana whispers close to her father's ear. "Papa, if I may, I would like to have a bath drawn to freshen up before supper."

Lord Stratford relays this request and the innkeeper's wife bobs her curtsy. "Right away, my lord."

Lord Stratford and his daughter are shown to their respective rooms next to each other while Lord Raby retires to the parlor before being shown to his room.

Ariana is looking forward to an uneventful evening. Her bath warms and relaxes. She envisions a viscount catching her with Lord Raby. She quickly dismisses this idea. What has come over her? She wants to bring events about so she'll not have to meet this bridegroom in the first place. Determined to be difficult, her point must be clear. She must find a way to discreetly discourage him from marrying her. The more she thinks, the more her subconscious is stuck like a pig in mud. Her brain is porridge. Her web is stuck.

Lord Raby may be able to help, but what will he think of her? It makes no difference. She doesn't want this marriage. How might she broach the subject? She may as well just tell him. Privately, of course.

Becky helps Ariana dress for supper. She wears her favorite India muslin of peach, trimmed with golden flounce. Becky dresses her hair with pearl fillets leaving soft wisps falling lightly to frame her face and neck. A simple string of pearls with matching earrings completes the look. She doesn't want to appear too wealthy for the company at the inn. But, of course, a lady must also be presentable. All the powers of persuasion she can muster will be put to good use. After all, there is no harm in using her feminine charms.

Ariana's entrance to the parlor elicits the response she is hoping for. Her father is less than astounded, Lord Raby topples his chair backwards.

"My laird, have I startled you?" Ariana gives him her most innocent smile.

"I, um, forgive me, my lady. I have been taken in by your loveliness this evening."

Lord Stratford looks at one and then the other, rolls his eyes to the ceiling, and bellows as loud as she imagines the Sultan in The Arabian Nights. "Can we get on with supper? I cannot wait a moment longer. I'm famished!"

Ariana's eyes are steady on Lord Raby while he repositions his chair on the opposite side of the table.

Lord Raby leans forward and lowers his voice to a whisper. "There must be an abundance of ale for it has been offered nonstop since we sat down."

"What's that?" The Sultan reels again. "Why, on God's green earth would you want more ale? They've been offering it nonstop since our arrival. I don't think I've consumed this much since my niptials..." A slew of hiccups follow.

Ariana tightens her lips. Giggles broil in her throat. She looks at her father and then to Lord Raby. Guilty glazes taunt her. "I see two gentlemen who seem to be having an enjoyable time."

"Enjoyable time indeed, my dear. It has been a long time. And, it has been a long time we are waiting on you to descend for supper!"

"Yes, papa, ye're correct." She covers her mouth to stifle the most persistent chortle. "Let us begin at once."

Her words are spoken and the attending servants appear with covered platters.

Supper is simple. Mutton and potatoes with mushy peas followed by banbury cakes.

Generous amount of mutton contribute to less intoxicated discussions on one of Ariana's father's favorite topics.

Lord Stratford wipes his mouth and lays the napkin on his plate. "I don't think I have asked you if you like to fish. Wentworth Hall is laced with lakes and streams offering a wealth of freshwater trout and wide-mouthed bass."

"It has been a long time since I had the pleasure of fishing. I fished quite often as a boy, but I own finding time now has been difficult. It's quite a different experience than hunting."

"That it is, my boy. That it is. Ariana can hook a fly better than any on cook's staff." Lord Stratford leans back in his chair and loops his thumbs in his belt in an attempt to loosen it. Ariana turns away to sip her wine. Maybe Lord Raby won't notice. Moments tick by. How can he not?

Lord Stratford taps the seconds with his fingers against his girth before he continues. Not her father's best impression by far. "I have found the best time is early in the morning or late in the evening. The most relaxing time is the evening, of course. Best results when fishing then. Best results."

"I can't recall when last I've fished, but I seem to recall catching bass in a stream not far from home."

"You must come and fish the lakes before you return home."

"I thank you and welcome the opportunity."

Lord Stratford sits up straight, places both palms flat on the table, and leans forward. "Yes, yes you must take me up on that offer. And, *wide-mouthed* bass it is, my boy, *wide-mouthed* bass." Lord Stratford raises one hand and slams it back down on the table. "Cook prepares the best trout cakes. You must come by and try them."

The evening slithers on. If she hears one more mention of the word fish she may become seasick. "I must apologize. As wonderful as this evening has been, I fear it is time. I must retire."

"Yes, yes, of course, my dear. I'm sure our talk of fishing and all such dribble is a great bore to you."

"No, papa, ye know I quite enjoy a lively conversation of sport, I'm only quite tired from the trip."

"Of course you are, my dear. We shall see you in the morning. Must get an early start, you know, if we're to make it there before nightfall."

Ariana stands and kisses her father on the cheek. "Yes, papa, good night."

She turns and acknowledges Lord Raby. "Good night, my laird."

Lord Raby stands to take her hand, this time keeping firm hold of his chair. He kisses the top and leaves his hand to linger a hint more than appropriate. His soft caress of her palm zips, zaps, and zings all the way up her arm. Her stomach jumps in a peculiar way, and she falters. Ariana steps back quick. Her father must not notice.

Lord Raby offers to escort her to her room. He must have had too much ale.

"No, no, my boy, not necessary. Not necessary." Lord Stratford shakes his head. "It's only one floor up. Ariana is quite capable of making it to her room unaided." Lord Stratford stands up. "I say, young folk and all your gallantries, for what?" He takes one step and wobbles. "I, on the other hand may need a set of helpful hands. I do think this ale is stronger than I had imagined."

Ariana's words are lost. She's never seen her father react in such a way. It *must* be the ale. He's not accustomed to drinking so much and, of course, with this atmosphere it's quite easy to overindulge.

It's good Lord Raby doesn't appear to be offended by the comments. His kind smile and silent reassurance he will take care her father makes it safely to his room revamps the zips, zaps, and zings from before into something soft, kind, and sweet.

Ariana settles down for the evening's rest in wonderment. Lord Raby's touch. Lord Raby's kiss on her hand. Lord Raby's smile. Such foolishness! Although it is pleasant to have one's senses enticed so.

Voices in the hall pull her back from further contemplation of his affect to her senses. One voice is familiar? Lord Raby? She stays in her bed. The voices continue. Maybe she should go to the door and ask them to keep their voices down. No, too coarse.

Curiosity overcomes sensibility. Ariana gets up to put an ear to the door. What are they saying?

"...will not marry her...." "...but you must understand..." Ariana can't hear. She cracks the door to see who it might be. The profile of a man with gray hair and pink livery is talking with Lord Raby. Hands are flapping in one direction and wigwagging the other. "I shall not return presently and I will not marry a woman just because it is arranged. I will no doubt see the earl on the morrow, in any event."

"But, sir..." Lord Raby raises his hand. The gray-haired man wearing pink stops speaking, stops flapping, stops wigwagging, and leaves. Lord Raby leaves last.

Ariana's mind is whirling.

Lord Raby? Marriage? Is he also plagued with an arranged marriage? Maybe he will agree to help her out of her predicament. And be helped out of his in the process!

CHAPTER SEVEN

Bath, England – Spring, 1798

Ariana's first thought when she wakes up the next morning is to find a moment alone with Lord Raby. Lord Stratford has other plans. He's tired from the road trip and wants to get an early start. He pushes to be at their townhouse in Bath by mid-afternoon.

No one speaks, the carriage trudges along as if in no apparent hurry. Ariana scopes out the landscapes through the window where the scenes bounce by. Resplendent visions line the road. An open meadow full of lush green grass springs past. A family of deer dance in the distance. "*Rein*deer" echoes between her ears. Her father's habitual clarifications amuse her. Fawns with their painted spots and cotton tails cling close to their mother while she swanks through the grass. Graceful creatures.

A creek with the rushing waters of white foam angle around and over rocks before passing below them, then spill off in the distance. The bridge creaks and groans with the weight of the carriage. Beautiful scenes and perfect memories she will include in her watercolor landscapes.

Groups of people are gathering in a clearing ahead. Carriages, curricles, and phaetons mow their way in that direction.

Ariana disrupts the silence. "Papa, what do ye think is going on over there? So many people are heading to that clearing?"

Lord Stratford pulls back the curtain on the window behind him. "It looks like a troupe of strollers!"

"Strollers! Can we stop and see their show? I would so enjoy an opportunity to see them perform."

Her father flips open his timepiece and raises one brow. "Do you really think it necessary, child? I had hoped to reach Bath before dark?"

"And, we shall!" Ariana slips forward in her seat. "I promise we willnae be long."

Lord Stratford looks at Lord Raby who shrugs his shoulders. He smiles at Ariana but says nothing. Ariana quizzes her father in the form of a pout. "Please?"

"Alright, child. But, only a short while."

"Thank you! Papa! It will be wonderful."

Lord Stratford signals the wheel-boy giving the direction of the performers.

All excitement aside, this is her chance. Her chance to speak with Lord Raby about her plans.

The closer they get, the more excitement replaces any plans. They're not strollers. They're an entire traveling circus! Ariana cannot wait to exit the carriage. She moves straight for the center. Elephants, tightrope walkers, trapeze performers, lions, and clowns. Their rehearsals draw onlookers from all directions. The colors, the sights, the sounds. Even more canvasses for her watercolors. How will she be able to remember them all? Surely these will be appropriate for such paintings. And who cares if they're not! She's going to paint them anyway. Vibrant hues of the circus will fill her pages with the emotion of it. She'll capture it all.

Horses canter in a circle with a team of young men balanced on their backs. A boy of about ten stands flat footed on the horse's back. He jumps in the air, does a somersault as the horse continues to canter, and he lands flat on the horse's back!

Ariana claps and yells. "Bravo! Well done!"

The boy sees her, loses his footing, falls backwards, bounces off the horse's rump, and falls buttocks first onto the ground.

"Oh, no!" Ariana covers her mouth as soon as the words are out. She runs toward him and Lord Raby follows. She kneels down next to the boy while Lord Raby slips his arms under each of his to help him sit up. He opens his eyes and stares right at her. The most intense green eyes she has ever seen. "Are ye hurt?"

"No worries, m'lady. I be fallin' off a time or two. Only ways to get learned on 'orse tricks." His smile is straight and white. Brilliant white.

Ariana helps him adjust his position to sit upright. Lord Stratford calls out to her. "Ariana? What are you on about down there? Get out of that ring!"

"But, it's my fault! The poor boy was distracted. If I hadnae made a cake of myself, he may not have fallen off."

Lord Stratford does not agree. "Nonsense. They do this kind of thing all the time. I'm quite sure it's not the first time he has taken a tumble, eh, lad?" Members of the circus surround them. "I say, Raby can you not help her see the way of things?"

Ariana doesn't sway. "What is your name?"

"Wendell, ma'am. Me ma calls me that a cuz it means wanderer and see'in as tho' I be doing that she's called me Wendell."

"Wendell. Tell me what I can do. I must do something to make up for causing ye to fall. Tell me."

Wendell shakes his head. "M'lady must come and see me show in Bath on the morrow. That'd be enough."

"Verra well. I promise." Ariana stands up. Wendell stands up too. "I shall come tomorrow to see your show." Ariana holds out her hand to shake Wendell's. "Maybe then I can persuade ye to accept something for your trouble."

Lord Stratford scuffs the gravel each time he paces in front of the entrance. Ariana can hear it all the way in the ring where she stands. "Ariana! Please, will you come out of there? I promise you will not like it if you make me come in there to get you."

Lord Raby offers his arm to Ariana. "My lady, I do believe it would be good if you allowed me to escort you back." She allows him to fold her arm in his. "Shall we?"

Ariana slows the pace. Now is her chance. She allows her father to gain distance in front of them. How to start the conversation?

The silence is strange. Solemn and thoughtful. Lord Raby's jaw is set firm. The muscle clenches. Why is he so tense?

ARIANA'S EYES. WENDELL has Ariana's eyes. The same color of green. The same shape. The same size. Unique. The two of them together just now, there is no mistaking it. Two sets of emeralds. Lord Raby racks through thoughts and scenarios. It's not unheard of for men of Lord Stratford's caliber to find comfort in the arms of a woman especially after the loss of his wife. Lord Stratford is particular about correct distinctions, how is it possible he didn't notice? It was *Lady* Stratford who had those eyes. The voice beside him beckons him back to present company.

"I wonder, my laird, if I may speak with ye on a matter of strict confidence."

He turns to face Ariana. He tries to hide what lurks in his thoughts. "Of course, my lady. You may rest assured of my discretion. What is it that distresses you?"

"I donna quite know how to say it. I am deeply distressed it's true. I find it difficult to put into words." She fidgets with the edges of her gloves and takes a deep breath. Maybe she did discern the same thing he had and is going to ask him his opinion on the matter. Certainly she doesn't expect him to speak of such things regarding her own father.

"Papa has arranged for me to be married to a man I donna know."

"I see." Not what he suspected.

"I understand ye're in a similar...that is to say— well, first, I must admit something." She bites her bottom lip. "I may have overheard ye speaking with an older man in the hall of the inn last night." She pulls at her gloves once more. "About not marrying a woman *you* have never met."

Lord Raby stops and faces her. "Go on." How much did she hear?

Ariana fists her hands at her sides. "There's no other way to say it. I mean to encourage this gentleman papa wants me to marry to call off the arrangement." She lifts her face to him and aims direct. Where exactly is this line of thought heading? "I'm wondering if there was a lady ye donna wish to marry. We could scheme together and create a *controlled* scandal. Something we can contain so we're not completely ruined or should I say, so *I* am not completely ruined." She inhales deep, shakes her hands at her sides, exhales, and stares at the ground. "There. I have said it. What do ye think?"

Lord Raby doesn't know what to say or do. He peers around them looking for context. He doesn't find it. He concentrates on the words, *controlled scandal.* Quite far from any idea he's come up with. "Let me clarify. You want me to contrive with you to compromise your honor?"

Ariana's face turns pale. Is she going to faint? He cannot have that. What will Lord Stratford think? Truth be told, this idea of hers is really quite brilliant. Why not? He lets out a roar of laughter and grabs Ariana to steady her. He certainly cannot have her faint from panic. "Why not? I don't know how we could pull it off without bringing a severe blow to your reputation. Have you a plan?"

Bright pink flushes back into Ariana's face and she joins him in his laughter. "It certainly is no worse than what was attempted in the aviary, might I remind ye."

"So, is this to be your compensation?"

"No, for it is to your benefit as well, or am I wrong?"

"Does it bother you I may be getting married?"

"Of course not." She bites her bottom lip. "I only thought it might be something we both could benefit from."

"Be assured, I do not plan on marrying any woman I have not met, do not share the same interests with, and for that matter, do not love. So, my lady, I would be delighted to help you in this adventure!"

"Adventure, indeed. If only a lady could choose for herself as do the gentlemen." The pink glow that was there lightens to soft white. Pink is better.

"It isn't fair. I do not agree with what society dictates in regard to these matters. Alas, you know there isn't much we can do and this scandal of yours could put us both in a compromised situation."

"Yes, I have thought of it, but I see no other way. I donna like it, but I must do what I can to stop it."

"And if you cannot?"

"I'll have no choice but to marry, but I willnae meet him until the wedding."

"Until the wedding?" He hears his voice crack. Absurd. What woman does not want to meet her betrothed before their wedding?

"I'm quite determined. Why should I? It makes no difference."

"You, my lady, are quite charming when you are determined."

"Charming? Papa would say exasperating. And, what are ye laughing at? It's not so entertaining— you with that grin of yours from ear to ear."

"Ear to ear is it? I'm not laughing, I assure you. It's only that I quite like the way you think."

"Ye mean ye're not put off by my display of *independence?* Or my hoydenish ways?" Ariana peeks up at him, a half smile tipping the corner of her lips.

"It is most definitely the opposite, I assure you. And I've noticed your accent. It's heavier when you're passionate about something. I cannot wait to hear what you've planned."

"Yes, I know." Pink flushes return to her cheeks. "I cannae help it. My mama was Scottish and so, I've learned her accent. Sometimes I can control it, but I donna try so much. She's part of me this way."

"As well she should be."

"As far as a plan, I've not thought that far ahead, but I'll enlist the help of my friend, Victoria, once we arrive in Bath. She'll help come up with a plan."

"Yes, I am sure she will."

"Ye know Lady Victoria, then? The Salisbury's?"

"Um, well, I only just met her a few days before they departed for Bath, but I could tell she is very clever."

"Clever, indeed. When we were but girls in the schoolroom Victoria was always scheming and coming up with tricks to play on our elders— for which there was not a shortage of punishment, I assure ye."

"So, you blame it all on Victoria? I find that hard to believe. I've no doubt you, too, were not lacking in insight on that account."

"Best not continue for the moment. The carriage awaits." Ariana proves just how clever she is by evading the question.

Lord Raby clenches his teeth. What did he agree to? Lord Stratford is already settled inside. "I say, why are you dawdling about? I do hope to reach Bath before nightfall, if you don't mind."

"Yes, papa, we're only enjoying the opportunity for a walk."

"A walk! Plenty of time for a walk when we get to Bath." Lord Stratford's growls rumble with the passing crowd.

Lord Raby hands Ariana up into the carriage. Her tippet falls from her shoulders and he can't help stealing a glimpse of the adorable dimple as he places it back around her shoulder. Clever minx. He can be clever too.

CHAPTER EIGHT

Bath, England – Spring, 1798

Radiant streams of first light fill the morning room with brilliant warmth. Ariana rejuvenates from her trip the previous evening. Eggs, bacon, and buttered toast is just the thing. Victoria calls at their house on the Royal Crescent within one hour of Ariana's note telling her of their arrival.

Victoria throws her hands around Ariana. Giddy enthusiasm encircles them both like playful puppies excited to meet a new friend. "Oh, my dear Aria. It's so good to see you! I have so much to tell." Ariana smiles. The pet names they have for each other remind her how much she enjoys Victoria's energetic and impulsive nature.

"It's been too long, Vicky. I've missed yer happy ways." Ariana guides them to sit together in front of the window. "Do tell me where ye've been to and what ye've been doing? Ye look radiant!" Victoria is not short on stories to tell her of the adventures she encountered in Brighton with her Aunt Cecily.

"My! It seems to me ye may not even make it to London for a Season!"

"Really, Aria, as if I would give up my chance for a Season."

Ariana welcomes the short silence that breaks out between them.

"So, Aria. What is going on with you? I know something is amiss. It's not like you to sit quite so silent while I go on about my adventures."

Ariana's nerves begin to toil like the vibration of a tuning fork. What will Victoria say? Will she support her? Will she help her? What if she tells her father? After hearing about Victoria's adventures in Brighton, she's not sure. Ariana can't hold back. Her nerves force her to blurt it all out in one sentence. "Papa's gone and arranged for me to be married to some viscount, the future Earl of Warwick."

Victoria squeals and gasps then squeals again. "Aria, how is it possible? He was always so indulgent on the subject of marriage. You always said he would never persuade you to marry someone you did not love."

Anxiety builds toward a crescendo as she speaks. "I dunno. It's all verra sudden. He has his reasons, I suppose, but I just cannot abide it. I donna even know the gentleman. I will have one thing to say in it, though. If I have to marry him, I willnae have him set eyes upon me until our wedding day in front of the vicar."

Victoria scrunches up her nose and her upper lip almost touches it. "Aria dear, I can see how this upsets you—your mama's words are coming through strong—how can you not meet him before you're married?"

"Vicky, ye can be so animated. Of course, I'm upset. If I have to marry him anyway, what difference does it make if I see him first or not? It willnae change a thing. I refuse to meet him until that day, if my plan doesn't work."

"Your plan? Of course you have a plan." Victoria's face shrinks back to rights. Her eyes widen with excitement.

Ariana moves closer to Victoria as she continues lowering her voice and anxiety level to the other side of the crescendo. No servants need hear what she's about to say. "I want to create a scandal."

Victoria presses her brow. "A what?"

"One that could be contained, of course. One that would most definitely cause him to refuse to marry me."

"How do you propose to contain a scandal?"

"I've not thought it through that far yet. But, that would solve the problem, would it not?"

Victoria sits still. "I suppose it would." Focused concentration reveal the cogs and wheels of her mind are rolling. "Wait a minute. You said the future Earl of Warwick? Do you mean Alexander? Is he the one your father has arranged for you to marry?"

Ariana nods her head. "I'm afraid so."

Victoria's eyes grow wide once again. "Aria, he's part of the group staying with our family. We received word of his plans to join us here in Bath. He should be here any day now. Lady Warwick and Mama have been friends since childhood. I cannot believe you would not wish to marry one such as Alexander. He is set to inherit the earldom. Aria, his title. His wealth. He is quite the catch *and* very handsome, indeed."

Ariana waits for her friend to take a breath. Victoria always the adventuress. She rarely over-exaggerates when it comes to male members of society. Ariana closes her eyes for an instant. She will not entertain any reconsideration of her resolve. Although, what will this new information mean for her plans with Lord Raby?

"Yes, dear, that may be all well and true, but I just cannot do it. I willnae be made to marry someone I donna love. Even if he is handsome."

"...and titled."

"And titled." Ariana repeats.

"...and rich."

"Yes, and rich. But he is probably a rake and will treat me like a possession."

"You don't know he will be that way. I must confess, Aria. As a girl, our families, mine and the viscount's, spent a lot of time together. He's not as gruesome as you may think. There was a time when I felt for him as I do my own brother. In fact, I do believe Mama holds hope his attentions may be directed toward me, but I own I do not wish it."

"So, ye think I should allow this?"

"I cannot tell you what to do and I know you will do as you wish, in any event. I say this as your good friend. He seems most agreeable and I do believe you would suit."

Ariana waits for more to be said as is her way, but instead Victoria folds her hands in her lap and says nothing more. Maybe it isn't all bad. Maybe he'll be an honorable man. Maybe he'll allow her some latitude in light of her past and her present circumstances. No. She cannot risk it. Nagging fear of being tied to a man she cannot love fills her insides. Losing all freedom of will. Never being allowed to do as she wishes. Never riding Vanora in the way she is accustomed. He'll probably be offended at the very thought of handing her the reins. "No! I willnae! I simply cannot!"

Victoria jumps a little in her seat.

"So, will ye help me with a scheme to pull this off?"

Victoria's reluctance is clear. Her lower lip gives her away. "Of course, I will. But, this is most assuredly against my better judgment."

It's Ariana's turn. She throws her arms around her friend and hugs her close. "I willnae forget it. I have already enlisted the help of one very delightful gentleman to help with the plot."

Victoria squeal-gasps again. "Aria, who could you have found to confide such things to? He cannot possibly be honorable if he agrees to such things."

Ariana laughs. "Vicky, it's quite innocent, I assure ye. I met him while I was out walking the grounds at Wentworth Hall."

"Walking the grounds? What was he doing there? Was he alone? Were you alone?" Before Ariana can respond, Victoria clasps her hands to her mouth. "I know you were alone for you always walk the grounds alone. Aria! You didn't!"

Ariana raises her hand to dismiss her friend's censure. "He was lost. I'm not sure exactly what he was doing. Papa is quite taken with him. He traveled with us here to Bath. In fact, ye probably know him as well for he, too, was staying at Harlaxton. Although, I dunno if he's part of those staying with ye here."

"What's his name?"

"Raby. Lord Raby."

Victoria flushes white. "Of course I know him! We've somewhat of an attachment."

"An attachment? Did ye not just moments ago tell me ye willnae give up your Season? And how can ye have *somewhat* of an attachment?"

"I can still have my Season. I'm sure he would not deny me that. I wanted to tell you as soon as I got here, but we started talking about your *scandal*. Aria, he's magnificent! The moment I laid eyes on him I felt my heart through my ears."

Ariana listens to another one of Victoria's long-winded stammers, this time about Lord Raby. It's difficult to hear. Why isn't she happy for Vicky? She can't shake the feelings. Feelings she had when she first met him herself. The storm. The sudden run for shelter. Her bare hand in his. The aviary. He almost kissed her. Maybe he's not an honorable man. Why would he treat her so if he's pursuing Victoria? She fell face first at his feet. It feels like her heart may have fallen too. They laughed together. He pressed her hand at the inn, the sensations it caused.

The conversation she overheard in the hall at the inn crashes through her thoughts. Her stomach whirls like a top. Is this his arranged marriage of that conversation? Surely Victoria would know such a thing. Or does she? She did say 'somewhat.'

Lord Raby did not actually say he had fallen prey to an arrangement.

"Vicky, how well do ye know him?

"Aria, have you not heard a word I've said? Woolgathering, were you?"

"I'm sorry. I may have been, a little." Ariana bites the inside of her lip. "It's a lot to ponder, ye know? With my arranged marriage I'm trying to get out of— and ye're trying to get into a marriage." Ariana only half smiles.

"I know, you're right. It is a lot. And you're so unhappy. But, papa has known him through some business dealings. I have on occasion been in attendance for different events when I believe he did pay particular attention to me. Only just this morning did I go out with him in his phaeton. Papa even offered to have him stay with us."

"Well, that certainly seems to indicate he may be interested. Are ye sure he feels the same? I mean, has he declared himself to ye?"

Victoria's face wilts. "He hasn't exactly declared himself, no. I feel very certain he will soon. Even Mama says he must be interested and she is very keen on how to know these things, Aria."

Ariana sighs relief the moment she hears 'no.' Guilt's heavy shadow crouches over her. She certainly doesn't want to get married. Why should she care if Vicky and Lord Raby marry? She's grown very fond of him and she loves Vicky as a sister. She'll have to keep him as a friend who has promised to help her with her scandal and that will be that.

Victoria is too silent. Regret about destroying her friend's hopes seeps in between Ariana's turmoil. "Come now, I'm sure ye're right. If Raby has fixed his interest on you, I'm sure he'll ask yer father to pay his addresses verra soon." Ariana wraps her arm around Victoria's shoulders and gives her a shake. "And, ye do still want a London Season. Maybe he's waiting for ye to have that Season?"

"I suppose. Now I cannot help but wonder if he has changed his mind. What kind of gentleman would do what you are asking?"

"Vicky, please, it is not as ye make it out to be. He's only trying to help. Can we focus on deciding what will work?"

"You're right. I will try not to be so low. Let's see, it will have to be somewhere public, not too public because we need to control it. Who do you want to discover you?"

"Discover me?"

"If your father discovers you, he may try to keep it a secret so that will not work, and if the wrong person discovers you then you could be ruined for all time."

"I see what ye mean. What do ye propose? I mean ye know the viscount and how he may react."

"I know him to be an honorable man. He would not wish to cause you to come to ruin— that is as long as it can be contained and his reputation is not affected in any way."

"So, what can we do? We need something that will allow him to discover us?"

"Well, he may decide to overlook it as long as no one else knows, so that may not work."

"Maybe this willnae work at all!"

"Just wait, Aria. Let me think." Victoria taps her forefinger against her chin. Ariana is ready to forget the entire idea.

"I know! I'll get papa to have a masquerade ball. We'll invite so many people that it will be easy to slip away without being noticed and we'll have masks to hide who you are when you need to. We can manipulate the situation using the masks."

"Splendid! I knew ye would come up with something." Who cares that she was seconds away from tossing the whole thing.

"You'll have to be careful, though, that you avoid those members of the *ton* who could pick up on our little scheme and ruin you for good. We can't have you forced to marry Lord Raby, can we?"

"Of course not, dear, surely that would be most unfortunate. Ye know I could never do anything to hurt you."

"I know that, which is why I trust you most implicitly."

"So, tell me what we are going to do."

"Well, first I was thinking..."

CHAPTER NINE

Bath, England – Spring, 1798

Soon after Victoria leaves, Lord Raby arrives. More than a little discomfort gurgles inside Ariana. She flips open her fan to cool the heat building on her cheeks and glances at the fireplace across the room. Low and steady flames. Not the likely cause of her discomfort. Victoria's attachment may make this harder than originally planned. Becky is now installed inside the parlor instead of sitting outside the door. Ariana must not give in to some innocent flirtations with him. To deny the attraction she feels is no longer a question. Victoria is her good friend. She must keep any feelings in check.

Lord Raby is quick to notice the change in Becky's placement as he enters the parlor. Ariana clips her fan closed and stands to welcome him. His eyes are aglow below his one raised eyebrow. She calls for refreshments and takes a seat across from him. How to approach the subject she wishes to discuss with him? Her tongue sticks to the top of her mouth. How much longer will they be with the tea? At this rate she may as well pour herself a brandy. Lord Raby surely will not be shocked since he is agreeable to her designs thus far.

Lord Raby smooths the path to her subject. "Tell me my dear, what have you and your friend come up with for our scandal?"

Ariana clears her throat and attempts a swallow. She begins to convey their plans, stopping momentarily to allow Hawthorne to bring in the long awaited tray of cucumber sandwiches, water and tea. In no time, one full glass of water is down complete and the empty glass back on the tray.

"Are you alright my dear?"

"Yes, quite." She presses the back of her hand to her forehead. "It must be the fire is too hot."

"Would you like it cooled?"

"No, no. I am fine, now."

"Are you sure?"

"Yes, yes. Here, may I offer ye some refreshments as well?"

"Yes, thank you." Ariana serves him a glass of water.

He sips and asks, "So, you were saying?"

"Yes, we have indeed decided it would be most desirable if we could contrive to have a masquerade ball."

"A mask, how delightful! Deceitfully splendid!"

Relief radiates reckless throughout her. Ariana heaves a breath and continues. "I thought so too. We're hoping to devise a way for it to be held in the country, maybe at Harlaxton, for most assuredly there would be less of the *ton* but still enough for our purpose. The scandal could be better contained, if ye will." Lord Raby's grin splashes across his face. Unexpected and sudden. Like a school boy who just hatched a plan. Dreadful man. Why must he do that? Uncertainty overwhelms her. Should she go through with it or not? Lord Raby equals nerves. Or does he?

"Such attention to detail. Leave it to the ladies to devise such concoctions of deceit. I must say I cannot wait for the distraction to begin! And what, pray tell, have you come up with that will put us in the compromising position?"

Ariana's face fumes hot.

"No, no, that will not do. If we are going to pull this off, you must not be so— *missish*. You must hold yourself as a lady confident in her flirtations."

"*Missish!* I've had many such flirtations as ye well know."

"Do I?"

The heat in her cheeks flashes its force straight down her neck. What on earth is going on? Her teeth grind. More water. She must drink more water. She reaches for the pitcher to pour a glass.

"What say you to a bit of practice then?"

"Practice? I'm sure I dunno what ye mean. Would ye like some more tea? Water?"

"Yes, thank you." Lord Raby stares closely as she adds to his glass. His eyes are glued to her every move, his lips in that upturned position. Is he mocking her? No. Maybe. Confound it. He does look quite pleasant and his face is kind. Except when it's not.

Lord Raby removes himself from the chair across from her and settles himself next to her on the couch. Heart palpitations. Close proximity to the man causes her to lose her wits. Ariana is in no doubt her cheeks are as scarlet as the couch they're sitting on.

"So, practice then?" He lowers his voice to a whisper. He's so close.

"Alright. Practice." She whispers back.

His presence, so close to her. She can feel the warmth of his breath. He removes the water glass from her hand and places it on the tray. Very cautious, he places his hand around her small waist. This act further complicates her raging pulse. She can feel his fingers as they mingle through the lace of her muslin.

"My laird, what..." her voice is barely audible, although her gaze is fixed on his lips. His face leans in closer, he is going to kiss her...but, instead, he turns to whisper in her ear.

"Yes, my lady? Or, shall I call you Ariana?"

The light touch of his breath sends a surge of tingling down her neck and back. Conflict clouds her mind at this moment between her friend's declaration of her feelings for this man and the ripples that begin fluttering in her stomach.

"Ye're sure this *practice* is most necessary?"

"Quite certain." His answer is soft and low. His hand skims along her cheek and down her neck to her left shoulder. "And you did not answer me..." His words end and he bends his head to cover her mouth with his own. Ariana presses herself against him. His grip is tight around her waist. He pulls her closer. Flutters intensify. Strange excitement fills her. We're just practicing and that is all it is. She settles the matter in her head and wraps her arms around his neck.

Becky coughs from her station by the door. Ariana motions her maid to leave the room. No need to stop their practice session. Lord Raby continues his attentions to her neck and the back of her ear, unaffected by the discreet reminder of her maid. The sensations this man's kiss is creating cause her to squirm in her seat. He parts her lips so they may share the luscious mysteries inside. Ariana melts against him. Willing and without reserve. All control is lost. Cool and tender, tongues dance. Feelings of breathless anticipation threaten to explode. Lord Raby pulls away and kisses her again on the corner of her mouth. He stops and stares back. His arm rests on the couch behind her. He says nothing. His eyes are a beautiful color, holly blue butterfly blue. Why did she let him kiss her? Why did he have to stop? She doesn't want him to stop. He steals one last taste of her lower lip before standing up.

Lord Raby turns away and walks toward the fireplace. His hands ruffle through the top of his hair in sequence one after the other. "I think we've made quite a good start. We won't be needing any more *practice*."

Ariana sits motionless. New feelings and sensations are out of control. The fire is the only movement in the room, intertwining its glow between them. She touches her lips. They feel bare and naked, somehow alive.

Together in silence, they listen to the fire crackle and pop. Ariana pours water and sips. Lord Raby takes the seat across from her and eats the last of the cucumber sandwiches. How does one manage appropriate conversation after that?

"Have ye come across any remarkable storms of late?"

Lord Raby chokes.

"Are ye alright?"

"I'm sorry. Yes." He wipes his mouth with a napkin. "I'm not accustomed to young ladies asking about erm... remarkable storms and no, unfortunately. I have not."

"Ye were out looking for clouds on our first meeting, were ye not?"

"Yes, that's right. You are correct."

"Do ye do that often? Look for storm clouds?"

"The truth is, I don't do it as often as I would like to."

"Whyever not?"

"Do you *really* want to know?" Lord Raby flashes his perfect smile and winks. "Or, are you just trying to make conversation?"

Ariana has no choice but to cool her heat-flushed cheeks once more with the flip of her fan. "Yes, I *really* want to know!"

She sits back and faces the window. "I find tempests quite fascinating actually." Ariana tries to focus on the rhythm of her fan rather than the beating of her heart.

"Hmm." Lord Raby loosens his cravat. "Since I came here to help you keep a promise, what say we go to the circus. We can talk more on the way."

"Wendell!" Ariana snaps her fan closed. "We must leave at once and, yes, we can talk on the way." She stands up, straightens her bodice, and adjusts her fichu. "Please excuse me while I go and change." She stops at the door. "Would ye like me to ask Hawthorne to replenish the tray?"

"Yes, I believe I can do with a bit more replenishment." Dark eyes meet hers. Is he angry? Surely, they did nothing wrong. Allowing Becky to leave— well, encouraging her to leave, not such a good idea. She must direct Hawthorne to offer him brandy.

Lord Raby's kisses are still vibrant on her lips. Ariana ascends the stairs to her room. She closes her eyes only for a minute, holding the banister as she steps. He is there behind her lids. His holly blues. She smiles and opens her eyes. She reaches the landing and calls for Becky to help her choose an ensemble. Becky is quiet. Something must be wrong. No doubt on what it is.

"I know ye have something to say, Becky. What is it?"

"My lady, 'tis just I think you ought not to 'ave 'ad me leave. I worry you might get yourself into a bit a trouble is all."

Becky's right. Ariana doesn't care. "Ye must not be concerned, Becky. I assure ye all will be fine. I'm sure ye know of papa's plans for me to wed this viscount. And Laird Raby has agreed to help me get out of it."

"Get ou' of it? Excuse me, m'lady, why would you want to get ou' of it?"

"Because— I donna want to be marrying someone I have never met, donna love, someone I have nothing in common with."

"But, my lady, isn't that wot all young ladies want? To be married?"

"Well, I donna want it! And, only recently has papa decided I must, but if I cannae get him to listen then I have no other choice except to get this viscount to call it off."

"Oh, so that's it. Well, I hope you'll not be regrettin' it later."

Becky's less than subtle caution is not what she needs right now. Truth be told, Ariana doesn't know exactly what she needs. One thing is for sure. A circus is in town and the gentleman who can ensure her future happiness is downstairs waiting to take her to see it. "Come Becky, we must hurry, Laird Raby is waiting downstairs to go to the circus!" A coquelicot and primrose striped caraco and petticoat of fine Merino cloth, a wide-brimmed hat with elaborate trimmings of flowers and feathers from her aviary will be just the thing.

Ariana descends the inner staircase. Lord Raby's eyes lock with hers. He shifts against the stair rail to steady himself. She giggles. Maybe he replenished himself with a bit of brandy after all. He offers her his arm and they proceed out and down the street toward the park where the circus is being performed. Becky follows discreetly behind.

The big top tent rises in appearance as they walk closer. The buzz of the circus surrounds them. The acrobats climb and balance as they showcase their talents. Such discipline. A cage full of lions slog in circles. Hunger, or maybe sadness brim through the bars of the cage. Just above the lions, the swinging trapeze. How can they hang upside down? Such trust in one another? To the left, a young girl walks a tightrope. So many sights to see, such unique talents. Ariana's eyes scan the scene searching for Wendell and instead fall upon Lord Raby. His blue eyes remain on her. The blue appears darker than before.

"My laird, are ye alright?"

"Yes. Why do you ask?"

"Ye did say we would discuss more of your remarkable storms on the way here and ye haven't said more than a sentence. And, all of this, well, I am quite taken with everything and still ye donna seem taken in at all."

"I can assure you, my lady, I am quite taken, not just by the circus."

Her dratted cheeks flame with now familiar heat.

"Is there nothing here that just amazes ye?"

"Yes, there are many things. I guess, perhaps I have seen them before. What would you like to see before we go see Wendell?"

Ariana whirls around. She spots Wendell across the ring. There. She tugs at Lord Raby. "I want to see him first." She pulls Lord Raby toward the horses and Wendell.

"M'lady, you came." Wendell drops the hoof pick and bows before her. Does he think she's royalty?

His animated actions regale her. He must have her most genuine curtsy. "Of course, I came. I promised I would and I must keep my promises, ye know. How are ye doing now that ye've had a chance to recover?"

"Oh, 'tis nothin. Fallin' be somethin' I do." Wendell directs his attention to Lord Raby. "How d'ya do sir?" Before Lord Raby can respond, the music begins and the ring master appears in the center of the ring.

"Ladies and Gentlemen!"

"Best be gettin t'yer seats. The show be a startin." Wendell takes a spot behind a curtain.

Ariana pulls Lord Raby to their seats. She must sit as close to the front as possible. The performance unfolds in excited anticipation. Wendell and his troupe do not disappoint. Ariana makes sure to clap louder than the first time she saw this scrawny lad do his 'tricks.' The troupe consists of six horses, inclusive of two ladies. They all ride bareback. A trick unique to each performer mesmerizes the audience. They jump to one side, then the other. The horses canter around the ring. Ariana stands up to see over the top of the few rows in front of them. Lord Raby stands up too. Excitement zips through her each time this troupe executes their tricks. She grabs Lord Raby's hand. Never has she seen horses do such things.

NEVER HAS HE KNOWN a woman such as this.

CHAPTER TEN

Bath, England – Spring, 1798

"I don't understand why I must always attend these last minute rendezvous." Lady Salisbury dabs rose scent behind each ear. The musty scent of the carriage is making her eyes water.

"You certainly do know. When Prinny calls we must attend." Lord Salisbury taps the back of the carriage to signal departure.

"Yes, but why do I always need to be present? Can you not inform me of the details? You know I have guests and Victoria to attend to." She replaces the scent bottle in her reticule.

"Yes, well, I've wanted to speak with you about that."

"About what?"

"I don't believe I like the way Victoria's head turns of late."

"What do you mean?"

"You know exactly my meaning."

"I prefer her interests lie toward someone less active in the service of the King."

"You mean you don't want to lose another operative."

"Of course, that's what I mean. Raby is an important agent and I don't want our daughter hurt in any way."

"And you think to retire him, should there be an attachment?"

"There will be no attachment because I cannot afford to retire him." He turns his head to peer out in the darkness crawling by.

"My love, I fear you're going to break our daughter's heart."

"It cannot be helped." Lord Salisbury looks at her again.

"Can he not be used in less dangerous situations?" Certainly her husband will make an exception for their daughter.

"Cathy, I know how important it is that she marry well, but do you think a baron is the best she can do?" He takes her hand in his, removes her glove one finger at a time. "And, not only that, do you want to risk her learning the truth of our work for the Crown?"

"Surely that is not the reason for your apprehension." Drat the man.

"What? That our daughter might learn of our covert operations these past years?" He kisses the tips of each finger.

"Well, is it?"

"Of course. And she can do better than a baron."

"Flumakin." Lady Sailsbury pulls her hand away and replaces her glove.

"What was that?"

"I said 'Flumakin'!"

"Wherever did you hear such a word?" His laughter booms through the carriage.

"Where I hear all my words, of course." Her hands are now properly clasped in her lap.

"My dear." He coughs. "I'm quite sure that is not a word."

"It most definitely is. You heard me say it, did you not?"

"Yes, but..."

"But nothing. I said 'flumakin.' I mean flumakin. I'm sure Prinny will agree it's a word."

"Prinny will agree to most anything you suggest to him as long as it doesn't involve the security of England. Even then there are times I believe he would only listen to you should you present him with the solution."

"Are you jealous, my lord?" She leans close to speak the words soft in his ears.

"What? Of the Prince of England? Why would I be jealous of him?" Lord Salisbury wraps his arm across her front and places his hand on her hip. She squeals. He whispers in her opposite ear. "Let's go and find out, shall we?"

The carriage stops outside.

"Yes, let's find out what's so outrageously important we need to be summoned at such an inconvenient hour."

"Outrageously important?" The spread of her husband's grin reaches to his ears.

"Yes, well." She swallows and sparkles. "You know how you fluster me, I declare."

The carriage door swings open. Lord Salisbury steps down first and then helps her out. Once inside the Prince's residence they are directed to the sitting room most favored by the Prince. Lord Salisbury bows. Lady Salisbury curtsies. The Prince nods and motions them to be seated on the gold-trimmed couch in front of him.

"We appreciate you coming on such short notice, but you will understand it could not be helped." The Prince snaps his fingers and a refreshment tray is rolled between them.

"Of course, Your Highness. We are at your service, as always." Lord Salisbury flips his tailcoat, sits at the edge of the chair, and leans one elbow on his knee.

"Please enjoy some of the best whisky in England." He motions the servant to pour. "And Lady Salisbury, what can we offer you? A glass of wine perhaps?"

"No, Your Highness. A glass of water will be fine, if you please." A further wave of His Royal Highness's ring-infested hand and the servant pours a glass of water and offers it to Lady Salisbury. One more circle of his hand and the servant leaves them alone.

"Now, the reason we called for you." The Prince leans to the side to open a drawer in the side table next to where he is sitting. He pulls out a document and hands it to Lord Salisbury. "Take a look at this and tell me what you think."

Lord Salisbury takes the document and puts on his Martin's Margins spectacles to review the paper. Lady Salisbury leans close to read over his shoulder. The pop from the fireplace breaks the silence. "It reads to be a standard business contract. I don't see anything amiss with it. You have had it reviewed by the solicitors?"

"Not yet. What if I told you this document is being executed between multiple Lords of Parliament and a certain Sir Andrew Watson?"

"Sir Andrew Watson? I know of him. I'm not sure I know much more than he leases an estate called Wentworth Abbey."

"Is that all? You are sure?"

"He made some such proposal about a new venture he is planning to Lord Warwick. Warwick's the one who mentioned it to me although he didn't go into much detail. I suspect Warwick may have been treading lightly to test the waters. Raby and I were both there, in fact."

"If I may interrupt for just a moment." Lady Salisbury places her empty glass on the tray in front of her, "I'm not sure why this is a matter of security for the Crown?"

"Yes, I would like a little clarity as well." Lord Salisbury removes his spectacles.

Prinny sits back deeper in his chair. He looks from one to the other. "It may not be. This is why we want you to investigate and see what you come up with."

"May I ask, what could be the possible security risks from this business transaction?"

"My dear lady, we have been informed many of these contracts have been executed in and around Wentworth Abbey. We believe that suspicious."

"Indeed." Lord Salisbury repositions his spectacles once more.

"Yes, as you can see from the contract, Salisbury, there intimates a certain amount of control over a large portion of the land...over a large portion of England!"

Lord Salisbury flips the document to the last page. "This document is unsigned."

Lady Salisbury removes the document from her husband's hands. "How do we know it is legitimate?"

"It was provided to us by an informant of the Crown. We are told it will be signed soon. We wish it not be so. These are lords of Parliament. We wish to ensure the government continues to be influenced in a way that is best for England."

"I see."

Lady Salisbury places the document on the table. "Simply put, you fear this may allow this group to have too much authority in Parliament."

"Precisely, madam."

"Flumakin."

Lord Salisbury stares at her with wide eyes and pursed lips. Wonderful. The trip back will be more entertaining than the trip here.

"You always have such a way with words, madam. We so enjoy having you join us for these meetings."

"And, we would not have it any other way, your highness." Giddy crackles trickle through Lord Salisbury's voice. He presses his hand to her thigh. She presses him back with her elbow.

"Ah! The second item we wish to discuss."

"Yes. We're listening."

"Of course you are!" He flails his arm in a circle above his head. "Have you heard of this group lately formed who go about observing clouds and storms and documenting such findings?"

"Yes! As a matter of fact, one of the members is staying with us at Harlaxton." Lord Salisbury's voice is steady now.

"Excellent news! We would like you to put a man with this group. We think it a worthwhile endeavor."

"Really, Your Highness? Cloud observations?" The prince's head turns in Lady Salisbury's direction. No smile.

"Absolutely, my lady. We are very interested to see if they can actually learn to predict the weather."

"Predict the weather?" What a silly notion.

The prince continues. Can he tell she thinks it silly? "Yes. It behooves us to support a worthy cause if it actually can be done. There are great benefits to avoiding major storms on the high seas. The catastrophe of 1756 may have been lessened greatly if we but knew what was coming."

"Imagine the shipwrecks that can be avoided, my dear." Salisbury has that tip in his voice again. How is she to know the prince is serious? Surely, he will get over it. He always does.

Lord Salisbury continues. "I have just the person." No. He's going to assign Raby. There must be a way to change his mind. Surely, there is someone else.

The prince's eyes widen. "Oh? Do we know him?"

"I've used him before..." She cups her hand around his elbow to interrupt.

"My lord, why not review the profile first before making a final decision?" Will he listen?

"My dear, I'm quite sure Lord Raby will be a perfect fit for this mission." He places his hand to cover hers and pats.

"As you wish, of course." She slumps half back.

"Good. That's settled. We'll let you get back to your day's events." The Prince stands. They rise and take their leave. They reach the hall entrance and Lady Salisbury whispers, "Does he even realize he summoned us at midnight?"

"Not likely. He did appear to be out of sorts." They enter the carriage waiting for them outside the palace.

"Don't you mean 'they'?" She covers her mouth to hide the giggle bubbling up.

"No. I mean 'He.' You know I am not one for the Royal 'We.'"

"Yes, I know. But, you also didn't believe 'flumakin' was a word."

"And I repeat. Out of sorts." As soon as the doors are closed and the carriage moves forward, he wraps both arms around his wife. She does the same.

"Oh, flumakin."

CHAPTER ELEVEN

Wentworth Abbey – Spring, 1798

Sir Andrew Watson's next move plagues his mind. The towers of Wentworth Abbey appear before him. Years of carefully planned stratagems are being deployed. England needs reform and everyone is in agreement, but no one dares initiate such maneuvers for fear of sedition. It has not been many years since the Jacobite Rebellion and many are still uneasy about any talk of change. Hmpf!

Watson alights from his carriage. Another carriage is parked at the stables. He enters the vestibule of Wentworth Abbey. Sir Lewis Rockingham greets him with a half empty bottle of whisky and flask in hand.

"Sir Andrew! I only just arrived. I hope you don't mind I ordered refreshments as I knew it would not be long before you came."

"Indeed, and should I have been detained, they would not have gone to waste I am sure."

"Uh, quite sure."

Settled at last in the study, Watson pours his own flask filled with the finest Scotch whisky available. Watson wastes no time getting to the point. "So, Rockingham, what news have we?"

"All is proceeding as planned. Assets are being liquidated as we speak due to the speculations on the part of our 'investors.' Speculations that we will maintain did not go as originally anticipated."

"Good. Glad to hear it. I, too, am proceeding with my plans to align the estates surrounding Wentworth Hall and there will be no alternatives. With the majority of lords aligned, we will have control of this part of England and the changes we propose will have certain success. We will be able to influence those we need to in order to procure change."

"Change?"

"Yes, change! Rockingham! We need to protect our land. It is times like these that try men's souls don't you know. Change is needed if England is to survive!" He takes a swig of his whisky. Rockingham does the same.

"Hell, change is needed if the very monarchy is to survive!" He takes another swig. Rockingham does the same.

"We are moving forward to a new century. A new monarchy." Watson finishes it off and pours another.

"Are you not informed? Are you not concerned about the possibilities of war with France? Are you not worried about Napoleon and all of his conquests, that he might bring war here?"

Watson stares. Half-slit eyeballs stare back. Yet, another glass is poured for him. The bottle is finished off. "Yes, yes. I do stay informed, but don't you think with the right diplomacy war can be avoided?"

"Precisely!" Watson stammers. He lifts his glass in the direction of Rockingham. They down their drinks and Watson walks to procure another bottle, offers a glass to Rockingham who accepts graciously. "That is why we need *parliamentary reform* and our alliance will get us just that. I am not talking about ending the existing political system. But, of course, if war is necessary to procure our advantage, then so be it. We must protect our assets, we must protect our wealth."

"I see. You mean to support a democracy?"

"No, no. Parliamentary reform! Demme! Aren't you listening?"

"I assure you I am, although you sound much like that Englishman who authored all those pamphlets a few years back, The American Crisis, don't you know."

"No, no. You mean that Thomas Paine fellow?"

"I don't know what his name was, but I remember reading something that sounded like what you're talking about. All souls being tried and all."

"Not in the least." Watson sits back in his armchair propping his feet up on the ottoman. "Although I hear he's in France at the moment stirring up who knows what over there with the French Revolution. I daresay I should not like to follow his philosophies for he would have us all living as paupers in service to the farm hands."

"Who, sir?"

"Thomas Paine! I swear you must be going deaf! Who do you think I'm talking about?"

"I don't quite know. I thought we were talking about reform. A new monarchy and such."

"Yes, right! Wait. A new monarchy? No, no. Don't be absurd. Although, if it is necessary, maybe." Watson pauses, scratches his chin, then bursts out, "This alliance, what should we call it?"

"Call it? Sounds to me like this alliance is in support of the Whigs?"

"Whigs? Maybe some of their ideals, possibly. The strength of England definitely depends on its wealth. I intend to do more than remove taxes on foreign exports. Let's see." Watson stares at the wall. "We need a name like those fellows, Society for Constitutional Information."

"I believe there already was a Society for Constitutional Information."

"Will you listen man!" Watson slams his hand on the armrest. "I am saying I want to call the alliance something! I'm not going to call it the Society for Constititional Formation—Demme!" Watson shakes his head and swirls his glass in his hand. "One cannot even pronounce such a monogram. I was only giving you an example of what I *want* to do."

He downs yet another glass and Rockingham clears his throat. "Right. You let me know once you come up with it."

"I shall." Watson removes the contents of one more glass, and Watson sinks lower into his chair. Rockingham does the same.

Moments pass. Thick silence hangs in the air. Watson announces clear, loud, and sudden. "Wentworth Hall will be merged with Wentworth Abbey as it should be and I will bestow upon you a most comfortable living for the rest of your days as we have agreed."

"Yes! At last." Rockingham sputters left over liquid from his mouth. "And have you decided on a name for this alliance?"

"What? —No, not yet. I will need to put more thought into it." Watson's fingers strum, strum, strum.

Rockingham stands. "I do believe it is time for me to take my leave. Before deciding to stop by, I was on my way to Bath on business."

"Bath? To take in a season I presume?" Watson inspects the tips of his nails.

"No, I assure you I have no designs on that account." Rockingham side-steps his way toward the door.

"I would suggest you begin designs on that account. Once Wentworth Hall is enjoined with the Abbey your living will more than compensate you for your efforts on my behalf. You'll need to ensure your legacy continues to grow. Elsewhere."

"Right, one step at a time." Hamilton walks in to hand Rockingham his hat and walking stick. "There's plenty of time for that." Rockingham places his hat on his head. "When do you need me to check back with you?"

"I'll send word." The man turns to leave. "And, Rockingham, there may not be as much time as you believe. We think we have plenty of time and before you know it..." Watson's long fingers snap once. *Click!* "...time has run out. Remember that."

Rockingham hangs his walking stick on his forearm. He whirls around and continues his side-step out the door while attempting to straighten his hat.

"Stupid man."

CHAPTER TWELVE

Bath, England – Spring, 1798

Breakfast at the Salisbury townhouse is not uneventful this morning. The guests and the family all gather for breakfast at the same time in the morning room. Coincidence? Maybe. Conversation abounds.

"Mama, I should like to hold a masquerade ball. What do you think? Would it not be a perfect diversion? It has been an age since we have held any such event and you know how society loves a mask."

"My dear, I think that to be a splendid idea! I quite like the sound of it."

Lady Salisbury proffers the idea to the marquess at the head of the table. "What say you, my love? A sterling prospect, is it not? It will be a crush I am sure."

He looks at his wife. He looks at his daughter. He looks around the table. All are waiting for him to respond. He looks, again, to his wife. "My dear, I prefer to leave the details of such entertainments to the ladies. If you wish such a ball to take place, then by all means you may make such arrangements. You know, of course, you will not be able to hide from me for I am always able to seek you out."

"Be assured I will figure it out and when I do..." Lady Salisbury stands up and walks over to the marquess and whispers something in his ear. She then proceeds to the sideboard to fill her plate, comes back, and sits down to continue with her breakfast. The marquess does the same.

Lord Warwick does not say anything during the entire discussion. His attention lies with the food piled on his plate. He finishes his last piece of bacon before directing his attention to Lady Warwick. "You know, my dear, since we are already planning a ball at Toddington Peaks, why not make it a masquerade ball? Eh, Victoria? Would you mind so, if we were to steal this ball idea of yours and take it to Toddington Peaks?"

Lady Warwick looks at him, eyes round in shock. "Of course, my dear, I do think I should like a masquerade ball. Only if there are no objections by our hosts."

Lady Salisbury stops her attempts at slicing the bacon on her plate. "Bella, of course, we have no objections." She picks up the bacon between her forefinger and thumb and pops it in her mouth.

Lady Warwick's eyes brighten. "Alexander, what say you to such an event? I've no doubt your bride-to-be will have no objection. Ladies so love a masquerade." Lady Warwick nods at Lady Salisbury across the table. Her closed-mouth smile spreads across her face. "Even married ladies still enjoy the wiles of a masquerade ball." Lady Warwick returns her attention to Alexander. "The two of you could plan to wear something to complement each other and create an intrigue— how romantic it could be..."

He rolls his eyes. "Mother, need I remind you..."

Victoria squeals before interrupting. "You know there is a traveling circus in town that could be asked to come and entertain the guests."

Lady Warwick is in complete agreement. "Oh, yes! And, a balloon ascension. There must be a balloon ascension."

"Dearest Cathy, are you sure you don't mind if we commandeer the mask and have it at Toddington Peaks?"

"Of course not! We've been friends far too long to stand on conventions. We're family. I should love a trip to your home for it has been ages! It would give me time to plot my strategy and finally level a win in my favor." Lady Salisbury nods toward the marquess.

The marquess lifts his glass to his lady. "Let the games begin!"

Plans for the event continue amidst Alexander's failed attempts to interject. He finally stands. He turns to his mother. "If you will excuse me, I am in need for exercise after such talk of entertainments and a wonderful breakfast. I shall leave the details for such a remarkable event in your most capable hands."

"Alexander, dear, there are no clouds on a day such as this seems to be." He ignores her attempts to get him to stay. He kisses her on the cheek and proceeds out to the gardens.

Victoria and Lord Raby join him not long after. He is about to venture into the knot gardens. He has not had occasion to see either of them much since arriving in Bath.

"Do you mind, dear Alexander, if we join you?"

"By all means. I enjoy a brisk walk now and again and company will add to the diversion."

"Splendid, and what better entertainment for a lady then to be escorted by not one, but two eligible bachelors of her acquaintance— at least for the present," Victoria purrs. She positions herself between them linking her arm with each.

"So, Victoria. How long have you known Lady Ariana?" Alexander had intended to be more discreet. No matter. Victoria doesn't appear to have put too much thought into his blunt request.

"I have known her my entire life. We played together growing up. We got into such mischief." Clearly she has fond memories.

"Oh? Pray tell what mischief could two young ladies possibly get into that rivals that of two rambunctious boys?" Nothing compared to his adventures with Edmund. A smile pastes across his face. Innocent, loud, and boisterous. Gone too fast.

"You must not compare young ladies' romps with those of young boys! You and Edmund were the most raucous of them all. We were more into the intrigue. Why, I recall, Aria and I were the most determined ghost hunters of Harlaxton House." Bright, immediate pleasure splashes across Victoria's face as she begins to explain.

"Ghost hunters?" Alexander and Lord Raby respond in unison.

"You must go on. I must hear more of this!" Lord Raby smiles down at Victoria. He reaches over and touches his hand to hers. The attachment is clear. No doubt Raby will be speaking with Victoria's father, if he hasn't already.

"Yes, this does sound good." Alexander must learn as much as he can about his soon-to-be bride.

"Well, my two energetic friends, let me continue with my story." She giggles.

"Have you not heard of the infamous ghost of Harlaxton House?"

"No, really?"

"Yes, 'tis true. Aria and I have seen him on many occasions, in fact. He wears a black cape and hood which makes it difficult to see his face, but he is most definitely very gruesome and sad. Many say they believe him to be John of Gaunt. And have you not noticed the portraits around the house suddenly appearing upside down or mixed up?"

"John of Gaunt!" Alexander listens, intent on every word. "Where on earth did that come from, may I ask? And, the portraits? I'm sure the servants somehow manage to replace them incorrectly during cleanings or some such incident." He'll pay more attention the next time a portrait is out of place. It's a most intriguing story.

"Well," she lowers her voice, as an infamous secret is about to be revealed. "You know our Harlaxton House is the second great house built. The first Harlaxton was built on a different site in the fourteenth century and was used as a hunting lodge, among other things." A small glint dances in her eye. "By John of Gaunt. And by 1475 it was deserted and then the house you now know as Harlaxton House was built."

"So, tell us, then, how you came to believe the ghost is John of Gaunt?"

"That's easy. The hunting lodge was where he and the greatest love of his life shared their er—interludes." Victoria's cheeks flush pink. This is the Victoria of his youth. Always caught up in the story until it's too late to digress. Both men wait while she catches her breath and end her tale in one last dramatic breath. "Since it was torn down and replaced by our Harlaxton House he is doomed to roam the halls of eternity pining to be with his greatest love."

"I say, Victoria, young ladies have the wildest of imaginations!" If Raby caught on to her discomfort, he hides it well.

"Dear me." Victoria presses her hand to her chest. "It was either that or the boring story that he was angry because of the rumors he was actually the son of a Ghent butcher. Aria and I decided we much preferred the story of a lost love."

"As do I, my dear." Lord Raby pats her hand. The glances being exchanged between Lord Raby and Victoria leave no doubt as to their feelings. Any ideas he may have had about rekindling something between them is no longer an option. Alexander decides to give them some privacy. Raby is a gentleman. He'll not take advantage.

"As much as I have enjoyed our conversation, my lady, I fear I must depart your company for a pressing matter in the city. I shall leave you in the capable hands of our Lord Raby who I'm sure will be most obliged to protect you from the ghost of John of Gaunt!"

"But I have only just begun with the stories of our meetings with him." Alexander smiles, kisses her hand, and turns to leave.

"Very well, if you must." Victoria wastes no time turning her attention back to Lord Raby.

Alexander is not blind to the very obvious affection on their faces. He cannot help but compare it to his own predicament and the circumstances of his "arrangement." How is he going to bring things about?

He walks to the gate where he meanders toward Abby Church yard. Lord Raby catches up to him and asks to join him on his trip to the baths.

"If you prefer the company of the baths as opposed to that of the lovely Lady Victoria, I welcome the company. How is it that you could leave her so soon?"

"I must be mindful of what is proper, you know."

A short time later they both find the baths are warm and inviting.

"Ah, one can think quite clearly while relaxing in water such as this."

"Quite, clearly, indeed." Alexander begins to close his eyes as the words are mumbled between his lips. He mentally removes himself from his current quagmire. Only for a minute. Lord Raby is interested in conversation.

The latest news down at the track keeps them occupied until the conversation comes to what most likely is the intended subject— Victoria. Lord Raby's eyes light up whenever he speaks of her.

"So, have you spoken to the marquess about paying your addresses?"

Raby hesitates. "I have not."

"If you love her, what's the hold up?"

"I do find myself increasingly fond of her and would be the happiest of men were she to accept an offer of marriage. I've not found the courage to approach the marquess. What if he does not see the financial benefit? I've never had difficulty in this arena. What I mean to say is, I've never felt such apprehension about approaching someone. What if he considers a baron too low for his daughter?"

"I own I have not had occasion to experience apprehension in this way. Truth be told, I have never met a lady I cared enough about to want to speak with her father. Now, as it is, I may never have to address that issue since arrangements have already been made."

"On the one hand, I envy your situation. I should much rather have it arranged for me. Although, of course, I should like to be in agreement as to the lady."

"Well, there you have it. Make up your mind you are going to approach him and think of nothing except for your lovely lady. From there you will find the courage to make it through." Alexander closes his eyes again. Maybe Raby will catch on. Truth be told, Alexander shares the same doubt on whether the marquess will accept a baron's offer. Lady Salisbury, on the other hand, will have no qualms to such an arrangement, especially when she knows her daughter's feelings on the subject. No doubt she'll communicate her inclinations in that regard to her husband. A relaxing, quiet snooze in the baths is not happening today. Lord Raby is intent on further discussions relative to his weather predictions. At least it bodes for more engaging conversation.

CHAPTER THIRTEEN

Bath, England – Spring, 1798

The circus performers are camped out in between performances as he approaches the field on the outskirts of Bath. His thoughts linger on Ariana and how he is going to come clean about his own deceptions. Ariana's reactions at the circus endeared her even more to him.

This is going to get complicated. How can he avoid the embarrassment? What if she finds out from someone else? How is he going to tell her after he agreed to help her scandalize her fiancé? A small diversion is about to culminate into something he fears. Regret. Ariana must have felt something during their *practice* session. Her response to him was pleasant and surprising. He must tell her soon. Not until he returns from this quest into the world of sleuth.

He must find out about Wendell and where he comes from. He walks toward the horses' tent and scans the faces of passersby. Someone must have the same brilliant green eyes. Wendell must have a mother or father in the midst of circus people. He enters the tent and Wendell is there talking to an older gentleman. This man is not from the circus. He's dressed quite fashionably from the top of his head to the white-gemmed, silver, buckles of his black shoes. He's familiar. What's the connection?

Wendell sees him and motions for him to come over where they stand. The older gentleman turns to look and moves to the side to allow him to join them.

"Hey, there, ain't you the gent wot was with the lady yesterday? You come to see me fall on me arse agin?" Wendell's wide-toothed smile ripples his cheeks.

He stares at the older gentleman who kicks at the ground with one shoe and then knocks his cane against the other. Wendell puts his hands in his pockets and looks at one and then the other. "This is me 'doptive uncle. Sir Lewis Rockingham. He's a banker who takes me money and 'vests it. I make money on me money so he says." That must be why he looks familiar. He's a banker. "Say, maybe he could 'vest yer money...Sir..."

Wendell turns around, "Sorry, Sir, I don't recall as I know yer name for proper 'troductions."

He can't help but smile. Wendell's attempt at a formal introduction amuses him. He turns to Rockingham to introduce himself. "Alexander Barrington, how do you do sir." Alexander bows. Rockingham does not pursue more conversation other than the usual niceties. In fact, he leaves immediately. Wendell, on the other hand continues his conversation in the same easy way. How did this young boy come to be in the circus? There must be more to his story.

"Watch this." Wendell begins a comedic imitation of the clown practicing in a nearby ring. The clown does not share in the amusement. It also doesn't help that Alexander is laughing more at Wendell than at the clown who is now chasing him around the ring with a bucket of water. The clown trips. The water does not reach its intended target, but rather the opposite. Wendell comes running back heaving air and laughing. He bends over and places his hands on his knees. "So, you wanna see me do me 'orse tricks?"

This is an opportunity. Alexander can learn more about Rockingham and the investments Wendell referred to. Wendell is spectacular. He must have trained from a very young age to be able to do all the things he can do on the back of a horse. In between the sets, Alexander asks him about his 'vestments.'

"See it goes like this, Uncle Lewis ain't really me uncle. He 'dopted me, see."

"Do you know from whom?"

"I can't say as I do. Uncle Lewis says 'twas some gent whose loved his lady very much but couldn't marry her, I come along and can't ladies of quality have kids and not be married— so Uncle Lewis takes me and gives me to me mama to raise— me 'doptive mama see. Uncle Lewis, he's good with money and he takes me money, from me and me mama, and 'vests it in his bank. He says in a few years I can go to one of them fancy boys' schools."

Alexander listens. He talks about his 'doptive uncle' and his 'doptive mama' and others. The more he learns, the more he believes his suspicions to be right. He needs to check one thing before leaving. Does Wendell have the same dimple over his left shoulder?

The ring master comes into the tent holding Wendell's costume for the show. Perfect. Wendell stands up and jogs over to grab it out of his hand.

"Thanks, sir, I best be gettin' ready now."

This is the opportunity Alexander wants.

"Wendell, can I see you do more of those horse tricks now in your costume before you go?"

Even Wendell's smile resembles hers. His teeth are straight despite where he lives. Wendell goes behind the curtain. In minutes he is riding out on his horse. He circles the ring in preparation. In seconds he jumps, rolls, and lands flat footed on the back of his black mare with ease and grace. He dismounts and comes over to Alexander to bid him farewell. Wendell turns his back to hold the reins of his horse— there it is.

Alexander is not surprised. He expected it. The clues are there. Wendell's eyes. His "uncle" with the investments. The explanation of where he came from. The dimple. There's still more he must discover. How does Wendell fit into the family of Stratford and who is Sir Lewis Rockingham?

ALEXANDER ARRIVES AT Ariana's townhouse at The Royal Crescent. He must speak privately with her. How will he start? It's best to come right to the point, but this is different. Will she be angry with him? Not want to see him again? They've taken such pains at creating their scandal. How will she react?

He knocks on the door. Hawthorne opens. "If you would be so good as to inform Lady Ariana that a visitor requests the favor of her company this afternoon. My card." Alexander hands the butler his hand-written card and walking stick.

"If you will wait here for a moment sir, I will see if Lady Ariana's at home."

A few moments pass before Hawthorne returns. "If you will follow me, sir."

Ariana accepts his call in the parlor.

"Laird Raby! How delighted I am ye've come!"

She is adorable this afternoon. Absolutely divine with her familiar out-of-place wisps of hair. They frame her face. The sparks from the fire flicker in her green eyes. He longs to pull her to him once again and kiss her silly. He holds himself back on this account. He envisions her speaking his name against his skin. His name. Not the blasted name he introduced himself as. Silent curses invade his thoughts. What has he done? He must now find a way to tell her he is not who he said he was. That they are actually betrothed. How will explain he introduced himself to her as Raby? Stupid!

Alexander doesn't have a good explanation. A foul mood during his observations of the storm formations over the parklands of Wentworth Hall? Hardly satisfactory. Frustration over the marriage arrangement? Also not good enough. At the time, he simply wanted to walk. An intense storm brewing always served to sort out any nerves or anxiety. Storms always put life in perspective. Put life in place. Not even the Regent himself nor any of his armies can stand against the slightest of whirlwinds. It's what moves him to march on. To march on in his quest to know them. To understand them. Be one with them. This overpowering quest for knowledge blinds him to time and distance in the pursuit of excitement, the adventure. All he wanted was distraction. Once he learned who she was? It was perfect. The perfect opportunity to learn about this woman. To know her. Is she a woman he can be happy with, fall in love with? Storms do not frighten her. It didn't occur to him what he would do if he did fall in love with her. This whirlwind of a woman. Can she love him knowing he deceived her?

"Please sit down, while I call for refreshments." Alexander can't stop the racing drub-drub of his heartbeat.

"What?"

"Please sit down?"

"Oh, yes, right, thank you. Apologies. I don't know what I was about just then. Must have been the walk."

"Ye had a bit of a walk, did ye?"

Alexander takes a seat across from her in front of the fire. The racing slows but the drub sounds loud in his head.

"Yes, I was, um, out over at the baths for a bit then took care of some other things, rather boring actually. You?"

"Nothing spectacular yet today."

Flames mesmerize with their dance of different colors and shapes swishing around the sparks making their way up the chimney.

Hawthorne brings the refreshments. "Do you have anything stronger? Whisky perhaps?" Hawthorne pours a whisky and hands it to Alexander.

He serves tea to Ariana. "Thank you, Hawthorne." Ariana turns to Alexander. "I must say, ye donna seem to be your usual self this evening. Ye must have a lot on yer mind. Are ye having second thoughts about our arrangement?" She sips her tea.

"Arrangement?" Alexander chokes. Whisky spews into the fire, producing an instant blue flame. Spots on his newly starched cravat will not be appreciated by his valet. Amber liquid drips down on top of his dark gray breeches.

"Are ye alright?" Ariana hands him a napkin from the tray and attempts to help him with clumsy hands to dry his clothes. Lavender scented hair teases his senses in the process. She brushes at his cravat. It nearly sends him climbing the walls. Next, she wipes his waistcoat. She doesn't stop there. Immediately, he stands and walks to the fire.

"That is quite enough." His voice is husky and short. "I shall stand for a moment in front of the fire and all will be dry in no time. I'm a bit distracted today." He recalls the reason for his discomposure and repeats her words. "Arrangement you say?"

"Yes, the *event* we're planning? What arrangement did ye think I meant?"

"Yes, yes, of course. And no, I am not having second thoughts. I must say I'm looking forward to the adventure!"

Alexander settles, once again, in his chair by the fire, glass refilled with whisky, and the blasted silence. Arrangement, indeed. He downs the glass in one gulp.

Calming flames of the fire swell up again. Ariana speaks first. "Ye know, I must divulge today has been most quiet. Papa has been about town doing what he does and I have done what ladies do to keep busy learning to be accomplished." Her green eyes sparkle over the top of her teacup as she sips.

"And what accomplishments have you worked on today, may I ask?"

"I practiced a bit of pianoforte. I find it a most agreeable pastime."

"*Practice* you say?" He cannot help but tease her. He really should not. He must focus on telling her the truth. But, here she is again. As if she wants him to practice with her again. Does she?

"Yes, *practice.* I find that practice is the key to success when working on one's accomplishments." She does.

"Indeed!"

Heavy footfalls echo in the hall. "Hello, Papa!" Her cheeks flash pink.

"Ariana, Lord Raby."

"How are you this evening Sir?"

"Very good. Very good. There are a few things I would like to discuss with you, if you don't mind. May I see you in my study?"

"Of course."

Today's lesson, postponed.

LORD STRATFORD TAKES a seat behind his mahogany desk.

"Sit down, my boy." He motions to the seat across from him.

Lord Stratford delivers his message terse and to the point. "I feel I must tell you that although I have great respect for you, your prospects here are not to be fruitful."

"Prospects? Sir?"

Lord Stratford clears his throat and continues less terse, still pointed. "Yes, prospects. You see, Ariana is betrothed and is to be married very soon."

Alexander sits silent for a moment before answering. Good timing. "Yes, sir, I am aware of the arrangement. I have some information I don't quite know how to impart."

"Well, out with it. Whatever it is will be better served once you've told it I always say." Lord Stratford sits patiently as Alexander proceeds to explain some details surrounding his arranged marriage, the frustration of that morning in the meadow ending with, "You see, sir, *I* am Alexander. Lord Warwick is my father."

Lord Stratford's eyes bore holes if boring holes were possible. He's probably imagining how best to slay him. A roar of laughter as infectious as his daughter's, minus the snort, erupts from the man sitting across from him while tears of revelry are wiped from Lord Stratford's eyes. Not what Alexander expects.

After starting and stopping again, Lord Stratford reveals his satisfied smile. "I must say I have not been this diverted this age." Alexander certainly did not expect his future father-in-law to find any amusement at all. "Here I am gently coaxing that mulish daughter of mine to Toddington Peaks to meet her intended, which she refuses to do I might add, when here you are helping her to get him to beg off."

"It does sound rather cheerful when you put it that way." Alexander cannot avoid joining his future in-law in another round of merriment. The seriousness of the situation calls them back to the issue. "I am not sure what to do right now. I wish to tell her the truth. I came here today for that very reason. I could not bring myself to the point."

Lord Stratford, still buzzing with hilarity sits back with one hand tucked in his coat pocket. "I think maybe we should let things be for now. Going to Toddington Peaks will be the best opportunity. It will be more difficult for her to remain angry in the midst of your relations. She may be upset for a time, but I called you in here because I know my daughter. She has a marked affection towards you. She'll come around after it all sets in. She may even grow to enjoy the event as we have."

Relief. He'll have time to work things out further. "I'm very glad to know at least you are no longer in the dark as to my intentions and as to who I am." Alexander rises to take his leave and cannot help but notice the portrait over the fireplace to his right.

Lord Stratford follows the line of his observation. "That is my late wife, Lady Arabella. I cannot bear to take a house where I do not have her lovely face look upon me."

"She's a great beauty, indeed. I'm quite enamored with the unique color of green bestowed upon her eyes. Might I ask if they truly were so or is that an artist's rendition?"

Stratford sighs and stays focused on the portrait. "Yes, those were the eyes I adored. That is as close to the brilliant color as could be possible. There is no injustice done to them by this artist. I was bewitched by them. I've known no other with eyes of that color in my lifetime although they are common to the Rutledge clan, I'm told."

"Is that so?"

"Ariana has inherited them too."

"The Rutledge clan out of Scotland?"

"Yes! No doubt you've noticed Ariana's Scottish timbre rise in intensity now and again. She gets that from her mother too. Thicker when she's roiled. I'd bet those eyes are what turned your head in her direction, eh, my boy?"

"One of her many fine qualities. They are remarkable. I, too, have never seen such as those in my life." One young circus performer continues to patch out thoughts in Alexander's brain. This piece of information is not to be told. Yet.

CHAPTER FOURTEEN

Bath, England – Spring, 1798

Lord Stratford sits alone in his study after Alexander leaves, eyes fixed on the portrait of his lovely Arabella. He drums his fingers on the dark wood of his desk. He misses her. She would have loved the beautiful woman Ariana has become. Would she approve entirely of the tolerance he shows to her? Probably not, but he can do no better than he has done. He blows out a deep breath and walks to the liquor cabinet to pour himself a glass a sherry. He flings himself low into his leather arm chair in front of the portrait and takes a long slow drink.

The last moments with Arabella as she lay there upon their bed continue to plague his thoughts. Childbirth. Not a few women give their last breath for the miracle of a precious new life. Tears spill down his cheeks. Joy for the impending birth turned to great sorrow spar with one another searching for the final piercing blow.

Dear Ariana, so young. How can he explain all that happened? No, he did the best he could for her. Believing her mother was very sick and succumbed to her illness was best for her. Protecting her was most important. How else was he expected to deal with the grief? Losing his son, his heir, and his wife in one night? Stratford downs his drink and pours another. He'll need to retire early tonight.

He sits for a brief moment before going to find Ariana. Alexander's revelation raises his spirits a bit when he locates his daughter in the parlor.

"Did Laird Raby leave?"

"Yes, he had some matter to discuss with the marquess or some such thing." Lord Stratford manages to stammer his response into his drink while raising it to his lips. "Ariana, I've had word from Lord Warwick. He intends to have a masquerade ball at Toddington Peaks. I mean for you and me to go. It is high time you met the man you will marry."

Ariana's back straightens. "I told you, papa, I willnae attend. Ye have arranged this marriage and I see no need to go anywhere to meet that man until I walk down the aisle to the altar. The arrangement is done. Ye must allow me this last request."

"My dear daughter, you must see how disagreeable and unrefined this is."

"Why? It's the way many arranged marriages of future Kings and Queens were done. They came from afar and only met at the altar. How is this different?"

"Ariana you must be reasonable. Those were the dark ages. We are far from that time now. What you are asking for is simply not done."

"No. What simply is not done is fathers forcing their daughters to marry men they donna love or know or even men who are twice their age!"

"Ariana, Alexander is not twice your age. He is only twenty-eight. Quite acceptable. You are three and twenty. And, you know full well arranged marriages are perfectly acceptable in society. *Expected,* I might add." Stratford's heart beats down hard in his chest. He never wanted this for her no matter what society expects.

"It verra well makes no difference and that is not the point. I willnae go!"

Hawthorne enters the parlor and clears his throat.

"Yes, Hawthorne, what it is?"

"Lady Victoria to see Lady Ariana, sir."

"Send her in, I was just leaving." Lord Stratford turns his attention back to his daughter, "We will discuss this further when you have calmed down," then stands up and takes his leave.

"ARIA, I CAME TO TAKE you riding. Papa has secured two horses for us to ride whenever we want."

"Vicky, it sounds just the thing. But where? There is certainly no equivalent to Hyde Park in Bath."

"No. Papa stabled them outside of town in the country. I'm sure we'll find some open space to ride. It can't all be steep hillsides."

Ariana takes a deep breath. "Why not? Even if it must be sidesaddle. Let me go change into my riding habit. I'll be down directly." Her limbs will not move fast enough. What she would give to have Vanora and the comfort of her other "habit." Such nonsense to require women to ride a good mount on the side. So be it. She will make do.

Vicky paces at the bottom of the staircase.

"Really Aria, how long does it take to put on a habit? It's not as if we're being presented at court you know."

"It has been some time since I had occasion to wear one, I will grant ye that."

The smile on her friend's face squeaks out as Ariana descends the stairs. "Oops," she raises her hand to her lips. "I had forgotten your penchant for riding in men's breeches."

Ariana locks her arm in her friend's to lead her out the front door. "Ye should try it sometime. Ye'll never want to ride sidesaddle again, I promise."

"Mama would have me under lock and key for ages if she ever caught me. I can't imagine what papa would do."

"Ladies should know how to ride astride in case they ever need to. Ye never know when it may be necessary."

"Necessary? Really, Aria. When would it ever be necessary for a lady to know how to ride astride?" The stable hand holding their mounts coughs. One is black and one is grey.

The horses stand ready as they are each assisted up. Ariana's experience with horseflesh at Wentworth Hall moves her to prefer the black. "This one is beautiful. What is he called?" She takes the reins in her hands and the horse begins to prance in place.

"Red."

"I'm sorry, did ye say Red?"

"Yes, ma'am."

"A black horse called 'Red.'" Ariana circles the courtyard.

"I'm afraid so."

"Ye must tell me the story behind that."

"Must we hear it now, Aria?"

"Yes, Vicky. I must know. Ye know verra well how I love to know the history of the horses I ride. It helps to know your mount. Its history."

"How you do go on at times. You would think you sell horseflesh for a living."

Ariana ignores her friend and nods to the stable hand to continue with his story.

"Well, my lady, Red here used to be a race horse whose owner didn't want him named Blaze or some common name so he named him Red for the color of fire. People never took him seriously until they saw him race. I hear tell he won a fine purse in his racing days."

"See Vicky? Is that not an amazing story? Would ye ever have guessed it of Red? There now. How delightful! A black race horse named Red." Ariana strokes the horse's muscular neck. Red prances in the circle ready for a run.

Victoria sits bolt upright while the stable hand continues to hold her mount at a standstill. "Alright, tell me the name of mine."

"Gray."

Ariana stumbles over her words in sing-song syllables. "Tell me there is a story with that."

"Afraid not, my lady. Different owner. No story." The stable hand coughs again. He releases the reins to Vicky.

Vicky rolls her eyes. "It about sums up our lives, does it not, Aria? You will always be riding a black horse named Red in men's' breeches while I shall be riding a gray horse named Gray, sidesaddled for the rest of my life."

"Vicky, that willnae always be so. It is what ye make of it or even how ye look at it."

"Yes, but I will always be ordinary and you will always be having adventures."

"Do ye really want to be having my adventure right now?"

"Yes, well. There is that."

"And, what about all the adventure of living in a house with the infamous ghost of John of Gaunt? I have always thought of you as the adventuress."

"Yes, well. That's another story to be told."

"Maybe. I believe there are adventures right before ye if ye take hold of them. Ye just need to find them. Like the one rising just over that hill."

There. Cast in silver and green across the sky. Purple flashes of light stab at the expanse. Ariana knew it the moment they started out. The weight in the air. A storm.

"Aria, we should turn around. I want adventure, but..."

"I donna think so. Not yet. We still have time."

"I don't like the idea of being out in the open in the midst of that. Where will we go for shelter if we get caught?"

Vicky is right. Where will they go? Ariana surveys the area. There is not much around them. They walk the horses around the back and out into the fields behind the stables to find the wide open space of the country. It does appear they will have to turn back soon. The storm is coming.

"Just a bit more time, Vicky. Ye know how invigorating it is to ride in open space. Let's go around once through that field over there then I promise we'll go back."

"One time, Aria. That is all, or it's sure to overcome us and we'll become dowsed in rain."

"Ye said ye wanted an adventure!" Ariana nudges Red with the heel of her foot and the horse shoots to a canter. "Blasted sidesaddle!" She wants a gallop. Vicky's gray moves to her side. "How can a person truly enjoy the ride and the feel of a horse in such a position? It is not the same."

"Aria, I believe you have been in men's breeches too long."

"I willnae change it for anything."

Ariana allows Red the reins. He does not disappoint.

Vicky's Gray matches pace with Red. They trail a blaze across the field to the path Ariana pointed out earlier. The horses are familiar with the route and fall into line with the opening Ariana spied from afar. This is exactly what Ariana needs. To get away from the turmoil of what will soon be. The odd silence rises up, not even a bird sounds. The horses are agitated. The rain is close.

"Aria, we need to return."

"I know. We've been out too long. We might need to find a place to shelter instead."

"What? Out here? Where can we possibly find to shelter out here? I knew this would happen. I told you," Victoria scolds. She tightens her fists holding the reins and Gray shakes his head to loosen her grip.

"I dunno, maybe there's a cabin or a resting spot. This is a trail of a sort, ye know."

"There is no cabin, Aria. I knew this would happen. Now we're going to be drenched."

"Ye wanted adventure, didn't ye? Let's enjoy it. Come!" Ariana kicks Red with the force of one leg.

"Where are you going?"

"I'm racing across the field in the middle of the storm to let the wind whisk me away!" Ariana watches Victoria disappear in the distance as she rides further out across the open green.

"Not this time Ariana!" Victoria's response is barely audible.

Ariana circles back. "What? Were ye not just saying how ye wanted adventure?"

"I don't care, I'm going back to the house. I don't wish to catch my death on such an adventure." Victoria's voice echoes in the space between them. No matter. Ariana returns to her original course, eyes set forward on nothing but the beauty of the overcast sky swirling above her. Flashes outline the swirls. The movement of Red as he canters then gallops, the movement of sky as it flows, then billows. She is so tiny in this vast open field among such strength of wind above and power of beast below. There is no rain yet, but the air is heavy and it is near. It is a wonder, but she has no fear. She inhales deep, full breaths of the humid air. The fragrance of the wood and moss from the trees is intense. Red's forceful run changes to a dead halt. Ariana is flung forward to sit "side-bottom" on his withers. Red is pacing in place. His head bobs up and down. His whinny cries storm. She clasps her hands around his neck to adjust her seat.

"Ariana! What are you doing out here alone? A storm is coming!" Alexander and two other gentlemen emerge from the edge of the woods running toward her with cannons the size of shotguns. At least they look the shape of cannons. What on earth are they?

Still awkward and side long across the horse's withers Ariana explains. "Of, course I know. Why do ye think I'm here?"

"I should have known, although what you don't know is how dangerous such an event could be on horseback, in an open field."

"Yes, well, that was not intended. I had only meant a short excursion, but ye and yer men are the ones that frightened my mount. We were fine until only a moment ago."

"My men and I? I doubt we had anything to do with it. More like that." Alexander motions upward at the silver still flashing around them.

"My laird, would ye be so kind as to hold the reins while I dismount?"

"Yes, yes, of course."

"There. I cannot tell ye how absolutely impractical sidesaddle riding is for the female gender."

Alexander's eyes lift in support of his smile. "Impractical?"

"Yes." Ariana smooths out her riding habit. What a mess. She adjusts her hat. It rests too far forward on her forehead.

"How so?"

"Have ye ever ridden sidesaddle?"

"Uh, no, I can't say that I have." His smile still slathered across his face.

"Until ye have, let's just say ye will have to take my word for it."

"You don't make a habit of riding sidesaddle, is that what I'm to make of it?"

"No, I donna. I hate it." Ariana strokes Red's withers while she talks. "After today, I willnae be riding for I cannot continue to ride like this."

"Come now, it cannot be all that bad for. All ladies ride sidesaddle." Alexander holds his cannon-rifle across his chest so it rests on his forearm.

"I donna ride sidesaddle. And, will ye please stop smiling so? Are ye telling me ye have never known a lady to ride in men's breeches?" Ariana crosses her arms.

"Not that she has ever admitted to."

"That is sad. Now ye have. And, please I must ask ye *not* to share this event with my papa. He willnae be pleased. Can ye hold the beast still at least?"

Alexander pushes the cannon-rifle to his side so the leather strap is diagonal across his front. "What are you doing?"

"I must remove this saddle. I cannae ride the horse astride with this saddle on it."

"But, Lady Ariana..." Alexander lowers his voice and nods in the direction of the others. "...you will be seen."

"Donna worry. Can ye not handle it for me? Please?" Ariana takes Red's reins to guide him to a patch of grass.

"What do you expect me to do?"

"I dunno. Send your friends away or something. Or take them somewhere. What are ye even here for? What are those horrific things ye're holding anyway?"

"These?" He pulls the cannon-rifle to the front and lifts it in the air. "These are actually designed for an event such as this. We are here to observe this storm."

"To observe this storm?"

"Yes. You see, these barrels are filled with large balls of colored cloth. We'll shoot them toward the clouds to see how far the wind will carry them." The wind is blowing harder now. Red is agitated.

"Amazing. Have ye done this before?"

"Yes, and no. We tried it once before with colored parchment, but the paper was burned when we fired it. So, this time we are trying it with lightweight cloth."

"How brilliant! What colors are the cloths?"

"What colors are the cloths?" Alexander's brow wrinkles.

"Yes, I mean can ye see it in the sky when ye fire them? Will it be like fireworks or stars floating across the sky?"

Alexander laughs. "No, I do not believe it will appear so. I'm not even sure if we can get them up high enough. I cannot believe such things are of interest to you. Would you like to stay and watch since you're already here?"

"Yes! Verra much."

"Come, let's get back to where we need to be and wait and see if the storm will develop." Alexander takes the reins from her and together they walk Red over to where the other horses are tied to a log and sheltered by a grove of trees. Alexander introduces her to his companion.

"This is Luke Howard. He's a young man who I've been pleased to work with in London. We have similar interests in weather."

"Surely Lady Ariana is not interested in the weather?" Mr. Howard's young voice cracks between the words of his question.

"Pleased to make your acquaintance, Mr. Howard. And, I assure ye, I am verra much interested in what is going on here. I find it most intriguing. Might I ask how it is ye became interested?"

"I've always been interested in weather and predictions and fortunately I have friends with similar interests to help me along in these pursuits." Mr. Howard looks at Alexander and pulls out a pocket watch to check the time. He's a young man of focus. "We're going to have to wait and see if anything develops worth pursuing."

Mr. Howard's next response is directed at Ariana. "That is always the nature of these things, you know."

Alexander looks around for the others. Mr. Howard centers his attention to the oncoming storm. "The others went to the far side of the field. Another lady, on that side appeared to be in distress so they ran to her aid."

"Vicky! She must not have made it back."

"Victoria was out with you? Why didn't you tell me?"

"Ye didn't ask. Does it matter?"

"No, I guess it doesn't, although do you think she will go straight back or want to be brought to you?" Alexander's irritation is clear.

"I doubt she will come here. She was adamant about going back. She didn't want to be drenched in the storm."

"But, you of course, do not mind?"

"I've no qualms about getting wet in a downpour. I wouldn't do it on purpose, but I donna fear it like many of my gender."

"Yes, I'm learning there is much you differ on with regard to many of your gender."

Mr. Howard pivots from one to the other. "Do you think we can focus on the task at hand? I do believe we have a development."

Mr. Howard points to the sky. The clouds cast gray-silver across most of the vast expanse. There is a long, white, spindle weaving across the sky. Ariana never envisioned something like this before. "What is it?"

"I have only heard of this told by sailors. Luke, have you ever seen one?"

"I have observed one such development near the beaches at Brighton."

"What do you call it?"

"Some call them waterspouts, but not when they happen over land. We're quite far inland for one to happen here."

"Are you ready to shoot the cloths?"

"Yes. Let's go." Alexander stares pointedly at Ariana. "Stay. Here. We need to get farther out into the field. I don't want you out in the open where we are."

The two men creep out into the open field, cannon-rifle in hand. Ariana follows. Does he think she will miss it? Stay back and miss the beauty of this spectacle? Absolutely not. The spinning above her reminds her of a potter molding his clay only this is happening on a much larger scale in the sky above. More wind intensifies around them. Not too harsh. The tip of the spout reaches out across the sky and wants to touch the ground, but pulls up like a woman testing the water before a bath. She is beautiful, spinning her weave across the sky. Shots explode into the air in segments, not unlike the rhythmic chime of a clock, but louder. Mr. Howard and Alexander both drop to the ground. Ariana runs to help them stand up. Colored splotches of cloth fill the air high around them. Gliding, swirling, falling, and trailing gusts of wind in various patterns, but in one general direction.

"I told you to stay back." Alexander is not pleased although his voice is not harsh.

Ariana stares at the designs the launched colors are creating in the sky. "What happened?" The wind is much stronger now. It shoves her hard against him, hard against his chest. He wraps his arm around her waist. Her palms are pressed flat to his chest and he holds one to his heart. The beat of it pumps fast against her wrist. His blue eyes are soft and gentle. "Are you alright?"

She looks up at him. She doesn't move. "Yes, I'm fine, but what happened to ye?"

"The recoil from the gun knocked us down is all."

"Oh, is that all. And, ye call that a gun? It's more like a small cannon. Ye should call it something, like gannon for gun and cannon."

"My lady, you do come up with such nonsensical notions." He kisses her forehead. He kisses the arched space between her eyes. He kisses the tip of her nose. He kisses her lips.

Luke Howard yells, "Run!"

CHAPTER FIFTEEN

Bath, England – Spring, 1798

Ariana's continued refusal to meet her future husband culls the guilt residing in Lord Stratford's chest. What is he going to do? A visit to the baths is what he needs. Drinking the waters in the pump room along with a brisk stroll always serves to relieve stress, clear his head. A decision of this caliber needs hardy contemplation.

"So, what brings you to Bath, dear cousin?" No. Not today. Not Rockingham. Sir Lewis Rockingham is the last person he needs to keep company with during his walk about the pump room.

"Taking in the waters, of course!" Lord Stratford doesn't make eye contact. Not exactly the cut direct, but maybe he will leave.

"Yes, yes, of course." Neither gentleman speaks for a few moments. Maybe Rockingham will leave him alone.

"You know, William, the investments were slightly up recently although they still are not up enough to pull us about. My offer still stands, my friend."

Lord Stratford groans. No such luck. How can he get the man to leave him without insulting him? He's family. "No, no. I have no intention of losing Wentworth Hall. I know it has always been your hope to acquire it, but we have discussed this at length and I thought you were in agreement that past feuds of our ancestors hardly have a place between us. Your side of the family was entailed Wentworth Abbey and my side received

Wentworth Hall. I'm not inclined to be forced to lease Wentworth Hall as you were forced to lease Wentworth Abbey to that Watson fellow." Lord Stratford remains with his chin high, eyes closed while he sips the waters. Pretend concentration on the task at hand.

Rockinghams' voice splinters through the air of the pump room. "Quite so. I only meant to put your mind at ease, cousin. To render assistance, if you will."

"As it stands, you may as well know, Ariana is now betrothed and I expect a very handsome marriage settlement within the month. That will put Wentworth Hall back to rights and into the positive."

Rockingham purrs. "Delightful! A marriage settlement. Splendid. Just in time, you know, because although I have been able to use my influence to keep the duns away, it only goes so far."

True. Lord Stratford needs to rein in his frustration with the man. If it wasn't for Rockingham he probably would have lost Wentworth Hall years ago. He really should show more appreciation for his efforts. However, now is not that time. Too much to contemplate.

"So when is this happy event to be announced?" Rockingham gulps down the water in his glass and grabs another.

"It is my hope to have it become public at a masquerade ball to be held at Toddington Peaks." Lord Stratford stops walking to allow Rockingham a minute to catch his breath.

"Ah, yes, Warwick. I've handled some investments for him from time to time. She is to marry Alexander, I presume?"

"Yes, that's correct. You'll no doubt receive an invitation to the ball if you have not already. All titled members of the family are to be included no matter how distant the relation."

"Distant, indeed. Our fathers were second cousins, I believe."

"Yes, I do believe that is so." Lord Stratford returns to his stroll around the pump room. Much better to keep family ties intact. He continues to sip the water from his glass unaware of the frantic body he leaves lingering behind him.

BLASTED STRATFORD! Idiot! Rockingham clenches his fist and punches the air at his side. He finishes off the glass of water and throws it to the floor. Is he really so daft? Stratford can't be allowed to undo what he has taken years to accomplish and prepare for. Rockingham ignores the few who are startled by the crash of his broken glass. Strategies, investments, prospecting will not have been for nothing. He will see to it. His alliance with Watson requires it. He will have Wentworth Hall. He's next in line after Stratford. Rejoining Wentworth Hall with the Abbey after Watson's lease is up must happen. He most certainly will attend the mask.

CHAPTER SIXTEEN

Bath, England – Spring, 1798

Small hail pellets rake across their faces. Ariana presses her face to Alexander's chest to shield it from the onslaught. The cloths shot into the air are sprinkled across the field. Fail. Alexander will have to rethink their strategy of how to get them high enough into the air to be pulled into the vortex.

"Don't just stand there!" Luke yells. He runs past them with his jacket over his head shielding his face. "We have to get the horses and ourselves to shelter. If it touches down to the ground it can mean disaster. At least it is when they touch water. These pellets hurt. We have to find shelter somewhere."

Ariana stands stiff, watching it. Unafraid. Alexander tugs her elbow to follow him.

"Come. We must go."

"It's so tremendous to see."

"I know, but Luke is right. We need cover."

"Can we watch it from the woods?"

"We'll see. Come." Alexander grabs her hand and they hurry back in the direction of the woods where the horses stomp and whinny. The animals yank at the reins to release them from the log they are tied to. Ariana, Luke and Alexander crouch down. The wind blows hard above them. The trees sway. Leaves blow, limbs break and fall to the ground.

"I don't think it's safe here either. What do you think Luke?"

"You're probably right. Let's go. Let's loose the horses and move in the opposite direction of the funnel."

Red stomps and paces to get free. Ariana holds him firm and tries to talk to him to steady his demeanor. Luke is already mounted and circling.

"I'm thinking the best direction is back to town. It's about an hour back, but either we find shelter or end up somewhere closer to shelter and if this thing heads in that direction we can let people know it's coming."

"Do you think it will last that long?"

"I don't know, but we can't stay here. Look at it now."

The point of it reaches down like a crooked finger to the ground. The tops of the trees spin off like blades of grass being trimmed with a scythe. Alexander has heard sailors talk about waterspouts on the water, but he has never seen anything on land like this. This is what he is on the lookout for. And here it is.

"We need to move. Now. Ariana, let me help you up." What is wrong with her? "Ariana!" Her face is frozen to the picture before her. He reels her around to face him. She stares at him.

"I donna think I can."

"What do you mean?"

Luke's mount whinnies and circles. He pulls at the reins to steady her. "You two need to get mounted and we need to go. I'm serious. This thing is getting very close."

"I mean that idiotic sidesaddle. I cannae ride in it. Not in this storm. I cannot maneuver properly." Her voice is strained. Something is wrong. All the ladies ride sidesaddle. There's no time for debate.

"Ariana. You need to get mounted, we need to go. If you can't ride in it take the thing off and ride bare back or however you need to."

"Really?"

"My dear, I don't care how you ride as long as we get moving. We need to go now." The change in Ariana's face causes his insides to stir. Her emerald green lights soften and he doesn't realize she lifts the stirrup to begin to unbuckle the saddle belt just before he steps in to stop her.

"Here. Let me help you." Alexander takes over and removes it to the ground.

"I have removed a saddle before."

"We have no time."

"Can ye give me a leg up?"

He places his hand around her ankle to help her on. Too much blasted fabric to contend with. No wonder she prefers men's breeches. Ariana quickly circles behind Alexander. Clearly she can handle herself bareback. He mounts his own horse and they take off back toward town. The whirlwind behind them continues to chop tree tops. It does not follow any discernible course. They gallop alongside one another until the wind cools to a gentle breeze. They almost reach town. Luke looks around and circles back behind them.

"It appears to be over." The sky behind shows clear. The silver and grey is gone. The sky in front of them is sunny as if nothing even occurred. "It's very odd. We should go back and see what is left and survey the results."

"Ariana, what do you want to do?"

"I'm not sure. How am I going to explain returning home with no saddle? I should go back with ye and get the saddle, but I donna want to ride it back."

"You could say you were caught in a whirlwind and the saddle was lost."

"No one would believe that and ye know it. It doesn't even look like the storm came near here."

"That is true. You'll have to ride sidesaddle and be done with it."

"*You* ride sidesaddle and be done with it!" Ariana's eyes narrow. She's angry.

"How do you expect *me* to ride sidesaddle? Men don't ride sidesaddle."

"Exactly! I should like to see a man ride sidesaddle one day. Why should ladies be required to ride such stupid things while men can ride astride, truly free?" She isn't mad, she's making a point. Clever minx. He doesn't disagree with her.

Laughter sputters out of Luke's mouth. "I should like to see you ride sidesaddle one day too, my lord."

"What? *I*, ride sidesaddle?" It can't be all that hard. "So, am I to understand you would like me to ride the lady's saddle, Luke? Is that what we're on about?"

A wide grin spreads across his young friend's face.

"And what exactly do I get if I do this?"

"I don't know, sir. I expect we could come up with something couldn't we?" Luke winks at Ariana.

Ariana giggles. "I'm sure we could come up with something too, my laird."

"Oh, so it's a wager we're talking about. I see how it is." What can it hurt? How difficult can it be? Luke is still a young buck. Why not have a bit of amusement with him? And, he can certainly find enjoyment with Ariana. "Alright. I'll do it. On one condition. It stays between us."

"Agreed."

"Yes, agreed."

They reach the spot where the saddle was left on the ground. Before they re-saddle the two men survey the damage to the area. Tree tops are chopped off at the tops. Wooden tree spikes shoot up into the air like blades where the trees were cut by the whirlwind. Colored pieces of cloths are scattered across the grasslands.

Alexander picks up a few pieces of the cloths and then drops them again. "It looks like we need to find a way to get the cloths higher into the wind."

"Yeah. We'll see if any turn up down the road. Maybe the whirlwind picked some up and we can measure the distance of how far it traveled. We'll see."

"That will be marvelous if it did. We should put numbers on the cloths next time so we can keep a more detailed record of how far they traveled and how they were dispersed."

Luke smiles wide. It fills his face. "Are you trying to get out of it?"

"Get out of what?"

"I do believe you have a wager to keep?"

Ariana appears with Red trailing behind. "Donna worry, Mr. Howard. I have Red saddled and ready to go."

"Very well, then. Any lady who takes it upon herself to saddle a horse deserves the reward. Let's go."

Alexander mounts the black. Red. Who names a black horse Red? He lifts his left leg so it may fit in the correct position ladies are expected to maintain in the side saddle. His leg is longer. It doesn't fit as easily as expected. The stirrup needs lowered. It doesn't matter. He can still do this. He sits up straight. So, what if his thigh feels like it bends against his chest.

THE VIEW OF HIM RIDING sidesaddle is not what she expects. He is very tall for the saddle. He almost looks like he sits with his legs crossed on the horse. He forgot to lower the stirrup. It occurs to Ariana that is the point of a sidesaddle. Chastity. A lady must remain chaste even while riding a horse. What nonsense. He's riding with his legs crossed on a horse all the while they have been practicing for a *scandal* together. She stifles a snort.

"Is everything alright, my laird?"

"Quite."

"If ye need to dismount, ye may."

"No, it's fine."

"Are ye sure?"

"Yes. I'm just a bit ... pinched."

Luke spits out a laugh. "How about we take it up to a trot?"

"Now ye know how the ladies feel."

"Ladies feel pinched?"

"Yes, of course they do. Especially when the muscles tense up in the calve area after a long ride." Ariana wants to offer to lower the stirrup but watching Alexander in his struggles is too diverting.

Luke's laughter spills out. "I don't think that is exactly where—"

"Luke!" Alexander stares at him.

"I'm sorry, my lord." Luke clears his throat. Children laughing can be heard from somewhere in the distance. They look around to see from which direction it is coming. They're not too far from town, but not far enough to be able to switch saddles and dismount before being seen by anyone.

"Look, Sara! That gentleman, he's riding a ladies' saddle." The little girls cover their mouths and giggle together. Three little boys join them.

"That lady with him, she's riding bareback." They fall to the ground laughing holding their sides. "We could make up a jolly rhyme about a lady and 'gent. Whoever heard of a gentleman riding sidesaddle?"

Alexander shifts in his seat. Luke's eyes crinkle at the side and Ariana bites the inside of her cheeks.

Alexander wiggles in the saddle. "How about we give them that rhyme?" Ariana looks at each of them. "Why not?"

CHAPTER SEVENTEEN

Bath, England – Spring, 1798

"I certainly willnae attend!" Ariana wails. Her father is holding an invitation to the masquerade ball to be held at Toddington Peaks.

"Ariana, I insist you go. All the relations from both sides will be there, not to mention select members of the *ton*. I have not bid you do my wishes before this and now I fear I have no choice. You will go to the mask! I demand it be so!" Lord Stratford's voice comes out in a tone Ariana rarely hears uttered from his mouth.

Ariana stands silent. Her father stares at her. She chokes back tears. She tries to remain firm in her convictions, but it appears there is no choice. The time has come for her to accept she has to marry.

Lord Stratford puts his arm around his daughter. "There, there, now. I did not mean to be so harsh. But, I will not hear any more of this. You must go to the ball. You will marry the viscount and if you insist on remaining hidden so be it, but at some point the masks will have to come off."

"Ye insist on this marriage and so it will be, but I insist it doesn't matter when I see the man and so I remain firm. I willnae see him until the day of our wedding!"

"Ariana, my dear, you are so like your mother in your defiance at times. I feel I have no desire to continue this conversation." He stands up. "We shall continue another time." Did she win? At least for now?

Lord Stratford leaves her. Now, she'll have to manage her own feelings. She sits in the parlor and Hawthorne notifies her Victoria awaits her to which Ariana directs she be shown in.

Victoria storms through the doors. "Aria, I was so worried about you. I am so glad you weren't hurt. I heard about the whirlwind in the country, how it trimmed the tree tops. Did you actually see it?"

"Yes, I'm fine and yes, I saw it. Are ye alright?"

"A little wet, that is all."

"I'm so sorry. I should've listened. Please sit down and let me order some refreshments."

"Not to worry. What did you do?" Victoria's eyes are round and ready to explode out of her head.

"I watched it for a few minutes until the hail started to fall and then I came back to town." Ariana doesn't share the fact Lord Raby was with her because she promised him to keep the saddle incident with the children a secret. Along with the rhyme, "The Lady, the Gent and the Sidesaddle Prince."

"There was hail? Large hail?"

"I dunno. Little, hard, pellets almost like hard snow, but bigger than snowflakes. The hail doesn't matter. Vicky, this whirlwind. It was beautiful and forceful, spinning and weaving, and yes. Ye're right. It was dangerous so I didn't stay and watch long."

"I'm glad to hear you do at least use some wisdom." Victoria sits back in her chair. "Only you could twist being pelted with hail in a whirlwind into an exciting adventure. Anyway, have you received it?" Victoria removes her gloves and places them in her lap.

"Received what?"

Victoria narrows her eyes. "Dearest, your eyes are red and puffy, why have you been crying?"

Tears well up again. "Papa is making me go to Toddington Peaks for that ball!"

Victoria leans forward and touches Ariana's hand. "But don't you see, Aria, this is exactly what we wanted? Don't you remember? Originally, we were going to plan it here. Instead, they decided on Toddington Peaks. This is the chance you were hoping for. We can put our plan into play. Have you spoken with Lord Raby yet?"

"No, I haven't seen him yet today. He may stop by later."

Victoria's cheeks flush. Her face scrunches and she pulls herself back. "You know, Aria, I should be quite upset with you. Nev— I mean Lord Raby— is courting me and here I am helping you plan a scandal with him."

Ariana knows she's right. Only yesterday he kissed her in the field. It wasn't practice. She bites her lip. Guilt churns her stomach. "I know, my dear, *dear* friend. Only the closest of friends would understand and do what ye are doing to help me out of this situation. Remember, though, when we started all of this, ye were not so close to your dear Nev as ye are now. If ye want me to call our scandal off, I will."

Victoria sits for a moment fidgeting with the lace on her muslin before glancing up at Ariana. An impatient huff spews out. "Of course you cannot! Besides, I love a mask, walking around guessing who is hidden behind the guise. Some people are obvious, you know. Yet others are a complete surprise. Mama and papa, for instance, have this game they play with one another where they try and guess the other partner. Papa always finds her, though, and she still cannot figure out how. I have my suspicions though I keep them to myself."

"It does sound wonderful and I know we will enjoy the festivities, but I cannot help feeling quite unsettled. I do hope we are able to pull it off."

"Tomorrow we will go shopping for our costumes and I know you will start to feel better. Don't worry, Lord Raby is quite a gentleman, and quite capable. He will not let things get out of hand. All will be well, you will see."

"I know ye're right. Ye've always been such a good friend. I dunno what I would do without ye."

"I almost forgot to tell you! Lord Warwick has enlisted the circus to perform."

"The circus? I'll get to see Wendell again!" That pulls her spirits up again.

"Wendell?"

"Yes, a circus performer we saw on our way to Bath. He's part of the most amazing troupe of horses and the performance is spectacular!"

"I can't wait to see it then. I must get back home now. I'm so glad you're better for I simply could not leave you in a state of distress."

"Thank you. I am much better." Ariana sniffs, dabbing the last of her tears with her handkerchief.

She shows her friend out. She can't help but smile, excited she will see Wendell and his delightful 'orses' again.

ALEXANDER NEEDS TO know Ariana is all right after their whirlwind experience. Her interest in the weather surprises him and pleases him. He is not fond of the sidesaddle incident although it was amusing watching her enjoy herself. He sees Victoria leave the Wentworth residence. It should be safe to call. Hawthorne directs him to the parlor where he finds Ariana, hands folded, and looking at the floor. This is not what he expects, nor the impression he intends to elicit from her. What caused the sullen look in her eyes? It rips him in his gut to see her this way.

"My laird, please sit down. Shall I call for refreshments?"

"No, no. I am fine. You, however, seem a bit ... er, distracted. Is everything all right?"

"Yes, quite all right." He doesn't believe her.

Ariana and her sweet scent of lavender is clouding his objective. He wants to confirm her attendance at the mask. He kissed her yesterday in the field. She didn't move or try to get away. It wasn't practice. It was the wind. It pushed her to him. It closed the gap between them. Should he attempt to talk about it with her? She's been crying. Aches in his chest urge him. Urge him to take her in his arms and kiss her pain away. He dare not go against her father. He must take care to play his role. Her father wants to keep her in the dark until the ball. He doesn't want to risk her refusal to attend. Blasted silence. "My dear, what is the matter? You look ill."

"Thank you. It's nice to know I look ill." She sniffs.

"That is not what I meant er...exactly. It's — wait. Are you being sarcastic?"

"I assure ye I donna do sarcasm." She flashes him a half smile.

"Really?"

"Yes, really."

"So, what is the matter then for I know something is amiss?"

She huffs once and spouts it all out. "I am not ill. I wish I was. Papa demands I attend the ball at Toddington Peaks to which I most fervently refused. But, of course, he insists and will brook no argument on my part."

"This *is* what you and Victoria wanted, was it not?"

"Yes, but I had not thought it to be at Toddington Peaks and I donna want to be present with *him.* It will be easy enough to conceal my identity for a time, but at some point they will call for us to be unmasked and— I dunno anymore. I'm so— please forgive me." Her voice trails off into a whimper. Tears begin to fall.

Now her full-on crying feeds the ache again. What can he say? What can he do to make it better? He moves to be closer to her on the settee and she instantly falls against him.

"There, there, please don't cry so." He puts his arm around her shoulder and gathers her in tight. He takes her hand in his. She looks up at him and reveals the turmoil of her inner spirit. Her brow purses together, tears pool in the corners of her eyes until cascades trail her cheeks. The ache in his chest presses up to his throat. He wants to make her pain invisible. Tell her who he is and that he won't marry her.

She accepts the handkerchief he offers. She wipes her tears. "I'm so sorry for breaking into a fit. There is nothing anyone can do, really. I'm sorry to have brought ye into this. If ye would like to bow out, I quite understand."

Alexander is astonished by her suggestion. "Bow out?" Then, a hint of amusement taps into his voice. "After practicing to perfect our performance? I am appalled, madam, you would think such a thing."

Ariana half smiles. "How shocking!" She encourages him to continue.

Cautious, Alexander moves his arm lower, wrapping it tight around her waist, and pulls her gently to his chest. He softly kisses the top of her head. "There, now, see? This is what I like. We will work this all out, my dear, I promise."

A fresh batch of tears overwhelm the corners of her eyes—not the response he is hoping for.

"Please don't continue on so or I will be forced to take you this minute and marry you myself to get you out of this mess!" The words were out before he has a minute to think of what he said.

Ariana doesn't move from him. She raises her head and locks into a warmth of calm he feels move between them. Intense and close.

Alexander raises his hand to wipe the tears still lingering at the edge of those glistening emeralds. Ariana lifts her hand to hold his and she kisses it, gently holding it there, close to her lips. The moment holds them immobile. She peeks up at him as he gazes down at her. She is lovely. He is enthralled by her beauty and the tears enhance the green even more. He can think of nothing he wants to do more than pull her closer still. She does not move back and allows him to kiss her lightly on her lips. She wraps her arms around his neck and pulls him down toward her.

Alexander kisses her harder and more intense. He cannot contain himself much longer. Maybe a little longer. His hands roam down her back, her side, and the top of her hips.

Gentle kisses, warm embraces, and the soft touches of skin to skin take great effort on his part to keep her in check. No thoughts. No one. Just her.

Ariana doesn't want him to stop. She wants more. What exactly? She doesn't know. Only that he be with *her*— not Victoria. "Oh, no! What are we doing? Victoria!" Ariana wails and pushes Alexander back in the same instant.

Alexander shoots up, disheveled and shocked, as if caught in some mischievous act. Not altogether false. "Victoria? What about Victoria?"

Alexander sits back silent. Ariana must be aware of the attachment between the true Lord Raby and Victoria. What can he say now? Nothing. He will have to let her tell him what she wants.

Ariana sits, Alexander sits. She stands, he stands. Alexander remains silent and watches while she works it out in her head.

She paces for a moment before focusing her attention back on him. "I must apologize to have involved ye in this. Please, we must not speak of it again and we must not *practice* so again. I believe we have it worked out quite well now. I think ye must leave immediately." Not what he expects in the least. "I'll see ye at the ball. I'm sure Victoria will apprise ye of our plans for arrival."

"Of course." So, she still doesn't know.

"And, by the way, about what happened in the field...please donna..."

"It was the storm that pushed us together, my lady. Think nothing of it."

"Thank you."

"Of course." Alexander leaves. The familiar ache returns. He hopes one day she truly will see an amusement of it all.

CHAPTER EIGHTEEN

Toddington Peaks – Spring, 1798

Toddington Peaks is a half day's journey from Bath. Ariana insists they arrive the day before so they do not become exhausted after their journey. How can she be expected to attend the ball that same night?

Lord Stratford begins to discuss the arrangements for overnighting with the family. "How, my dear, do you plan to keep yourself from the viscount since you will have an entire day and night to avoid making his acquaintance?"

"We willnae stay at Toddington, Papa! We shall stay at the inn in town."

"At the inn in town? You must be addled! Warwick will consider it an insult. It is perfectly proper to stay at Toddington. He is your intended and there will be no chance for you to be alone with all the guests around I am sure."

"Papa, ye're missing the point. While ye are correct it is perfectly proper, ye forget I fully intend to adhere to my convictions on this account. I willnae meet the man until the day of our wedding! If that means we are to stay at an inn in town so be it. It is *also* quite proper."

"Ariana, your persistence in this matter has worn me out. If it is an inn you want, then we shall stay at an inn and hope Lady Warwick does not consider it an insult. I am quite curious, however, to see how you plan to carry on with this pretension."

"I assure ye I'm quite determined."

ARIANA ARRANGES FOR Victoria to stay at the inn with her. The journey to the inn is not so eventful, but excitement about the event is building. They arrive and are shown to their rooms. Not as lavish as they are accustomed to.

Lord Stratford is not pleased and makes sure they all are aware of his inconvenience. "Ariana, this notion of yours is absurd. We are remaining in these lower accommodations when all we need do is stay at the home of your future husband."

"I told ye papa. I willnae. Lower accommodations or not, I will have this one last request from ye."

"You will have, will you?" His voice booms through the hall.

"Would ye truly deny this of me?" Ariana's question is firm and calm. "After all ye're asking of me, donna deny me this when I'm to do your bidding." Her cautious plead earns results.

Lord Stratford softens slightly. "I do not understand why it is you do not wish to marry." He turns her to face him. "All young ladies of your station marry, and marry those gentlemen their parents choose for them."

"It's not that I donna wish to marry. I wish to marry one *I* choose to marry. I know it's not how things are done. I donna want to be pushed off on a man whose only interest is in my fortune. I want to love and be loved. To share the same kind of love ye had with my mama. Is that so hard to understand?"

"No, my dear, it is not, but I have explained that while I have always allowed you your indulgences, this marriage must take place. If we must stay in this dreadful place, I will allow you that." Lord Stratford kisses her cheek.

"Thank you, papa, I knew ye wouldn't deny me."

"Yes, yes, I believe you did. Now, let's get ourselves to rights so we may be rested for this ball tomorrow!"

LORD STRATFORD HAS the carriage brought around. Preparations are finally complete.

"Oh Aria, I never dreamed at how alike we look! Even our hair and eyes can almost pass as the same person"

"I know! Such merriment can be had with our appearance," Ariana snorts. "Ah, but there is no doubt *your* Nev will know ye immediately."

"You didn't even want to come. You must own you are glad, are you not?"

Ariana refuses to give in completely. "I still would prefer it to have been my own choosing, but I willnae linger any longer on the subject and will make every effort to enjoy myself! Look, we've almost arrived. Let me adjust your mask. We cannot have anyone recognizing us yet ye know. How is mine?"

Victoria reaches over to provide a slight adjustment to her friend's mask. "You look exquisite!"

"We both do!"

The carriage draws closer to the entrance and Ariana pulls out a pair of green scent bottles adorned with purple flowers. She gives one to Victoria. "Here, dear, take this. They're lavender scented. Put some on now before we go in and I'm sure we'll need some later on after the dancing commences."

"Good of you to remember this. Mama usually remembers the scent bottles when we go out. Her favorite scent is roses though. I hadn't thought to bring a bottle with me. But, no mind, we shall even smell the same. No one will be able to tell us apart for sure." Victoria giggles.

They get out of the carriage to enter the ballroom of Toddington Peaks. Lord Stratford offers one arm to each of them. Excitement. Amazement. Anxiety. Ariana experiences all of it. Everyone is dressed in the most elaborate of ways for the event. There are sailors, chimney sweepers, flower girls, Egyptians, clowns, and a number of gypsies like herself and Victoria.

They enter the great hall of Toddington Peaks and instead of admiring the splendor of the great house, Ariana's eyes immediately begin scanning the room. Where is Lord Raby?

ALEXANDER RECOGNIZES Ariana immediately. Her slender form and the curve of her jaw. The color of her green costume compliments her skin very well. Its golden hues glisten in the light as she moves about. She wears her hair up with one lone curl hanging down over her shoulder. He wants to touch it.

He approaches, but she turns to look the other way. The dimple on her left shoulder leaves no question. *This* gypsy is Ariana.

Alexander reaches out to claim her attention just as Lord Raby comes from the opposite direction and steals her away. What is he thinking? Why wouldn't Raby ask Victoria for the first two dances?

Alexander heads for the punch bowl. Maybe liquored punch can quell his annoyance. He bumps into Victoria in the process.

"How very kind you are sir, is that for me?" Her voice is sweet, too sweet. Alexander stares at her. What the deuce is she asking? He follows the direction of her gaze to the punch he's holding in his hand. Alexander offers it to her and proceeds to pour another for himself. Victoria's yammering on takes second to his attention to the dance floor and the sight of the two people dancing. Ariana moves across the floor with grace and elegance, completely in rhythm with the orchestra.

Alexander is left with no choice but to ask Victoria to join him on the floor. He wants to be near Ariana. A minuet will not help. Although, he may be able to steal her attention for a moment as she moves about him on the floor.

The music ends and Alexander thanks Victoria for the privilege of dancing with her and tries to claim the next dance with Ariana. A second opportunity is fumbled when Victoria's brother, Edmund, steps in front of him to claim her for his next dance. *Blast! Edmund.* Alexander is determined to get the next dance with Ariana. There is somewhat of a consolation to be had. It's a waltz. He can be close to her at length.

Alexander and Ariana glide along the edge of the room. He does not miss this favorable circumstance to pull her as close as possible without causing too much notice by those who may consider it inappropriate behavior. What he'd like to do is whisk her away, out the door to the veranda, and into the gardens where he might once again taste the sweetness of her lips against his. This time he will show her the beauties of the evening in the gardens of *Toddington Peaks.*

He is determined to quell the silence that always challenges them. "I trust you are comfortable at the inn in town?"

"Quite."

"I hope you did not have to wait too long in line before making an entrance tonight?"

"No more than is customary."

"Did you sleep well?"

"I'm sorry?"

"Forgive me, I did not mean to offend." Sleep well? What caused that inane question to come out? "You seem a bit out of sorts this evening. Are you sure you are well? Is there anything you need?"

"I assure ye, sir, I am quite all right."

Despite his attempts at conversation, the dratted silence begins to build between them. It's almost as if she's straining to get away from him. Had they not agreed to stick together through the events of the night? They're only minutes away from the fireworks display. She is sure to enjoy this event. "Shall we move toward the veranda ahead of the crowd so that we may have a most excellent view of the fireworks?"

"Of course. I would like that. I so love fireworks!"

As they make their way to the door, the major-domo makes the announcement everyone is waiting for. "Honorable guests, it is time for the fireworks to begin!"

Ariana maneuvers silently as Alexander gently guides her from behind. What can be the matter with her tonight? This is not the Ariana he is accustomed to. They must speak privately so he can get to the bottom of it. However, once outside, the fireworks detonate with great force. The colors explode into the sky filling it with brilliant colors of purple, green, blue, white, pink and red with loud and sudden cracks then a delayed *boom!* echoes through the night air. One cannot help but be in awe of the display as they culminate in one last burst of color, sound, and brilliance signaling the time when they will remove their masks and reveal who they are. Ariana slips away in the direction of the gardens.

CHAPTER NINETEEN

Toddington Peaks – Spring, 1798

Ariana's impending nuptials plague her thoughts. She cannot deny her feelings for Lord Raby. He kissed her in the field that storm-filled day and it wasn't practice. She didn't stop him either. How can she justify this to Victoria? How can she justify it to herself?

Her dance partner interrupts her contemplations. "My dear, you departed so quickly it was all I could do to keep up with you."

"I'm sure it was not that difficult. Ye are much more active than I am."

"Yes, well you are much faster than you let on. I know from experience, unless you have forgotten the first time we met and our trek through the parks?"

No. She has not forgotten. She will never forget. Ariana wants it indelibly etched in her memory forever. Memories sure to sustain her in the coming days and those after her wedding. Memories she will keep close to her heart for the rest of her life. Once married, monotony and loss of her freedom will be her lot.

"Might you enjoy a walk in the gardens where we unmask privately?" His question reminds her of his presence.

The heat of her face tingles behind her mask. "I shall, indeed." Lord Raby's meaning is clear. She wants to be angry with him but she has no right to be. She wants the memories. Can they be friends?

Anger kindles inside. Not because he's marrying Vicky. Anger with herself. Did he really say he would marry her if she didn't stop crying? Is that all it takes?

Ariana's stomach turns to acid. The marriage arrangements are done. They'll move on with their lives albeit separate. All that's left is hope. Hope she may keep him as the friend she so deeply desires. Lord Raby will make Vicky an exceptional husband. Silence coupled with heavy sighs of deep concentration accompany them into the hedge maze.

"You know, my dear, we may actually get lost. Maybe I should make a trail so we know how to get back."

"That is, if we want to get back." Why did she say that? This is the last night. Then it's over.

"So, when shall we attempt our plan? Any second thoughts?"

"No, no second thoughts..."

"I only ask because you seem a bit preoccupied this evening."

This is her moment. Tell him. Tell him how much his friendship means. How much their time together has touched her heart. Share with him how she truly feels. Will he think her too forward? Declaring her love for him before he acknowledges to her his own? No. It will ruin what's left of a lovely night. A lovely memory. Lovely freedom soon to end.

"I own to be a bit quiet, yes, but I have only been thinking about what the future holds. Tonight will most definitely be a turning point, but it must be done."

THE GARDEN PATHWAYS are quiet. Ariana is solemn and different tonight. Alexander's heart wrenches to see her suffer.

He wants to tell her at this moment he is Alexander, not Lord Raby. Tell her there is no need to continue with their plans— He can't. The words won't come. Will she hate his deception? Will she break the engagement? He doesn't want to risk not having her close to him. With him. He *loves* her. He cannot bear to see her suffer. He cannot bear to be without her in his life.

"Come, my dear, let us not be so solemn for it is a beautiful evening. Tell me, truthfully, Toddington Peaks is a grand estate, is it not? Would it be so awful to be his viscountess?"

"Viscountess? No. It wouldn't, but I have never thought of myself as a viscountess. And I find I still cannot abide marrying for title, having someone else decide for me who will be my life partner. I want to marry for love and I want to know I am loved."

"How do you know you will not come to love him in time?" Did he actually say those words? He needs to hear her say she can love him. Even in this context.

"It will not change the circumstances upon which the arrangements were made and, besides, what if my heart is otherwise engaged?"

"Otherwise engaged?"

"Yes, otherwise engaged! What if? A young lady should be able to have the freedom to choose for herself whom she will spend the rest of her life with. Doesn't the man choose? Why can't a lady be afforded the same right to choose? I cannot accept it!"

"Just like she should be able to choose what saddle to ride, yes?"

"Absolutely!"

At least that brought a smile to her lips. "That is indeed the truth, in most circumstances. You forget. Gentlemen suffer from arrangements as well."

"I am sorry. Ye must think me wretched. Here I am distressing over my own situation when ye're suffering much the same fate. Although ye must admit it's much more favorable for a gentleman. A lady becomes a possession and loses all sense of self."

"My dear, you do make it sound grave."

"Is *your* arranged marriage so awful? I cannot help but wonder."

Here it is. The moment to tell her. "No, actually it is not awful." He can't decide to tell her.

He waits too long. The moment is passed. Ariana folds her arm into his. "Come, let's change this line of thinking for as you said. It is a beautiful evening. Let us think of more pleasant thoughts, shall we? I'm sure ye wouldn't like to be reminded of either incident any more than I would."

Alexander laughs out loud. If she only knew how many times he does remember. Every incident. With her. "No, I do not believe I would like a repeat performance of 'The Lady, The Gent and Sidesaddle Prince.'"

"Is that what they called it?"

"I believe so. We'll have to ask Luke. He's the one who documented it."

"Oh, no. If he documented it, then it will become a historical archive." It pleases him to hear her laugh. A laugh not so hearty now. If only she could laugh with him always.

Ariana straightens up. Serious and somber. Thankful to be able to enjoy the attentions of this gentleman, if only for this short time. The moonlit pathway spreads out before them while they walk. Cries of excitement from the guests channel out over the lawn. The announcement to unmask is the only explanation.

Ariana pauses and lifts her hand to begin to remove her mask. His hand blocks her. He holds it in his, lingering for a moment, before leaning down to softly kiss her lips. Lips asking to be kissed all night. Close and breathless, he touches her cheek; he whispers her name in her ear. "Ariana."

Ariana's breath is hot against his neck, his pulse races. He finds her lips. Ariana folds against him. He tightens his embrace. She raises her hand to run her fingers through his wavy hair. She doesn't allow him to bring his head up.

Ariana knows what she's doing is against propriety, but she is free with this man. He awakens her and she is safe and protected. Protected from the storm.

He raises his head to look at her for a second in time and kisses her again. He winds the one ringlet of her hair around his finger to move it to the side behind her shoulder. His lips move cautiously down her neck, across her shoulder. She will be ravished for sure. She doesn't care.

"THE NIGHT IS CLEAR, is it not Edmund? I am so glad to be free of that mask. I thought I might suffocate from it."

"Yes. It was rather warm. It is only too bad I must walk the maze with my sister. I would much rather have the arm of a lovely young lady intent on my every word." Victoria slaps his arm with her fan for teasing her. They enjoy each other's company many evenings. He will one day find a young lady truly deserving of his affections. In fact, she has plans to help him in that regard.

Her stomach lurches to the top of her neck.

"Vicky, what's the matter?" Edmund walks in front of her and holds each of her arms on the side. She covers her mouth with her hand. She's going to be sick. They *are* in love! She recognizes the two people in front of them on the path. Lord Raby and Ariana in an intimate embrace. Tears fill her eyes.

"Vicky, come now. What is it? You know I was only teasing."

Victoria swipes the tear that scales her cheek. "How could he? How could she?" She turns around and runs back toward the house. Edmund watches her go. He looks at the couple on the path ahead and then runs to follow his sister.

VICTORIA HEADS STRAIGHT to an antechamber tucked around a corner. Edmund follows close behind. "You must take me this *minute* back to Harlaxton. I cannot bear to stay here another moment!" She presses her face into his shoulder. Her voice is stifled against his chest.

She will not be consoled. "Victoria, you must know that is not possible. It is late and you do not wish to miss the balloon ascension, do you? I promise you we can leave right after. Please tell me what is wrong?"

Lady Salisbury enters the room. Victoria turns to her mother and falls into her arms. Lady Salisbury wraps her arms around her. "Mama! He is not interested in me. I saw them in the garden— together."

Edmund pulls off one glove. "This is about a man? Who is he? I'll make him name his seconds!"

Lady Salisbury shakes her head at her son and motions for him to follow while she leads her daughter from the antechamber. Victoria nuzzles into her mother's embrace. The eyes of the *ton* are everywhere. This distraction will wag their tongues. Victoria moves with her mother through the corridors back to the Salisbury guest room and sits down on the bed.

"Now, Victoria. What is all this about?" Her mother's voice is calm and soothing. She pushes stray hairs back from her forehead and wipes her tears from her eyes.

"Mama," she sniffs. "I saw him with Aria in the garden. I thought he was in love with me and that he was going to talk to papa about paying his addresses." Edmund hands her his handkerchief.

"Victoria, whomever are you talking about?"

"Oh, mama, I saw Nev— I mean, Lord Raby in the garden with Aria! He was... *kissing* her."

Lady Salisbury pulls her daughter close. "My dear, you must be mistaken for not five minutes before I came across you running to the antechamber, I saw Lord Raby in deep conversation with your papa in the corner of the assembly hall."

Victoria peeks up over the handkerchief given to her by Edmund and pauses for a moment. She saw them in the garden. In the maze. They were kissing. "But, I'm sure it was him. I had been with him almost the entire night up until the minuet when he asked Ariana to dance, which irked me to the core. I saw them go out to the veranda during the fireworks. I tried to go to him, but I was sidetracked by the viscount. I don't know what he was all about, trying to entice me to go with him privately. Oh mama, what should I do? I simply adore him and I'm sure he feels the same. That is, up until what I just saw."

"Entice you to go with him privately?" Lady Salisbury leans back and raises an eyebrow directed at her daughter.

"You know, of course, I would never entertain such an idea!" Victoria blows her nose.

"No, dear, of course not."

Lady Salisbury sits for a moment and then calls for her lady's maid.

"We will get a note to your father. We must get to the bottom of this. We will find out if Lord Raby asked his permission or not. That will settle this once and for all. As to why he was in the garden with Ariana is another matter. I am sure something is amiss."

CHAPTER TWENTY

Toddington Peaks – Spring, 1798

"This directive is straight from the Prince." Bollocks. Salisbury wants to discuss assignments. Courage. It's easy when it comes to protecting the Crown. To speak to the father of the woman you love? Not so much. Now, it will have to wait.

"So tell me then. What do you know of this alliance?" Salisbury's mask covers most of his face and is decorated with red and purple sequins. Lady Salisbury no doubt selected it. Only his eyes and lower half of his face show. The rest is covered. Best to unmask after their discussion in case anyone inadvertently hears.

"I don't know anything more than I have told you. We need you to investigate further. I want you to infiltrate this group. Find out what their plan is."

"That may prove to be difficult as it currently stands."

The mask on Salisbury's face lifts upward in a slight movement. "How so?"

"They may be reluctant to approach a lowly baron." This assignment may be a good opportunity. A chance to get into a better position, a better position for Victoria.

"I see your point." Lord Salisbury leans back in his chair and rubs the line of his jaw with his forefinger and thumb. The only facial expression, the blink of his eyes.

"We may need to use another operative or somehow raise your status."

This *is* good. "It may be possible to play the role of earl."

"I'm not sure we should risk it. You are already known in the general circles at this point. I'm not sure we can pull it off."

"There is, of course, other alternatives. Obscure titles." Will he allow it? An obscure title hardly known about in polite society?

"It's true. There are a few we haven't used in quite some time, but I'm still not convinced it is a good idea to do so now. We need to be selective."

"Didn't you say Prinny is concerned there may be issues with the protection of the Crown?"

"Yes, but I also have a second assignment for which I need you promptly and some of the same members are involved. They already know you in your present position."

"I see." What is that word Lady Salisbury says?

"Yes, let's consider how we might get you an invitation into this new venture while you begin work on the second assignment."

"And, that is?" Must keep a steady face. Courage. Victoria is counting on it.

"These weather predictors."

"I'm sorry, did you say *weather predictors*?"

"Yes. Pay attention Raby. Were you not in conversation the other evening with Warwick's heir about the possibilities of weather prediction?"

"Well, yes. We did have a conversation about what he does and how he goes about it. I found it fascinating. I've even started some of my own observations, although I can't imagine what would interest Prinny?"

"Can you not?" A slow and drawn out smile creeps across the bottom half of Salisbury's face from one cheek to the other.

"Think of the possibilities. Lives lost that could be saved both on land and at sea. The assets lost could be minimized, if not eradicated." Very good points.

"And this group has come under the nose of His Royal Highness?"

"Yes. And, I happen to agree. First, I thought it quite odd. But upon further reflection I realized how important the science of weather prediction is."

"So, how do you want to proceed?"

"On this, I will leave it up to you. I noticed you had a particular interest so I doubt it will be a difficult undertaking."

"No. No, it won't. I have already been in touch with Alexander, and his colleagues have agreed I might accompany them on some of their expeditions." The most recent almost blew them away, literally.

"Excellent! I knew you were the right choice for this one. Just keep us informed of how things go. If it looks to be a worthwhile pursuit, I will advise the Prince that he may proceed with his plans on the subject."

"And do you know what those might be?"

"No. Unfortunately, he does not always share his plans although I am sure in this regard he means to support their efforts to success."

"Very good." Raby swallows hard to prepare for what he means to discuss next. "If that will be all on the matters of government, I should like to speak with you on an entirely different matter."

"And what matter is that?" Does he already suspect the subject? What kind of spymaster would he be if he does not?

"It's Victoria."

"Victoria? What has she gone and done now?" Maybe he doesn't.

"Nothing. That is, well, you see we, she and I, well, I love her and..."

"Let me stop you right there." Salisbury raises his hand and looks around. Some other guests have started to join them near their spot in the corner.

"My lord?"

Salisbury lowers his voice to a whisper. "Before you go any further with this discussion, you must see that such an arrangement cannot be made."

Raby swallows the lump in his throat. Courage. "Actually, I don't."

"It's very simple. I should like to see Victoria matched with someone more her equal." What is he talking about?

"More her equal? How so?"

"You know how so. Do I really need to spell it out?" Please do.

"I'm afraid you do, because I do not see it."

"It's like this." Salisbury takes a deep breath. "I'm concerned for her happiness."

"As am I." The lump will not move. He picks up the glass of whisky sitting in front of him and swallows a large sip.

Salisbury watches him. His eyes follow the glass from Raby's lips to the table. "Let me rephrase it. I am concerned for her continued happiness."

"How so?"

"I do not wish for my only daughter to be wed to a spy." Salisbury hands him the same glass again. "Would you like another drink of my whisky?"

"I see. And no thank you." Blast the man. How can he be so calm? "And the fact that her father is the spymaster does not concern you?"

"Of course it does, which is why I should like to see her situated in a different circumstance other than that of her mother and I."

"Have you not had a happy and fulfilling marriage and would you not want the same for your daughter?"

"Yes, but it is different."

"I don't see how."

"You will when you become a father."

"I don't know how that might occur if I am refused permission to marry the only woman I could ever love."

"I understand how you must feel." Salisbury hands back his drink from the table.

"No, I don't think you do." Raby swirls the glass and stares at the liquid inside.

"Raby..."

"No. Please. Don't continue." He raises his hand as if to block any sound coming from Salisbury's direction. "Tell me this."

"Yes?"

"If I were to leave the organization, would you grant your permission?"

"You cannot be serious. We cannot afford to lose you. Your service is too valuable and you know it."

"Answer the question. Would you grant me permission then?"

"I don't know."

Raby continues to swirl. "You refuse to answer me?"

"I refuse to be given what is, in essence, an ultimatum."

Raby swallows what's left and replaces the now empty glass back on the table. "So be it."

CHAPTER TWENTY-ONE

Toddington Peaks – Spring, 1798

"Aargh! Sir."

"Yes, Aargh! Such nonsense." Can they not just go into the house? Rockingham moves outside in search of the area where the servants are to light the fuses for the fireworks. He cannot very well set his up with everyone prancing around in their costumes. The eye patch itches above his brow line. He tugs at the fake earring. It pinches his ear. How do the ladies endure these bobbles? Dressed as a pirate, a cloth around his head, a hat and eye patch completes his costume. It may have been easier to just wear a mask. In the back of the manor he finds the place he's looking for. Here is where he will set his fuses. Perfect spot. Just behind these bushes. A clear view of the house and the veranda. No question the guests will flock to view them from there. Rockingham lifts the eye patch. A clear shot to the house. There she is. Ariana. He pulls the fuses from the inside of his cape lining and sets them in the direction of the veranda where she stands. He lights the candles and steps back to watch. One of the fuses begins to flicker. He leans over to adjust it, but the fuse burns hot. Rockingham jumps back, but the candle tip catches in his cravat and the fuse continues to burn.

"Blast it!" Shrill noises roll from his tongue. The swan fountain. He runs for it. Rockingham lands face first in the cold water. He hears the comments of those passing by. He stays motionless for a few minutes. It soothes him after such a bloody mishap.

The size of one's rump in comparison to Prinny's becomes the topic of conversation for those passing by. Rockingham becomes even more determined to see his plan through. We'll see whose rump should be roasted once Watson's plans are implemented in full.

Rockingham sits on the side of the swan's bath. His clothes are soaked. He pulls his eye patch out. It slips back and slaps him in the eye. "Aargh!" He fumbles and tries to remove it, but it's tangled and stuck in between his ears and the cloth on his head. He moves it to the center of his forehead. He must look like a cyclops. He rubs his hands on his face. The earbob itches. He pulls at it until it comes off and he throws it in the pool of water in front of him. No one is around now. The dancing is continuing inside. He can hear the music. The laughing. The fireworks are done. His plans to take out the blockade to his future muddled. The unmasking is done. Now what?

There. There is the opportunity he now needs. The guests want to see a balloon ascension. They'll see a balloon ascension. One they've never seen before. Rockingham climbs out of the fountain, ducks behind a bush, and waits.

TIME ALONE. ARIANA'S walk in the hedge maze did not make her feel better. Lord Raby left to get refreshments. She strolls around more of the outer gardens of Toddington Peaks. What is she going to do? She is in love. He must feel the same about her. And Victoria? Nowhere to be seen since before the fireworks display. What if she and Lord Raby are off somewhere together? He did say his arrangement wasn't so awful. The scandal they so wanted to procure is illusive now. If only someone had discovered them in the hedge maze, all this would be over. Will she be able to achieve her objective? She must. Life with a man she is not in love with and the man she does love married to her closest friend. This is her future. She may as well unmask and do as her father asks. No! She will see it through. The viscount will not meet her until the wedding. She even took care to avoid the portrait room where the family portraits are displayed.

Ariana stops. There in front of her stands something magnificent. The balloon with its massive envelope and the burner hot underneath. It's going to ascend for the guests tomorrow. It's amazing and bold. How beautiful this will be to view in the light. It's massive compared to the small basket where the burner is and where the pilot and passengers will be.

Tomorrow is too late. What can it hurt to take a peek inside? It's tied down. She opens the side door of the basket and steps in. The red velvet cushion seating lines the edge for the passengers and the pilot. She leans forward and looks up inside the envelope. It's hard to see. The dark conceals much, but it reminds her of the big top tent from the circus. Wendell! He must be here practicing for tomorrow's show. She must go and look for him.

She turns to step back out of the basket. The door slams shut. A dark figure squats around the edges. The basket wobbles. Ariana loses her balance and falls backward. The sandbags that hold it down thump to the side. A sharp stab of fear grabs her around the neck and punches her stomach.

"What are ye doing! Stop! I am in here! Please! Don't release the balloon! Please, stop!" She hears her own sharp shrieks like an echo in her head. The judder under her feet can only mean the balloon is beginning to rise. Liftoff is like nothing she has experienced before. Her stomach falls to her feet and she fears she might swoon. She is alone on this ascension. Terror engulfs her completely. Piercing cries for help ring out from below. The balloon continues to go up.

Ariana carefully leans over to see the ground below her. A dark figure stands there watching. His face is upturned in her direction. She cannot make out who it is, except for a dark black circle on his forehead. The balloon continues to move away.

The basket bobs. She hears Lord Raby yell directions to the men at the bottom. They pull. They drop. Lord Raby grabs onto a rope still dangling off the basket and heaves hard to pull it down, to no avail. Others also join in the attempt to pull it down to earth. Ariana lapses into silence. She squats down into the basket. The basket tugs from side to side in the air. It's too heavy.

Ariana hears a group gasp below and looks up from where she has fallen. A man's arm reaches over the side. She gathers herself up to see who it is. Lord Raby clings to the side of the basket. She reaches over to grab his free arm dangling on the side. He clasps her wrist. She takes a hold of the other side of the basket so she will not be pulled out. She braces her feet and heaves. He quickly moves his grip to the edge of the basket. Cries drift up from below.

Ariana catches her breath, braces herself again, and he throws a leg over the basket's edge. She grabs his body and he draws himself up into the basket. He slips back. With one arm he reaches for her shoulder, tugs at the sleeve of her dress, and rips it clear to the bodice. Ariana doesn't care. She must get him aboard. Her mask falls to the ground below in the process. At last, he is with her. She wraps her arms around Lord Raby's waist. He pulls her close to his chest and burrows his hand in her hair.

His breathing is hard, but he holds her tight. Tears run rampant down her cheeks.

"I dunno why that man did this."

"What man? You mean someone forced you in here?"

"No," she sniffs. "I saw the balloon just sitting there and I was curious to know what it looked like on the inside. They must have been readying it for tomorrow, but I just stepped in for a moment. Then, as I turned to leave, someone locked me in the basket and loosened the sandbags. Oh..." she falls against him weeps violently.

Raby holds her close until she heaves a deep sigh. "What are we to do?"

He looks over the edge. He folds her close to him and moves her to sit down on the bench. Goosebumps appear down the sides of Ariana's arms and she begins to shiver. She can't control it. He tightens his grip around her and rubs her arms up and down, warming her with his touch. It's cold. Or maybe it's the anxiety of their predicament. Either way, his strength and his protection engulfs her. For the moment, he is her stronghold moderating any panic.

She cautiously moves her hand across the front pocket where he keeps his book. Will he ever share with her what it contains? Will there be time? Ariana's thoughts flash to the day they first met. His strong and confident appearance. Until her birds sprinkled him with their charm. She smiles for a second before lifting her head to him. His focus? Out over the top of the basket and into the sky, brows pulled together, observing his clouds.

THE BALLOON CONTINUES in the same direction. It must be the direction of the wind. Alexander conceives it must be although which way he cannot tell. If only his sense of direction were better trained. It appears as though they are no longer rising and steadier now. In more controlled circumstances, with a pilot, he might enjoy this adventure. What an excellent way to study the clouds. How advantageous it may be to ascend into a cloud. To shoot their cloths into one if they can manage to be close enough to a wind formation. Would it be safe? He leans over to see below and Ariana does the same, clasping his arm in the process. They are over a large field. The view is spectacular.

The moon is full and it is a clear night. Thank God for small favors. Alexander latches Ariana close to his side. He does not speak. She looks right up at him. Her eyes show tenderness. Will this be their last night on this great earth? It feels as if their thoughts are one. No words pass between them, just the inherent knowledge of their situation. What is going to happen, or how, he does not know. He knows one thing. He loves her and she loves him.

ARIANA RAISES HER EYES to his. Somehow his farcical mask remains on his face. Hers is long gone. She raises her hand to remove his mask, his lips claim hers. Sudden and urgent. Alexander draws her as close to him as he can and glides her back to the bench.

This may be their last moments of breath. Her hold around his neck tightens. She presses against him and she feels him shiver. It's still cold but his arms are around her creating a warmth that envelopes her. His breath on her cheek, the softness of his mouth, his kisses trace the tears and chase her fears away. The very ground is shaking below their feet, the earth is shattering around them. They aren't on the ground! What's shaking? Lord Raby unlocks first. The light of the moon is bright around them. The basket holding them above the earth still moves! They stand up and look below. Wendell and his troupe are there with their horses matching pace with the balloon above them.

Ariana gasps. Fear and delight mix. "What are they going to do?"

The scene below captivates its audience of two. The troupe positions themselves each one below a rope. On cue, like their performance, they all stand up on the back of their mounts, continuing at the same pace. Ariana watches, terrified. What might happen would be disaster.

Wendell yells upwards. "Don't ya worry now m'lady. We've done this trick many times jus 'a bit differnt than this. Hold on cuz it might be rough."

A few more strides, a series of whistles and whoops, the troupe simultaneously jump in the air towards the rope ahead of them and grab on. The balloon jolts in a downward direction from the extreme weight of them all lunging and grabbing on at once.

The performers hang on the ropes below the basket. The horses continue to match their pace. Wendell motions and, synchronized, they lower themselves to the end of the rope wrapping their hands around the ends for a good grip. Another series of whistles, the horses position themselves under their respective riders still running their paces. The weight of the six performers succeed in pulling the balloon down to where the troupe can tie the ropes around the saddle horn of each horse. The additional weight of the horses added to it allows them to slowly bring the balloon to a halt.

The pilot and guests, including Lord Warwick, Lord Salisbury, and Lord Stratford come running to the aid of the troupe. Ariana watches them from above pulling the balloon down and securing it to the ground. Their ladies, of course, stand silent. They watch their men pull the great mass to be sandbagged once more. The one called Etienne must be the pilot. He pulls up with a cart of sandbags. He's shouting most of the directions to the men tethering the ropes. French bursts of outrage do not fall on deaf ears. Lord Salisbury speaks to him in French, but Ariana's French is not good enough to understand what is being said although *mon Dieu* does not escape her.

The crowd murmurs. The field is aglow with moonlight where normally it is dark. A spectacular scene emerges in slow motion. A roar of applause ensues. "What heroism!" Lady Salisbury pierces through the crowd, parting it as she moves forward.

Etienne reaches in to open the door to the basket and help Ariana out first.

Lord Raby follows. "There you are, my lady."

Etienne shakes his head to the gentleman on his right. Another *mon Dieu* sequence ensues. "We are very fortunate zis day. No one waz hurt. Ze balloon waz not damaged. Whatever waz she thinking, entering ze basket unattended and alone wiz a gentleman?"

Ariana cannot begin to respond.

The earl and Lady Warwick reach them first.

"We are quite all right, I assure you."

"Yes, thanks to the troupe and Lord Raby's strength and agility at rope climbing." Ariana's eyes are half closed. Her knees are weak and she can barely laugh at her own attempt to lighten the seriousness of the event. An arm wraps around her waist and holds her close to steady her. She rests her head against his shoulder and closes her eyes. For a minute.

Lord Stratford arrives next. He removes his coat and closes it around her shoulders to cover her.

"Come, my dear. We must get you inside immediately, to your room at the inn." He removes her from Lord Raby's hold. She doesn't want to leave his side. Her arm lingers against him. His hand trails along her waist to her elbow, forearm, and grasps her hand in his as she is towed away from him. Ariana reaches back for him. Raby holds onto her until she can no longer touch the tip of his fingers.

"But, Papa, I must speak with Wendell, first. I must speak with Laird Raby. They risked their lives!"

"Now, now, there will be time enough for that. We must get you back to the inn and warmed up. You certainly are not," he clears his throat, "presentable as you are." Lord Stratford blinks a quick glance at the front of her dress. Ariana looks down at the front of her dress. Her mouth shuts tight and she clenches her teeth. Her appearance when she stepped out of the basket and what will be said by the crowd plays in her head. She tightens the coat her father wrapped over her shoulders and quietly allows him to direct her to his waiting carriage. They leave immediately. Ariana is not as chilled as her father believes. She leans her head back. A comfortable smile crosses her lips. The balloon trip was not completely awful. The man who shared it with her, he warms her heart and her soul.

CHAPTER TWENTY-TWO

Toddington Peaks – Spring, 1798

Lady Salisbury stands watching the commotion. Alexander removes the mask he is still wearing.

Lord Raby rushes up to him. "I say, what an ordeal! Do you need any assistance? Are you all right?"

"No, I am quite all right I assure you." Alexander watches Ariana's father escort her into their carriage.

"You know, I had feared Victoria was also aboard because I can't seem to find her anywhere and you know how those two ladies love an adventure. I was tied up for some time in conversation with the marquess and I haven't seen her since. Even missed the call to remove the masks."

Lady Salisbury moves nearer to them. "Alexander, my dear, thank God you are all right. I daresay you gave us a great scare. Whatever were you thinking, taking a *lady* up in that contraption *alone.*"

Alexander glares at her, his irritation is fueled by her accusation. "My dear lady, I assure you I had no designs of the sort. In fact, I heard a lady screaming and discovered it was Lady Ariana alone in the balloon as it was ascending, I could think of nothing but pulling it down which, of course, failed. Subsequently, I was pulled up and had no choice but to climb up into the basket with her. Surely, this is an exception!"

Lady Salisbury gasps and places her hand on her chest. "My dear boy, it is a wonder you did not fall to your death. You must know what it means when a lady of quality is found alone with a man. One can never know how society may choose to spin a tale."

Lady Warwick and the earl join them and Alexander's mother throws her arms around him with tear filled eyes. "It is no matter, for as you may or may not know, Alexander and Lady Ariana are betrothed. We will just move the date ahead." She turns her attention to Lord Warwick. "Is that not so, my lord?"

"Quite. We shall simply move up the date."

Lady Salisbury steps back and peruses the two men from top to bottom. "Apparently, you have not looked at your attire and you have not yet heard the inklings of what is being said. The two of you are dressed exactly alike except that you are wearing navy blue and you, Lord Raby, are wearing black." The two men in question exchange looks of confusion. Realization follows.

Lady Salisbury does not stop there. "You know I have already heard the whisperings that Lord Raby was in the balloon with Lady Ariana alone for a whole hour before being rescued by the troupe. I daresay even my own daughter thought it was Lord Raby with Lady Ariana earlier this evening."

Lord Raby steps forward. "But, I assure you— I was with the marquess since the fireworks."

Lady Salisbury nods her head. "I know. I saw you speaking very intently in the assembly room, but the fact is, the two of you look very much the same, especially masked. This situation has the potential for scandal which I am sure none of our families want. We must get this sorted out." She lowers her voice and continues. "Ariana's most revealing display caught the eye of many."

"My lady..." Alexander is past irritation. "...I assure you that happened during my attempts to climb aboard. I was hanging outside the basket with one arm!"

"I have no doubt and I sympathize, I do."

This may be used to advantage. Ariana compromised. It is what she wanted. But, the *ton* thinks it *was* Lord Raby in the basket. *Flumakin!*

UPON ARRIVAL AT THE inn, Lord Stratford instructs the innkeeper. "Please see that a bath is drawn for my daughter and that the physician is called upon forthwith. We must take care that my dear girl is looked after. She has suffered a great ordeal indeed."

"Immediately, my lord." The man's roaming eyes do not overlook Ariana's torn gown.

"Ariana, my dear, go on up now to your room and take care to keep yourself covered!"

"Yes, Papa, of course, but ye must know this is purely innocent! There was no wrongdoing on Laird Raby's part. Ye must believe me!"

"Now, now, my dear. Do not fret so." Lord Stratford pats the top of Ariana's hand. "All will be forgotten soon enough. I know you're a good gel. Run along and get yourself warmed up and clean so you may see the doctor as soon as he arrives."

Ariana jerks her hand away. "What do ye mean, ye know I am a good gel?"

"Ariana, you must know what people will say."

"*No*, what will people say?" She pulls the coat closer around her neck.

"My dear girl, you were in that contraption close to an hour and alone with a man who is not your husband."

"Papa, he was trying to help me! Ye must know this! The *ton* must know this! If I hadn't pulled him into the basket he surely would have fallen to his death! There was no choice in the matter. Surely, ye must see this."

"Yes, yes, my dear. I know and we are most grateful to the young man. Eh, Lord Raby, you say?"

"Yes. Laird Raby. Did ye not see him when we landed?"

"My attention was on you. To get you covered up and into the carriage as soon as could be. We cannot have you taking a chill, my dear girl."

"Donna tell me people are condemning his actions? That they somehow see him as compromising me?"

"Ariana, that will be quite enough. You were seen and that is all I will say on the matter. Now, move along up to your room so you can get warm. We cannot have you catching a cold. The bath is probably already drawn. And you must see that the maid takes those clothes for cleaning and mending, if they can be mended." Lord Stratford finishes his sentence worn and tired, turns, and walks down the hall.

IT'S NOT LONG BEFORE Alexander joins Lord Stratford in a private parlor of the inn.

"Sir, have you had an opportunity to talk to Ariana about what happened?"

"Only briefly. I'm quite determined she get some rest and a warm bath."

"Quite proper, sir."

"The doctor arrived a few moments before you and is with her now. I expect all will be well and nothing a good night's rest won't cure, but I must take every precaution, you know."

"Absolutely, sir. I must relay to you sad news, however."

"What's that?"

"Someone deliberately set the balloon to ascend."

"Deliberately, you say! Why on earth would someone do this?

"I cannot know, sir, but Lady Ariana most assuredly claims there was a man who saw her enter the basket and shortly after cut the sandbags setting the balloon to flight. She is quite certain, although it was too dark to make out the blackguard's face."

"What foolery is this! Who would do such a thing? I cannot imagine anyone wishing my dear girl harm."

"I'll be damned if I can see the right of it. I must ask if there is any way that *you* might have been the intended target."

"Me?" The bushy white brow of Lord Stratford twitches.

"Do you know of anyone who would want to hurt you?

"Hurt me?" Lord Stratford rubs his hands across his girth. "Hogwash. I can't imagine who and to what end?"

"Ariana *is* your only daughter and it stands to reason someone may try to get to you through her."

"I had not thought of that, but I cannot think of anyone at this moment. I am quite distressed over the matter. Quite. And, you, of course know what is being said by members of the *ton*."

"Excuse me, sir." The doctor clears his throat and enters the parlor. "I apologize for intruding. I assume you want an update on the young lady's health as soon as possible."

"Yes, come in." Lord Stratford motions to the doctor to join them. "How goes my dear girl?"

"All is well. I see no need to overly concern yourself. I have given her strict instructions to remain in bed the rest of the evening. I gave her an elixir to help her relax and rest easy tonight. She is to take it as needed in the coming days. Physically, she is fine but after an experience such as this she may feel distress and should take to her bed until it is passed." Dr. Preston shrugs on his dark coat.

"Thank God. I shall see to it she does just that. Shall I see you out?"

"No, no, I am quite familiar with the establishment. I'll leave my bill at the front. Take care."

Lord Stratford turns back to Alexander. "Well, that is one less thing to worry our heads over."

"May I ask what your plans are now, sir?"

"Why we must away to Wentworth Hall at first light, I'm sure!"

"I agree. I cannot like the idea of someone lurking around who wants to do you harm. Now, on to the other matter of concern between us."

"What's that you say? Oh, yes, right. That. We must tell her now because she was quite distressed at the thought she now may be forced to marry Lord Raby as society believes it was he in the balloon and not you."

"I have been thinking about that and the possible outcomes. I cannot disagree we must make known my indiscretion at her expense, I believe it may serve a purpose to keep my identity a secret still until we find out who is at the bottom of this. It will be much easier for me to discover who is behind it if I am not considered to be her betrothed. In fact, it may serve us well to encourage a union between Lord Raby and your daughter in light of these events. We do not know the intended target yet. Amidst the turmoil, the planned announcement of our betrothal was forgone for the evening. I say we let this play out and I'll enlist the help of my mother to that end. She knows very well how to manipulate those of the *ton* into seeing things her way. She'll not object to such designs, I am sure."

The earl rubs his midriff and contemplates the matter "I believe you may be right. Let's give it a little time, mind you. To see what can be discovered."

"Excellent! I've already taken the liberty of sending inquiries to my man of business in London. We may need to involve Bow Street on this. I'll not tolerate such insolence in my home. I must know who was behind it and why. We cannot take any chances of some other event occurring."

"Good. It's settled."

"I shall be in touch. Before I go, may I give my regards to Lady Ariana?"

Lord Stratford smiles a half grin. His countenance is strained from the events. "My boy, I know how you must feel, but I must decline allowing it at this time. I'm sure she's in bed on doctor's orders and I believe we have already created quite enough gossip for one night, wouldn't you say?"

Alexander is not pleased. He wants to reassure himself she is safe. An ordeal like this can have unknown consequences. He's not sure *he* won't be disturbed by the evening's events. "If you think it is best, although it would only be for a few minutes."

"I do. Think it best."

CHAPTER TWENTY-THREE

Wentworth Hall – Spring, 1798

Once at Wentworth Hall, Lord Stratford wastes no time enlisting the help of the constable to watch over the grounds and Ariana.

Ariana follows the doctor's orders and keeps to her room for a few days but it's been too long. Too long shut off from the outside world. Ariana ventures out and decides to take dinner with her father instead of in her room.

"My dear, it's wonderful to see you looking so well again. You look positively radiant this evening. How do you feel?"

"Much improved, papa." Her calm voice stuns her. She cannot shake the unsettled feelings that plague her. Someone might want to harm her. This sends her insides ajar. Lord Raby has not been to see her in many days. This, too, leaves her unnerved. Will he ever call on her again? If not for him, and for Wendell with his troupe, she would have been killed. Shivers trail down her spine.

Her father's voice returns her to the present. "Are you sure? You seem cold." Not waiting for her response, he instructs the butler. "Hawthorne, see that more wood is added to the fire."

"Papa, I'm fine. Believe me."

"It still would do well to warm the place up a bit. I say, I cannot wait for the summer months to arrive. The drafts in this house will be the end of me."

Ariana smiles at her father knowing the fire is being stoked on her account. She picks at her food. Picks at memories with

Lord Raby even amidst imminent danger. Thinking of him warms her enough. She must be glowing. What will she do now? Her dearest friend will be heartbroken and it is these thoughts her father intercepts. "Are you sure you are well, my dear? You look flushed and you are hardly eating."

"I am not unwell. I admit I do still have feelings of uneasiness from time to time."

"That is quite understandable given the circumstances. I daresay it could have been much worse. You are taking that elixir the doctor prescribed?"

"Yes, of course."

"Try not to worry so, my dear. The viscount has enlisted the help of a skilled investigator adept at handling such things... shall we say... discreetly?"

"The viscount? Whyever is he involved?"

"Of course, he would be involved. Why would he not be? The transgression occurred at Toddington Peaks did it not? And have you forgotten? He is interested in protecting your welfare."

"Of course, papa. I only meant that given the recent turn of events— what I mean is the scandal—"

"No, no, no, there is no such thing. Scandal, indeed. There is no scandal. Lady Warwick and Lady Salisbury have been most helpful in discussing the matter with— shall we say— certain *influential* members of the *ton*."

"What exactly have they been discussing?"

"You know, whatever it is that ladies discuss to dispel such incorrect notions without giving rise to *more* incorrect notions."

"That certainly clears things up." It seems she does do sarcasm too.

"Ladies of such rank are quite schooled in the manner of acceptable decorum, I've no doubt they set matters straight in a way most appropriate to these types of circumstances. I do not know exactly what was said, only that the matter has been cleared up and you have nothing to worry about." Lord Stratford takes a bite from his plate and taps his glass to be refilled.

Lovely. No Scandal. All her plans for naught. At least she is alive, thanks to Wendell. "Papa, ye know we must do something for Wendell and the troupe. They did save my life. Could we invite them for an evening at Wentworth Hall as honored guests?"

"I think that to be a good idea, indeed. Of course, we must do something. But, dear, there is a matter I must discuss with you." Lord Stratford's tone turns somber. "You know that while I did my best to avoid what I feared could happen, you were in the balloon with him for close to an hour *alone*. There has been talk of it being inappropriate."

"Inappropriate? Ye just told me Lady Salisbury and Lady Warwick were taking care of the matter discreetly. Whatever are they saying?" Ariana remembers her *inappropriate* behavior and blushes.

Her father closes his eyes when he says her name. "Ariana, you were *seen*."

"What do ye mean *seen*?" Her voice stammers, her head hurts.

"I've heard from different sources that you were seen in the arms of the man in the balloon with you and, well, I fear you have been compromised."

"Compromised? Papa, I am confused. Didn't ye just say all would be taken care of and there would be no *scandal*?"

"Yes, that is exactly what I am saying. What all of us seemed to forget, until Lady Salisbury most befittingly pointed out, amidst all the confusion and uproar of the evening's events there was no announcement of your betrothal."

"No announcement? I'm still at a loss as to what ye mean?"

"Simply put, my dear, the viscount must agree to break the engagement and you must marry Lord Raby."

"Are ye saying Laird Raby has offered to marry me? And, didn't ye just say the viscount was interested in my welfare?"

Attempting to contain the confounded slip, Lord Stratford responds quick and clean. "Offered to marry you? Not in so many words. We've discussed the matter at length and there is no alternative. You were seen with Lord Raby and so, in order for all our families to remain free of reproach, it's decided you must marry him. And, yes, the viscount and his father, I might add, are most concerned about your welfare for you were victimized as a guest at their estate." There. A proud recovery.

"It was decided? Again? Without consulting me?"

"Are you unhappy with the result? I was under the distinct impression you may be pleased with this strange turn of events. I don't mind telling you I had thought you developed a certain tendre for Raby."

"Tendre?" She can't say more. Inside, she's reeling. Confused excitement conflicts with guilt and sorrow. Dear Victoria. Can she forgive her?

Ariana needs to compose herself. It will not do. Finally, she finds her voice again. "Victoria and Nev— I mean— Laird Raby is in love with Victoria! *They* are to be married. I cannae do that to Vicky. No! I willnae." Ariana covers her face with her hands. "How did this happen?" She places her hands in her lap. "I must marry the viscount." Ariana can't believe she said those words. Her heart is tight in her chest. She cannot break the heart of her dearest friend.

"Well, my dear. We've gotten ourselves into a fine mess, that is for sure, but there is nothing to be done. You must marry Lord Raby. There is no alternative. Victoria will get over it. She is young and she has many suitors I am sure."

What he is not sure of, however, is how they are going to turn this around *again* once they solve the mystery of who the true target of this villainy is. Lord Stratford taps his glass for another refill. His lovely Arabella would never agree to deceiving their daughter this way. There is no other solution.

He misses his lady's soft word and kind help. She would know how to best handle it all where Ariana is concerned. All he can do is what he deems best. For her.

CHAPTER TWENTY-FOUR

Wentworth Hall – Spring, 1798

Ariana's plans for their dinner guests proceed quite smoothly except for her efforts to speak with Vicky. Why is she avoiding her? The invitation has been sent. Why no response? Ariana decides to call at Harlaxton and invite her personally. This is important. She must thank Wendell and his troupe for saving her life and what better way to honor them. Vicky must be there too. Ariana pulls up to Harlaxton in her father's carriage and is met by their Butler. His black eyes and line for lips is odd. Chadwick knows her. Why won't he step aside and let her in?

"Chadwick, I am sure ye must be mistaken."

"I am sorry, m'lady, but Lady Victoria is not available to callers today." Not available to callers? Anyone but her. Vicky always takes her call.

"Ye donna understand. I must see her. Come now, Chadwick, ye know me. I must speak with her. She willnae refuse. Ye know this." Chadwick's lip line turns white. "Will ye just ask her if she will see me?"

"I am sorry, miss. I cannot." The door closes and Ariana returns to the carriage and slumps in her seat.

She returns to Wentworth Hall and sees Lord Raby's horse being cared for by the stable boy. She meets Hawthorne at the door. "Laird Raby?"

"Eh, the gentlemen are in the study at the moment. Shall I announce your arrival and wish to join them?"

"No, I donna think so. I'm a bit tired at the moment. I'll not disturb them." They may be discussing wedding contracts. Ariana sorely wants to see him. She has not spent any time with him since their adventure in the skies. Vicky's refusal to accept her is too upsetting. Too much left to do to prepare for the evening's event. She'll see him then.

LORD STRATFORD AND Alexander are indeed in the study. Their conversation is not of the nature Ariana imagined.

"Sir, I have spoken with the marquess and Lord Raby. I explained to them the nature of our situation. Lady Salisbury has also agreed to allow the charade to play out according to our plans. Victoria has agreed to decline seeing Ariana until the day of our wedding, even in the wake of Ariana's persistence at speaking with her."

"Very good."

"I must ask, do you still think it wise to continue this charade? I am beginning to feel we should tell her the truth."

Lord Stratford shakes his head. "I do not see we have any alternative. Now this has become public, people must believe she is marrying Lord Raby and we must uncover who it was that set that balloon off."

"But, really, can we not find some other way?"

"No, no. I feel this is the best course. After you're married, your mother and Lady Salisbury will do what they do so well and hopefully it will be seen as a necessary ruse to discover the identity of who would do such an abominable thing to my dear girl."

Alexander taps his finger against his temple. "Yes, the ladies do know how to turn a tale."

"I've also arranged for Constable Daniels, whom I have known and respected for many years, to stay as security for the evening's events. I feel we have done all we can do unless you are able to come up with any other alternatives?"

"I have racked my brain for days on this and I cannot see another way to approach it. We must get the cad to reveal himself."

"Constable Daniels assures me if the man has tried once, he will try again. We must be on guard." Lord Stratford leans back in his chair.

"Agreed, although, I still cannot like this deception."

"Nor do I, but it is necessary."

Alexander pulls out a pocket watch to check the time and stands up. "I must be off. But, before I go, might I see Lady Ariana?"

Lord Stratford stands up. "You'll not let on about our designs, I hope?"

"Of course not!"

"You must take care in her presence, my boy, she's a sharp one." Lord Stratford walks around his desk. "I've slipped a couple of times and thought all was lost."

"While I don't pretend to be exempt from her quick wit, I will only be a few minutes. I must admit I've missed her horribly."

"As well you should!" Lord Stratford claps him on the back as he walks toward the door. "Take care you keep your senses. I will not tolerate indiscretion." Lord Stratford's eyes mark a target right through Alexander as he tightens his grip on his shoulder.

Lord Stratford calls for Hawthorne. "Please direct Lord Bar— uh— Lord Raby to the parlor." He winks at Alexander now that his point is made and clips him on the back one last time. "And let Ariana know she has a caller."

KNOTS. NO, ROCKS. MAYBE some magical creature clawing at her insides? So much for relaxing with a good book. Miss Charlotte Smith's *Emmeline* does not help Ariana's nerves or serve to remove her thoughts from her current situation. It only serves to remind her of it. Lord Raby is in the parlor waiting for her. How will her story end? It has been days since she has visited with him. Vicky will not see her. The scandal she wished to accomplish has proven more successful than she anticipated. But at the expense of her good friend. She has longed to see him for days and now he is here. What is she waiting for? She straightens her dress, pinches her cheeks, and lifts her skirt a bit from the floor. No repeats of their first encounter. She enters the parlor stifling a snort.

Alexander reaches out for her and in seconds hauls her close, nuzzling his face against her cheek. "I missed you these past few days. How have you been?"

Ariana nudges him away and turns to walk toward the window, arms folded as she looks out across her gardens. "I've missed you too. Why has it taken so long for ye to come and see me?"

He follows her to the window and stands behind her. His voice is a whisper touching her ear. "I am sorry, love, but I have been very much involved with finding the person or persons responsible for setting that balloon aloft— with you in it!"

He called me *love*. "Do ye think we will find the person responsible?"

"We are doing everything possible. Do not worry, my dear, we'll find him."

Raby caresses her arms up and down. Shivers run rampant throughout her body. Can he see them? She needs them to stop. Conversation. Keep speaking. She turns to face him. "No doubt ye've heard what is being reported about us?"

"Yes, it appears our *scandal* worked as planned." His smile is wide and happy.

"Not exactly, for I am still to be married— as are you!"

"Certainly you are not completely displeased about the turn of events? I think you have some inkling as to my feelings for you? As I believe you feel the same?" Is this possible?

"The same? Ye've not expressed to me your feelings, sir, nor have I."

"Have I not? I thought it was clear." His smile does not leave his face and he bends closer to nibble on her ear. Now the chills go down her neck. Why does he keep doing this to her?

"Clear?" Her voice sounds like a squeak. Certainly Emmeline would not be reacting like this. She is not Emmeline. Infernal drivel. Not what she should be thinking at a time like this.

"Yes, clear." He continues tapping kisses on the corner of her lips before settling warmly in the center. There, now. He needn't stop.

"My laird, please, we must stop." She manages to whisper stop only because she must.

"Do you still have doubts as to my feelings for you?"

"Why should I not? Ye have never expressed yer intentions other than helping me with my dilemma, seeing as it suited ye as well. I thought we..."

He interrupts her midway. "Ariana, how can you still be at a loss as to my affections for you? I have loved you from the moment you fell face first at my feet."

He remembers too. His eyes do not leave her face. Her cheeks burn. "But, I thought..."

"Do not think— *know*— I love you and I am most happy at the thought of taking you as my wife. Say you will agree and not continue to be upset at how this all happened. I *love* you. Will you marry me?"

Words will not reach Ariana's mouth. Thoughts from her head are clashing with her feelings. War is raging in her stomach. These words are unexpected. She does *love* him. Still, the words will not spill out. She stands frozen looking at his handsome face waiting for her response.

"Well, my dear? If you say no, I promise I will go to your father and tell him we do not suit. It is up to you."

"Ye would do that for me?" She doesn't want him to do that.

"I would do that for you." This will allow Vicky her happiness.

"But, what about the scandal? What will be said?"

"Do not worry. We'll come up with something on that end. My mo... I am sure I can encourage Lady Salisbury and Lady Warwick to spin a tale of some credit. I will not allow you to be compromised in any way. It's your choice. I will not marry a woman who does not feel the same for me as I do for her."

Ariana's senses and emotions are spinning out of control. This man standing in front of her is *asking* her to marry him. It is what she has been fighting for. A choice. Her choice. He makes her feel things. New things. They laugh together. The man risked his life for her! He is her shelter from the storm.

"I see." The soft break in his voice as he turns to leave snaps her back to the present.

"What? Oh, no, ye donna see." She jerks him back to her. "Yes, I will marry ye." Her arms wrap around him forcing him down to kiss her once again.

He sweeps her up holding her dangling off the ground. This time, it is Ariana who kisses him intensely, spiking his hair with her fingers. He sets her down so her feet touch the ground. His hold never loosens as he strums her back with his touch. This is the longest he has ever kissed her. Let him be the one to stop. He is her *one*.

His holly blue eyes finally stare back. She is breathless. "I guess I *have* fallen head over heels for ye— literally."

"Indeed." His breaths are short too. His smile is warm. She reaches to touch his lips. He kisses her fingers. "I wonder how your birds would view me now?"

"My birds?" Laughter gurgles out. "Max? Ye remember him? Now?"

Alexander's eyes crinkle in the corners from the reach of his smile. "Yes, of course, I remember!"

"Ye were so irritated, but wanted to hide it. I had a devil of a time holding back the fits."

"Fits?"

"My laughter, of course."

"Right. Yes, well I guess I was slightly irritated. Your laughing didn't help." He kisses her again. "That is nothing to what I would endure for you, my love." And, again, one more kiss on her lower lip before breaking their embrace.

Alexander turns to sit on the couch opposite the fireplace. "So, about this dinner. I have already sent word to Wendell and the troupe that I will send my carriage to pick them up. I've also arranged for them to stay at the inn for the night. They should be well on their way by now, I expect."

"How lovely! You have thought of everything! I cannot wait for us to see Wendell and his troupe to thank them for all they have done for us. I still donna want to think what would have happened had they not rescued us." She cannot bear the distance Alexander put between them and plants herself next to him on the couch.

He wraps his arm around her shoulders as she leans into him. "Yes, my love, anything could have happened. I am sure it will be a delightful evening for you are a charming hostess." He finds her neck once again and starts nibbling. "Mmm." Sensations are rekindled. Does he know what he is doing? He must.

Her stomach lurches. Everything halts. She stands up. "But, what about Vicky? We have not even thought about the pain it will cause her."

"Ariana, please do not worry so. Come, sit back down." His hand reaches and grabs onto hers. "It is true there is a measure of affection between us, but there is nothing more. She will come about, I am sure." His kind words and soft touch maneuver her back down beside him.

"I dunno. She refuses to see me for days and willnae return my invitations. I went there personally and Chadwick refused admittance."

"My love, I promise you all will be forgotten soon. You will see."

"I hope ye're right. Vicky and I have been friends our entire lives and I cannae bear to lose her."

"Trust me, my dear." His arm tightens around her and she leans back once more against his chest. She plays with the buttons on his waistcoat.

"How can ye be sure?"

"Because I believe there may be another person who has caught her eye and she may be moving on as we speak."

Ariana straightens up again and turns to face him. "I have not spoken with her so I dunno, what is his name? What is he like? I want her to find someone to make her as happy as I am."

"Are you happy?"

Ariana snuggles down against him once more. "Yes, verra happy."

He bends his head flurrying soft kisses across her lips. His embrace envelops her drawing her down on top of him as he leans back, lying flat on the couch. She lets out a light squeal. The intimacy of their position. The hardness of his body under her. He circles his arms tight around her.

"What is it?" This closeness feels awkward. But, still she is safe.

"You are the most beautiful woman I have ever known and I cannot wait for us to be married. In fact, I am quite thankful now for the scandal so we have good reason not to wait. I don't think I can wait much longer to make you mine."

"I have already said yes, my love, so I am most definitely yours." She lays her head down on his chest.

She called me *love.* "That, my dear, is not quite my meaning."

Ariana knocks on the hard cover of his book in his front jacket pocket. "Will ye ever tell me what this dreadful book is for?"

"Dreadful book? I had not thought you to be interested in my *dreadful* book." Is she jealous? The frown on her face is not something he enjoys seeing. It needs promptly removed. He reaches to pull the book from its place.

"I have often wondered what it is that ye carry with ye everywhere ye go." Hmm. Females. Not unlike felines.

"Well, here it is. Take a look."

Cute. She's holding the book in her hands while balancing her elbows on his chest. A little uncomfortable. It's worth it. Ariana leafs through the pages. She stops at the purple storm. One of his favorites. "I recognize the shapes and textures. These are illustrations of clouds. They're beautiful. Did ye draw them?"

"Yes."

"What are the numbers?"

"They're calculations. We're trying to develop a tracking system. Some of the numbers represent how powerful we anticipate it to be and then how it may end up. Sometimes we're right, sometimes we're not. It's in development." She continues to study the pages and illustrations.

Her interest in his drawings delights him. "So what do you think?"

Ariana examines the book and its pages. "I think they are phenomenal. I've seen all these clouds before. Do ye have names for them?"

"There is currently some disagreement in the field as to what to call them. Luke is actually working on that now."

"Luke? Isn't he a bit young?"

"Not so young as he appears. There's not much data right now and Luke seems to have a talent for collecting it. He's part of a group trying to gather information so we can better understand the clouds and storms. It may all help to better predict the weather."

"How fascinating! Are there any ladies in this group of yours?" Her elbows poke into his ribcage and he adjusts her arms to compensate.

"Ladies? Um, no. I'm afraid not." He twirls a wayward strand of her hair around his finger. Her eyes are aglow. Page by page she peruses his book.

"I would love to be able to follow these clouds with ye. Tell me I can. Please? Ye know I am quite adept with watercolors, I can paint them as ye record your data."

Her enthusiasm thrills him. "I would be delighted to have you join me while I chase the clouds." He promptly removes the book from her hands and deposits another kiss to her cheek, returns it to its place in his jacket, and encircles her afresh in his solid embrace. He cannot believe it. A woman who does not fear his interests, who will support him, who will join him. He has found her. There truly is a female such as this.

The rhythmic sound of their breathing is relaxing, they are alone too long. He is about to mention this fact himself, but Ariana does so instead. "My laird, I am afraid it is time for ye to go." He cannot help but nuzzle close to her one more time. Her lavender scent, he likes how it unsettles him.

"If I must." He is slow to move. Lazy. He enjoys feeling lazy with her.

"Yes, I believe ye should for we still have much to do to prepare for tonight." She nuzzles closer to him. Does she know what her closeness does to him? Probably not. She soon will.

His voice is rough. "If you want me to leave, you will have to get up first." She doesn't move.

"Ariana?"

"I'm thinking..."

"You're *thinking*?" The minx. "Well, you better not think too long or we *will* have a compromising situation." Still not moving. He stretches and tickles her ribcage. She squeals. He stands up with her and then secures her back on the couch. Mischief looks back. "I can see we will have many diversions together, you and I."

Alexander bends forward, plants an arm on the back of the couch on either side of her, pinning her down. He looks her squarely in the mossy green of her eyes. He bestows her one last parting kiss, exquisite in flavor and affection, before making his way to the door.

CHAPTER TWENTY-FIVE

Harlaxton House and Thereabout – Spring, 1798

"I am sorry, m'lady, but Lady Victoria is not available to callers today."

"Victoria!" Lady Salisbury hisses. "Move away. She will see you." Lady Salisbury pulls Victoria into the first floor sitting room at Harlaxton House.

"What about you, Mama? Do you not think she will hear you?"

"Don't be daft. She cannot possibly hear me from this distance and Chadwick barely has the door open." Victoria looks back through the doorway as her mother pulls her closer to the fire in the sitting room. "Come, let's sit down and you can tell me how things are going." Lady Salisbury sits and pats the settee cushion for Victoria to place herself next to her.

"Mama, I can't bear it! I just can't." Her mother purses her lips.

"What is it exactly you cannot bear?"

"Aria, of course." How can her mother not know this? "It has been days since the balloon accident and I haven't even been to see her once."

As if her lips could get any thinner. "You know very well why. We must do this for her. And, you know very well it wasn't an accident."

"Yes, well, isn't that what the ladies of the *ton* are calling it?"

"That may be, as it was needed to help muffle any perceived scandal. And, Lady Warwick would be most displeased if it were known to be an attempted murder at one of their gatherings."

"*Nooo*, we couldn't possibly have that..."

"Victoria Rhea! I will have none of that. It is also for the benefit of your friend that we do this."

"I still don't understand how it benefits Aria to keep all this a secret." She slouches and draws a big breath, twirling a lock of her hair around the length of one finger.

"First and foremost, we want to flush out the culprits. It's very important, Victoria. Lord Raby understands the importance as should you."

Victoria sits straight up. "But, to not be involved in the planning of her own wedding? Mama, I feel awful."

"It is as it must be, dear. As it is now, society believes there has been a scandal. There must be a wedding. This is why your role is so important." Her mother moves to sit closer and takes her hand to hold it in her own.

"I don't see it."

"My dear." Lady Salisbury begins by patting her daughter's hand. "You know Ariana. This way you, with my help of course, can plan a beautiful wedding for her while we... Ahem." Lady Salisbury clears her throat. "That is, the authorities figure out who would do such a thing." She coughs.

"Are you all right, mama?"

"Yes, dear. Quite all right." Her mother turns to face the wall and coughs again.

"Do they have any ideas about who could have done this? Has papa told you anything?" What is her mother looking at so intently? Lady Salisbury stands and walks to the window.

But instead of peering out, she removes a watercolor landscape hanging on the wall beside the window. Lady Salisbury stares at the picture.

"None that I have heard." Lady Salisbury turns the portrait around and hangs it back on the wall. Now, it makes sense. Upside down again. "What motive is there? Was this attack directed at Ariana? Or, maybe even Alexander?"

"Alexander? Mama, why would hurting Ariana be viewed as an attack on Alexander?"

"I am not an investigator by any stretch, but all these questions are unanswered. I cannot imagine what reason anyone would have for doing such a thing."

"It's awful to think someone could hate that much. Can you imagine if they weren't successful pulling them down?"

Lady Salisbury returns to sit next to Victoria. "Yes, well, all this needs to be fleshed out. And, then there's the issue of Ariana believing Alexander is Lord Raby."

Victoria turns to face her mother. "Yes, I don't understand why we can't just tell her?"

Lady Salisbury begins to brush stray wisps of hair from her daughter's face and gently holds her chin. "I just explained it. Lord Stratford wants things to go on as they are for now and we must follow his direction." Her mother releases the hold on her chin and Victoria looks down at her lap. Uneven wrinkles in the fabric of her dress pull at her attention and she attempts to smooth them.

"Aria has been through a lot." The wrinkles will not smooth out so Victoria decides to leave them for now. She pulls a pillow on her lap and holds it tight.

"There is no doubt. This is the best way to catch the person responsible and it works well with our plans to diffuse the scandal."

"How so?"

"Victoria, please stop fidgeting. The servants will think you are calling for them with that constant thumping of your foot to the floor."

"I'm sorry, mama. I didn't realize."

"I declare, you mustn't worry so. Things will work out. You'll see. We're going to put it all to a ruse used to find the offender. The gossips will eat it up."

"La, Mama! It's all so mind-boggling. To think of everything poor Aria is dealing with now."

"That is why it's important she have the support of her friends, yes?"

"Well, I'm going to make sure she has the best wedding possible."

"And how are those plans going?"

"I have almost everything arranged, but I must get with Alexander the moment he returns to review a few details in the plans."

"I know you will arrange for her everything that is beautiful and appropriate which is why I'm allowing you to take the lead. You must remember, though, society must see me as helping with the arrangements. Yes?" Lady Salisbury replaces the pillow to the corner of the couch and twists to lean her back against it.

"Yes, I know. You've told me hundreds of times. It's all very exciting, but I can't help feeling sad it's not my own. Has papa said anything to you about *my* Lord Raby asking permission to pay his addresses?"

Her mother's eyes widen. "*Your* Lord Raby?"

"Yes, well, I'm feeling a bit possessive of late."

"My dear. I know it's hard, but you must be patient. You cannot rush your father in these things."

"Rush him? So, they have discussed it?" Victoria scoots forward to grab her mother's hands.

"Truthfully, I don't know. That is, I cannot be sure."

Victoria pulls her hands back. "What do you mean?"

Lady Salisbury turns to face her. "The few times I tried to speak of it, we were interrupted and I haven't been able to find out."

Victoria twists forward and pulls the pillow in a tight hug, again.

"Are you sure of Lord Raby's affections for you, dear?"

"There is no doubt on that account."

"Victoria, I hope you have conducted yourself as a proper lady should!"

That crack in the ceiling has been there for years. They really need to do something to have it repaired.

"Victoria, tell me. Tell me you did not compromise yourself!"

Victoria returns her attention to her mother's white face. Lovely. More tight lips. "Of course I didn't compromise myself and I always conduct myself as a proper lady should."

"I certainly hope so. And, please. The thumping? Can you not learn to control that?"

"I can't help it. Waiting is frustrating and it's hard to plan someone else's wedding when you want to be planning your own. And to be clear. I only meant there is no doubt of his particular affection for me."

"Is that so? Then you won't mind telling me more about it?"

"Really, mama! I certainly do not have time to give you such details, but be assured I have conducted myself properly."

"Victoria, I think I might need a little more clarification."

"Not now, Mama, I really need to get back to this wedding I'm planning so I can be ready for Alexander when he returns." Clarification? Not a chance. Victoria begins to walk out of the sitting room. The doors open and Chadwick enters.

"Pardon the intrusion, my lady, but there was an odd knocking and I wanted to check to be sure you were not in need of assistance."

Perfect timing. Victoria sprays her palm with giggles. She walks past to leave. "No need for alarm, Chadwick. Just our resident ghost." Chadwick rolls his eyes to the ceiling. Victoria roars her laughter through the door as she leaves.

"Victoria? We're not finished with this discussion. Flumakin!"

WHERE THE DEVIL IS he going? "*Shh*...easy boy." Raby pats Dante's neck. They pick sideways along the trail following the dark figure ahead. Dante's tail swats to the side. His rear end struggles to remain straight. "Calm. We're going to stay close, but not too close to be seen." *Thump. Thump, thump, thump.* Hooves beat hard on the dirt. Raby circles a few times to steady the horse.

Raby looks around and behind. No one. Something clearly has Dante spooked. Truth be told, it doesn't take much to spook Dante. Raby reaches in his front coat pocket to pull out his telescope. He rolls it into focus and scans the area. Good. His mark is still ahead. At least it's not him who doubled back. It must be an animal. Maybe Dante was not the best choice for this expedition.

"Steady on." He clicks his tongue in his cheeks to encourage a cantor. Dante will not have it. His ears pull back and he rears. Raby loosens the reins and grabs at the pommel to stay mounted but is on his backside in seconds. Dante's black tail flicks him in the face on the way.

"Bloody hell!" Raby stands, swipes his forehead with the back of his hand, and flicks the dust from his legs and the back of his breeches. Dante is nothing but a spot of bay and black color moving off in the distance now.

Raby spins around in the opposite direction. His target will be long gone. He picks up the telescope and inspects the lenses. Still intact. He peers through the small end. Nothing. He will not be able to find out the identity of Watson's visitor today. The telescope is returned to his front coat pocket. Raby picks up his hat, brushes it off, and replaces it on his head. The rim is torn and dangling above his ear. Wonderful. The surveillance of Watson is complete, for today anyway. He heads back in the direction of the stables. Salisbury will not be pleased with today's results.

Raby pulls out his timepiece to see what time it is. Good. No scratches and it's still intact. There is still time to meet up with the weather predictors Alexander introduced him to. Maybe he can yet salvage the day to Salisbury's satisfaction.

CHAPTER TWENTY-SIX

Harlaxton House – Spring, 1798

Alexander mounts his stallion to return to Harlaxton. The day of his wedding cannot be here too soon. The dinner party tonight will be another opportunity to see Ariana. His stallion perks his head to listen. Something moves in the woods. Nothing appears. Alexander turns around to look behind. Nothing. Wait. Is that a Cleveland Bay with no rider? It's hard to tell from this distance. Someone may be hurt. Alexander surveys the area. No one.

"There, boy. Ease yourself. It's nothing." Alexander tightens the reins to steady his stallion. An unexpected jolt will land him on his backside. He won't fall nearly as efficient as Wendell was thrown from the horse in the ring. His excuse will not be nearly as good either. Wendell! He knows his true identity. How will he keep Ariana from discovering their secret from Wendell? If only her father would permit him to tell her the truth. He has no option, but to be called away from the event entirely. He is not pleased. Ariana will not be either. He hates to see her sad.

No one is about at Harlaxton. This gives him the opportunity to pen word to Lord Stratford for the arrangement of his absence at dinner. Hawthorne will give him a note the moment they arrive stating he is called away on urgent business that cannot be delayed.

It's not long before Lord Stratford sends word back agreeing to the suggestion. Alexander is quick to review the contents of the letter. He further requests Alexander help keep a watchful eye outside the house for anything that may appear amiss—discreetly, of course. "Of course."

Alexander readies himself quickly for the evening is already close. He will need to borrow an additional carriage from Salisbury in order to get the troupe to Wentworth Hall. The inn is not too far so it will not take long.

Wendell and his troupe are ready and waiting. Wendell's smile is plastered across his face. Alexander ushers them into the waiting carriages. As they approach Wentworth Hall, repetitive comments of grandeur and splendor are expressed for the meticulous gardens. His own reaction when he first set eyes on this spectacular home was not unlike theirs.

Each member steps out of the carriage with their head uplifted at the immensity of what stands before them. They are all dressed in their best attire, timid in their approach to the door. Hawthorne blasts past the guests straight to Alexander and hands him a piece of paper.

"My lord, an urgent message just arrived."

"Thank you, Hawthorne." Alexander reads the note and turns to Wendell. "My dear boy, I must beg your pardon, but I have been called away on urgent business that cannot be put off. I will leave the one carriage here to take you and your company home. Please accept my humble apologies." Alexander nods his head and takes his leave.

"Ye must take care of bus'ness, o'course, sir. Hope ever'thin works out." Vacant stares from Wendell and his troupe follow him back to his carriage. Too bad he will not be able to be there for Wendell. He'll need an encouraging comment or two to help him feel at ease, but then Ariana will make them feel comfortable.

"WENDELL, I AM SO HAPPY to see ye! Welcome to Wentworth Hall!" Arms wide open, Ariana greets each member with the same enthusiasm she bestows upon all her guests. They deserve so much more for their brave rescue of her. This is the least she can do.

"Please come in. Be comfortable. Let Hawthorne take your coats." She motions them further into the hall. They're all looking around, up, and down when Wendell begins to introduce them. Wentworth Hall has always been her home. To see so much interest in it is strange, though it's true they've probably never seen the inside of an estate like Wentworth. Ariana allows them to enjoy the experience.

"I would be delighted to give a tour after dinner, would ye like that?"

"Yes, ma'am. That would be nice." The one called Polly answered.

"Wendell, where is Lord Raby?"

Wendell looks around and repeats the subject of her question. "Lord Raby?"

Lord Stratford enters the vestibule from his study in time to answer Ariana's question. "Oh, yes, my dear, please do not worry yourself on that account. He received word of some urgent business that could not be held off. He hopes to return later this evening unless the matter cannot be settled. Now, my dear, let us all go in and begin the evening festivities, shall we?"

They move in further to the parlor, Wendell mentions the portrait of Lady Arabella hanging over the fireplace through the doors of the study. "Is that ya'mum, m'lady?"

Ariana stops to look where his attention is drawn. "Why, yes, Wendell, that is Lady Arabella. She is my mother."

Wendell examines the picture. Everyone gathers around him to view the portrait. Lord Stratford stands next to Ariana in calm contemplation as he places his arm across her shoulder.

Polly splits the silence with her voice. "Wendell she 'as the same color as in your eyes, she does! Ain't never seen eyes like yours 'till now." Polly taps her forefinger against her chin. "Come to think of it, Lady Ariana has a same color. Guess there's more of ya then we thought, eh Wendell?"

Lord Stratford looks at Wendell and then steps back to look at his daughter.

"What do ye think, Papa?"

"They are bright, like yours my dear."

"So, mama has some long lost brother or sister in the circus?"

"Ariana! Do not say such nonsense." Creased lines appear between ruffled gray brows. "We don't need any more talk."

"Ye know I'm being silly."

"Yes, well, not everyone understands your humor."

Wendell and Polly remain silent, looking first at Ariana and then her father.

"Let's go for dinner and continue the conversation there. I'm sure our guests are hungry."

"That is something we agree on my dear." Lord Stratford reaches in to close the door to his study, turns around, and motions them all to continue on to the dining parlor. He flips his hands behind his back and slaps one on top of the other. The crease between his brow deepens.

ALEXANDER WALKS THE grounds of Wentworth Hall. This evening is never ending. He peeks in the window. Lord Stratford's scowl and pacing is worrisome. The sun is down now and dinner will be starting soon. Ariana is radiant in her evening gown of burgundy. He ducks back between the windows to avoid being noticed by one of Wendell's troupe looking through the window. The last thing he needs is to be seen roaming the grounds outside. He'd much rather be inside. By Ariana's side. His methodical watch of the gardens around the house is more important. His efforts are more suited to insure all goes well and Ariana is safe.

He takes a seat on one of the stone benches. He notices their strategic placement throughout the area. Possibly for garden parties or resting during a walk about the estate. His first encounter with Ariana included a walk through this very stretch.

What was that? A movement to the left of that shrub. Very sudden. Maybe the shadows from nocturnal animals in the moonlight? It was just a glint, but he must be sure. There it is again! He cautiously moves in that direction. It's good he is wearing dark clothing. He can be hidden in the dark. There is definitely someone roaming the grounds. No animal. It's too steadfast, too calculating. Constable Daniels? No, he's in the direction of the stables. This person is moving in the opposite direction. Alexander crouches and moves slowly across the green lawn, quiet and determined. He ducks decisive behind the topiaries. There is a stir in the bush next to him. He moves to reach around the bush. Adrenaline surges through his veins and the pounding of his heart thumps between his ears. He reaches his arm out, a branch breaks behind him. He turns to face his attacker. The first thing he sees are black shoes and silver buckles decorated with white pearls. He lets out a deep breath. He knows their owner. Searing pain across the side of his head follows. Pinholes of light flicker against the darkness of the ground merging into pitch black.

CHAPTER TWENTY-SEVEN

Wentworth Hall – Spring, 1798

Hawthorne enters the dining hall just as dessert is being served and heads straight for him. Lord Stratford is familiar with the look of concern his butler displays. Ariana questions him silently with a tilt of her head.

"I shall just be a moment, dear, please continue in my absence." He pats her hand before leaving to dissuade any concern she may have. He can see her from the corner of his vision, watching him all the way to the door. She doesn't believe him. No matter. It's important.

Lord Stratford enters his study. The footmen are carrying Alexander in and laying him on the couch in front of the fire. "My God, man! What happened?" This is important, indeed! "Call for Millie to bring her ointments and tell Hawthorne to call for the doctor immediately!"

Alexander moans and touches his hand to his head.

"Lie still. We've sent word for the doctor and Millie will bring something to help with the pain." Lord Stratford whirls around to address the footmen. "What the deuce happened anyway?"

Lord Stratford slants an eye from one to the other, waiting for a response. "Well?"

One is offered by the one closest to the door. "Constable Daniels was returning from the stables when he noticed a commotion in the corner of the garden by the entrance to the hedge maze. He called to us to follow him when we saw a man club the gentlemen over his head and then take off. Constable told us to get him inside and then he took off after the trespasser on foot. That's all I know, sir."

Lord Stratford paces the room. Will the Constable catch the man? Should he send for reinforcements? Doors slam in the area outside the study. Loud voices bounce off the walls. Lord Stratford opens the door to the study. The dinner party emerges from the other end of the hallway. Constable Daniels is holding a tight-fisted and bound Sir Lewis Rockingham.

Lord Stratford speaks first. "Sir Lewis?" He turns to the lawman. "Constable? What is the meaning of this?"

Wendell pushes to the front of the group. His eyes are wide and round. His voice is higher than normal. "What are *you* doin' 'ere, sir?"

Lord Stratford steps back and stares at Wendell. "You *know* this man?

"He's me uncle, sir. He takes care of me and me mama...sir." Ariana is silent. Her confused stare hops from Wendell to her father.

Lord Stratford glares at the man struggling to free himself. "Constable Daniels, please explain."

He motions them through the door. "Let us go into the study." Wendell follows too. Ariana and the others remain dumbfounded. The doors to the study close leaving them alone in the hall.

Constable Daniels begins. "After I sent the footmen in with Lord Warwick, I ran after this man who was trying to get away. I finally caught up with him and he had this hacksaw." The Constable yanks it from the hand of one of the men with him.

"A hacksaw!" Lord Stratford turns on his cousin, Sir Lewis. The man he thought he knew. "What stupid, fool-minded stunt is this?" Silent poison projects from Rockingham.

The Constable continues. "Upon further inspection, I found that under the viscount's carriage, the wheel rod had been sawed halfway through. There is no doubt this man meant there to be an accident."

Now the poison projects from Lord Stratford. "Rockingham, I ask again. What is the meaning of this? Why?"

Rockingham snarls. The burning rage of a volcano stifled for years erupts. "Why? You ask *me* why? Wentworth Hall, of course! I've worked a lifetime for this."

"You have worked a lifetime? What exactly do you mean by that?" Lord Wentworth returns ice.

"I will be flogged if, when it finally will be mine, any estate assets are to be allotted elsewhere. Wentworth Hall and Wentworth Abbey both belong to me! I shall join the two estates as they should always have been. I'm next in line."

The ice is beginning to crack. "What is this fiddle-faddle? Join the two Estates? Wentworth Hall is doomed without this marriage.

The volcano oozes. "And, who, dear cousin, do you think are your creditors?" Lord Stratford looks at his cousin. The ice breaks. "You mean *you* caused this? And, Ariana? *You* released her alone in the balloon? To what ends?"

"No one has a right to any assets, cash or otherwise. Except me."

"Cash assets? Wentworth Hall is near bankruptcy. You're mad."

Rockingham smiles a frothy, mad grin fit for Balaam. "You think so, cousin? I had it all planned out... all of it... until you had to go and get her betrothed."

Rockingham sits silent now. The Constable urges him to continue, but Rockingham has said all he is going to say.

Lord Stratford sits down behind his desk. He looks at the faces in the room staring at him, waiting for his reaction to this situation. He needs to get Rockingham to talk. "And how do you know Wendell? Since when did you adopt a boy?"

Rockingham purses his lips tight and turns his face to the wall. Obstinate ass. *Jack*ass to be precise.

Alexander grumbles on the couch and sits up. His color is better, but he still must be in pain.

"Alexander, we've found the man responsible for clubbing you over the head, among other things."

"So, I've heard. If I may, my lord..." He flinches as he speaks. "I may have some information you will find most exceptional."

Rockingham now directs his venom at Alexander.

Lord Stratford observes the malice in Rockingham. Good. He's afraid. "Yes? Well, out with it! I must know the extent of my dear cousin's endeavor."

"Yes, right." Alexander grunts and adjusts his position on the couch to face them all more direct. "I must admit, as should you, Wendell has a marked resemblance to Ariana and, well, if I may be so bold, to your wife." Alexander nods his head to Wendell and then to the portrait. All eyes in the room follow.

Alexander continues his account. "I noticed it the first day I saw the boy at the circus. Even now, look as he stands by the mantel alongside your lovely Lady Arabella."

So, someone else has noticed. Since Polly pointed it out earlier, Lord Stratford has not been able to stop thinking about it. "His eyes— you are quite correct. He has Arabella's eyes, and Ariana's as well."

Alexander continues with his deductions. He explains how he suspected Wendell also has the same dimple as Ariana on his left shoulder.

Lord Stratford raises his eyes. "So, you are privy to my daughter's shoulders, lad?"

Alexander mumbles and touches his head where he was clubbed. "I assure you nothing indecent has passed between Ariana and myself. My intentions toward your daughter are completely honorable."

"Yes, yes, I know." Lord Stratford then directs his attention to Wendell. "My dear, boy, would you be so kind as to oblige an old gentleman and show me your left shoulder?"

Wendell, silent and wide-eyed through all this discussion, continues to be so. He takes his hands out of his pockets and nods in silent acceptance, proceeding to unbutton his shirt.

There it is. Just as Alexander had said. It's true. Ariana isn't the only one to have this dimple. He himself has it. The mark of a Stratford. All will need to be further verified, of course. But Stratford already knows the truth of it.

Lord Stratford reels around toward Rockingham. Blades shoot between them. "What is the meaning of this?! You.... YOU!" If he had his dirk he would slay the man where he stands. Fitting too that it be done by the weapon of his late wife.

"All this time, all this time— my son has been alive?!" Still unable to fathom the reality. Lord Stratford repeats. "You knew it! You caused it! All these years? How could you do such an abominable thing!"

The slithering vermin. Rockingham recoils. "How could *I*? I should have let the boy die. I was a younger, more inexperienced man then. Wentworth Hall and Wentworth Abbey belong together. My father should have inherited both. You will not change what I have done! You will not!" Long, pointed fingers poke in the air. "Do you hear me? It makes no difference if the boy is alive or dead. I will have Wentworth Hall and I will be heir of both!"

His frenzied words are lost. His offensive gestures, pokes and spit out words of wrath are lost. Lord Stratford listens without hearing. "Get him out of my sight. I can't stand the stink of him." Stratford waves to Constable Daniels to remove the animal. Only an animal can do such things. The man has wits to let.

All these years, his son is actually alive. It fits together now. Rockingham was there when his son was born. Rockingham arranged for the midwife, arranged for the burial. Stratford could not bring himself to do it, but Rockingham did. He thought it done out of kindness. Trusted Rockingham to manage his finances. He managed to make Wentworth Hall appear bankrupt, all to acquire it!

Wendell. His son. Where is he in the room amidst the chaos? There. Standing there. Alone. What to say? What to do? Lord Stratford heaves him close and envelops him with all the years of emotion a father has for a son thought lost to him forever. His son. His only boy. His heir. The heir to Wentworth Hall.

"WHAT IS IT?" WATSON swivels around in his chair behind his desk. Hamilton's face, bleary-eyes and black shadows, returns his glare.

"Sir, I'm sorry to interrupt."

"Yes, well you have so I'm of the assurance it is of great importance? Hmm?"

Hamilton steps forward one pace and looks straight ahead, clears his throat and coughs. "I'm sorry to inform you there has been an incidence."

"An *incidence*?"

"Yes, sir."

"Can you not elaborate on this so called 'incidence' you are referring to?"

Hamilton coughs again. "Eh..."

Blithering idiot. "That is the reason for your interruption, is it not?" Watson's fingers strum the desk in repetitious motion from pinky to forefinger.

"Uh, yes. Well, you see I have heard from my cousin." Hamilton folds his hands behind his back, raises up on his tip toes once, back down again, and stares at the wall.

"Your cousin?" Is the man a lunatic?

"Yes, you know. The one you asked that we have installed at Wentworth Hall."

"Oh, yes. That cousin." Hamilton stands at attention waiting further instruction. "Shall I postulate on what was heard or shall you present the information to me?"

Hamilton coughs once more and circles his fingers over his mouth as he does so leaving one pinky straight up, he bends forward and continues. "Right. Yes, well, a note was brought around by a boy sent to town for a doctor. It seems someone has been hurt at the estate."

"Hurt." Watson pounds his fist to the desk. "I say, man! Will you get on with it? This one sentence dribble is infuriating! Tell me what it is you have to tell me. Who was hurt and what exactly did the note state?" Insolent clod!

"I don't know exactly who was hurt." Watson circles to the front, fists tight at his side. Hamilton steps back, moves to the side and behind a chair.

Watson follows. "Will you please just tell me? What. It. Said."

"Rockingham has been arrested by Constable Daniels, sir."

One fist meets one jaw. Hamilton drops to the floor. "I just can't find good help these days."

CHAPTER TWENTY-EIGHT

Wentworth Hall – Spring 1798

The doctor arrives at Wentworth Hall not long after the Constable leaves. He examines Alexander and recommends bed rest. Alexander jumps to his feet. "I shall not remain an invalid. I am perfectly fine..." He falters backwards. "...although, I must say I do feel quite tired." His voice trails off. He lowers himself once more on the couch while holding his head.

The doctor surveys his patient, his brows knitted together. "Young man! I fear you may have a concussion and you must try to stay awake for a few hours until we are certain there are no complications. I must insist you remain calm." The doctor places his hand on Alexander's wrist to check his pulse then places the back of his hand on Alexander's forehead to check for fever. He packs his bag to leave and hands Alexander a bottle. "I will leave you with this tonic to take which should relieve some of the pain, but under no circumstances are you to go gallivanting around."

Lord Stratford calls for a room to be prepared.

Alexander sits up straight speaking to Lord Stratford in a hushed voice. "You must not prepare anything, for I must return to Harlaxton as soon as possible. If you wish to keep up this facade, I must not remain here with Wendell and the troupe, for they know my true identity."

"Yes, I see your point. But, the doctor does not wish you to travel and I don't want you to take a turn for the worse."

Alexander coughs. "Sir, I begin to have a strong belief we should inform Ariana of the situation immediately. I cannot like continuing to keep this kind of thing from my future wife."

Lord Stratford shakes his head and pats him on the back. "Now, now, my boy. You must be still. I assure you it is for the best. We must keep up appearances until the wedding."

What could possibly be the reason to keep up the charade now?

"I know we have apprehended the man responsible for the balloon mishap, but must I remind you we still need to address the impending scandal? Or did you forget the compromising situation between you and my daughter? Trust me. It's best to continue as planned."

Lord Stratford's tone makes him wary. Alexander is tired. He decides to leave the subject for now. The hammer in his head is relentless. His own bed is all he wants. "I must get back to Harlaxton before I am discovered. I cannot let Ariana find me here. Pray have my carriage prepared for me to leave at once."

"No, no. That will not do. May I remind you of the wheel rod Rockingham so intently prepared for your demise? I suggest you take my carriage until yours is repaired."

"Right. Please make it be so, for I most assuredly must leave as soon as may be possible."

The doctor clears his throat to interrupt. "Gentlemen, I implore you. I cannot recommend this. There is need for caution. I don't know what this is all about, but my first and foremost concern is for the patient. I must insist he not be moved."

Alexander speaks first. "I beg you understand. I cannot stay here. Might I trespass upon you to accompany me to Harlaxton?

It is but a stone's throw from here. Surely my injuries are not so serious I cannot travel if you are with me."

The doctor looks at one and then the other. "I cannot recommend such an attempt, but if you are determined I will accompany you to be sure you are safely installed elsewhere."

"Thank you. We must leave promptly."

ARIANA SITS IN THE parlor with the troupe. It is difficult to keep spirits positive after witnessing the commotion in the hall. The Constable and her father will get things sorted. What is Wendell's involvement? Conversation is all but nil when her father walks in the room.

"I have an announcement of great import!"

Ariana vaults up to stand beside him. "Papa? What is it? Is everything all right?"

Lord Stratford looks down at her by his side. He angles Wendell around to his other side. Her father's smile is wide and long. He hasn't smiled this smile in a very long time. He stretches his arms across both their shoulders and then looks out at the rest of those gathered in the room.

"This day I have found something or should I say some*one* I thought to have lost many years ago." He shifts and looks at Wendell. "It is my great joy to tell you all that my *son,* Wendell, has been discovered after all these years, I thought him dead at birth, but now he is found!"

What? Wendell doesn't say a word. He stares at Ariana. She covers her mouth with her hand to stifle the cry bustling to come out. News of this magnitude, she cannot fathom it. Polly is the first to speak.

"Gha! Wendell, who would have thought this morning you woke up a circus performer and tonight you'll go to bed an heir to the likes o' this!" She circles around the room. The troupe begins to mill around them, offering their congratulations to Wendell on his new prospects. Wendell stands motionless, a flicker of a smile begins to form.

Ariana cannot believe it. What does all this mean? Her father has a son? She has a brother? How could something like this be kept from her? She wants answers. "Papa, I donna understand. I mean, when? How long have ye known?"

"I will answer all your questions, my dear. And yours, Wendell. But, what say we put that off for tomorrow, eh?"

"I dunno how to wait until tomorrow. I mean, how do ye announce this and not be able to discuss it?"

"It has been an eventful evening and I am sure everyone is very tired."

"How can anyone be tired, now, sir?" Polly pipes up. "The excitement and all."

"Yes, well, be that as it may, in light of the evening's events I invite you all to stay here."

The troupe begins murmuring between themselves.

"Papa, why not ask them if they wish to stay. Maybe they prefer going back to the inn."

"Nonsense. I'll not accept no for an answer. In the meantime, while we wait for the rooms to be readied, since no one is tired, shall we go back to the parlor and continue with the evening's events? Ariana, why not play a bit on the harp. Maybe one of our guests should like to sing?"

"Really, papa. Now?"

"I would love to hear you play, my lady." Polly interrupts. "And, Bess here has a lovely singing voice." Polly grabs the hand of a tiny blond girl and drags her to the front. "She practices all the time with her mama back at the camp."

Lord Stratford calls for Hawthorne.

Ariana is not sure playing the harp and singing is best at a time like this. Wendell hasn't said a word. He must be in shock. She is in shock.

Lord Stratford claps his hands and encourages everyone into the parlor.

"Come now, let's have a bit of entertainment while the servants prepare the rooms. It won't be long. You'll see."

Ariana positions herself behind her harp and strums a warm up set. Hawthorne arrives in response to Lord Stratford's call. Polly shoves Bess forward. The room is silent waiting to hear the girl sing. Ariana tries to help out by playing a commonly known song. Bess doesn't know it. She stands there, hands clasped in front of her.

"I'm so sorry, I can't do it." Bess covers her face with her hands and shakes her head.

"Sure you can." Polly comes forward and places her arms around her. "Just sing like you do for your mama. We're all friends."

"It's not that, exactly."

"What is it, dear?" Ariana removes herself from the harp and comes near Bess.

"It's that I don't know that song and I've never sang to a harp 'afore."

"Ah, I see. Well, how about the harpsichord? My talents lie more with the harp, but I can play moderately well on the harpsichord."

Bess nods in agreement and they move closer to the instrument sitting in a different corner of the room.

"There. Now, tell me what ye might like to sing."

Ariana sees Hawthorne speaking to her father in the back of the room. Her father leaves with him. Wonderful. The last thing she wishes to do at this moment is sing. Wendell is the same. No expression. Too many unanswered questions they both have and the only person who can answer them has just left. Why is he making them wait until tomorrow?

"HERE IS WHAT I NEED. Come." Lord Stratford walks back to the study.

"Yes, my lord."

"Given the evening's events, the guests will need to remain for the night since they no longer have transport back to the inn." He walks to the cabinet to pour himself a drink and sits in the leather armchair in front of the fireplace.

"Of course."

"I'll need to have rooms prepared in the servants' quarters."

"And, for the boy?"

"The boy?"

Hawthorne clears his throat covering his mouth with his white gloved hand. "Ah, Wendell, sir. Do you wish to have him accommodated in the servants' rooms?"

Good question. How much is too much? It is clear he doesn't know what to make of it all. Maybe installing him in one of the family's apartments will be too much too soon. Lord Stratford swirls his drink in the glass staring at the amber color. He can't have the boy in the servants' rooms. He needs cared for properly.

"No. Have him installed in one of the guest rooms for now. We will see about moving him to one of the family apartments later."

"As you wish, sir."

"And, Hawthorne, see that none of the servants speak about the night's events. I should not like for Ariana to have any increased anxiety. She is still recovering from the balloon fiasco."

"Right, my lord. I shall inform Millie and the footmen directly."

"Thank you, and make sure Becky is not inclined to tell her anything either."

"Yes, my lord."

Lord Stratford sits looking at the portrait, listening to the sounds from across the hall and sipping his whisky. He lifts his glass to her smiling face looking down at him from above the mantel. "I have found him."

A knock at the door returns him to reality.

"Yes?"

"Papa, may we come in?"

Lord Stratford meets them halfway. "Yes, what is it?" Ariana and Wendell walk in slowly. The poor boy still looks shaken.

"It's nothing, really." Ariana has her arm around her brother. Her brother.

"We would like to come in for a few moments before retiring for the evening. There are a lot of questions, ye know."

"Yes, yes. I know. Come in. Sit down." Ariana and Wendell sit together on the small sofa in front of the fireplace. Lord Stratford returns to his chair.

"Can we have a discussion now?"

They really do resemble each other. Much will still have to be verified, but the truth is clear. How sad they could not have known each other all the years before. Grown up together. He would not have force Ariana to be married. All because of that charlatan Rockingham! Fury and white hot anger builds in his chest. He finishes the remaining liquid in his glass. "I can't. I can't tonight."

"But, why? I donna understand"

"Of course, you don't! Look, Ariana. Quite a bit transpired this evening that you don't know about." The clamoring in his chest is loud.

"That's the point. Tell us."

"No. Not now." She needs to stop pushing. He can't speak any more about it tonight. "I can't. Tomorrow. We'll discuss it more tomorrow." He loosens his cravat.

"But—"

Wendell places his hand on Ariana's. "Stop. It's fine. We can wait." Ariana places hers on top of his.

"What is it? Are ye not the least bit pleased to know ye have a family? I have lived half my entire life here with papa and only a picture of my mama." She smiles and looks from Wendell and then back to her father. "And, now I learn I have a brother. I am most pleased. I just would like to know more details."

Lord Stratford heaves a deep sigh, rests his head back on the chair and studies the ceiling. Wendell looks at him and then back at his newly found sister. He takes a deep breath, pulls at his ear, and scrunches his nose. Air whiffs through his teeth before he responds. "But, m'lady, see I had me mum and I had me family, the troupe, all these years. We was 'appy. What's to become of 'em? What'll I do now?"

Lord Stratford raises his head up to see them both. Ariana puts her arm around her brother. Silent. Two sets of glassy emeralds beam up at their mother's portrait above the fireplace.

CHAPTER TWENTY-NINE

Wentworth Hall – Spring, 1798

The sun shimmering through the curtains in Ariana's room casts shadows low across her bedposts. It's late. Last night is the first thing she remembers. Was it a dream? She sits up, stretches, and yawns. Of course, it's real. What will Lord Raby think? Surely, he will be as pleased as she is. It's not like Wendell is an *illegitimate* child. She can barely remember her mama now. She remembers brief moments in time. Like the lavender patch. Brushing her hair. And of when her father told her of her mother's passing. An ache swells in her stomach then wiggles up her chest. Why didn't he tell her about her brother? How could Ariana not know her mother was with child and died because of it? So many questions she must have answers to.

Ariana joins her father for breakfast. Her stomach growls. "Good morning. Where is everyone?" She goes to the sideboard to see what is prepared. Eggs, kippers, bacon, potatoes, and some kind of cold meat. Her father folds the newspaper he is reading and takes a sip of tea. She fills her plate with eggs and bacon and returns to the table.

"My dear, it is quite late. The troupe has already left for Bath."

She fills a cup with tea and sips.

"All?"

"Yes, I'm afraid, all. Wendell was not of a mind to stay. It is all so very new to him." Her father's eyes wilt. His cheeks hang low. Her own feelings are softened toward him. He finds a son he thought was lost to him, and that son chooses to leave. Still, she needs answers.

Lord Stratford vents a deep breath. "It's all so very sudden, you see, and he felt it best to let some time pass to let it all sink in. He needs time. He's worried about his mother. I don't blame him."

Ariana picks at her food around the edges of her plate. The eggs are dry and the bacon is cold. "I donna disagree, but I would have liked to say goodbye."

"Do not fret, my dear. I believe he will be back. He needs time, I think, although I hope he doesn't take too much time for I cannot wait to learn more of him, set him up for tutoring, then possibly Eton. Show him my hunting dogs, fish for some wide-mouthed bass, teach him to hunt reindeer." Lord Stratford leans back in his chair and gazes out across the gardens through the windows of the breakfast room.

Maybe now is not the time for questions. How can she stifle his hope and pride? The twinge in her stomach will not go away until she knows. "Papa, why is it that ye never told me about my brother? Why did ye keep it hidden all these years?"

Lord Stratford breaks from his reflections and gives his firm attention to his daughter. He says nothing. Maybe Wendell is misbegotten.

"Well, I own it was a mistake."

Her worst fears are coming true.

"You see, my girl, I was so lost and heartbroken I could not bear to speak of it."

Wait. What?

Her father's eyes begin to glisten and she moves closer to him. He continues to speak. His voice is soft and cracks. "At first,

I told myself I needed some time to get over it myself and then I would tell you."

He stops speaking. His lips tighten and he looks around the room. He takes her hand in his and pats it a few times before he continues. "Then, time passed and it never seemed to be the right moment. I never seemed to 'get over it' and now it has come to this. I know many years have passed, my dear, but to me it is still as fresh as yesterday." He stops and holds her hand briefly then shrugs back into his chair looking into the gardens anew. All these years. Her poor father. If only she knew. She could have borne the pain with him.

She leans forward and strokes his forearm gently. "We willnae speak of it for now we have found a great blessing indeed. Where we thought we had lost, we have found, yes?"

Lord Stratford takes her hand in his and kisses her fingers and the top of her head. "Yes, my dear, a great blessing indeed!"

Lord Stratford stands up, unshed tears in his eyes and slings the paper under his arm. He moves to the sideboard to place a tart on his plate. "Well, now what are we to do about your upcoming nuptials?"

Her wedding! She completely forgot. Almost.

"Oh, Papa! What are we to tell Laird Raby?" He turns to sit back down at the table. "What will he say? What if he doesn't want to marry me now?"

Her father chortles and he wipes his mouth with a napkin. "What? Not marry you? Why ever would he not marry you?"

The twinge in her stomach starts again. "Because maybe he'll think people may say Wendell is illegitimate?"

Lord Stratford roars. "*Illegitimate?* Ariana, where do you come up with such nonsense! Everyone can see the uncanny resemblance between you and Wendell *and* your mother for that matter. I'll have my solicitor handle all the necessary paperwork and verifications. We have Rockingham's confession as proof, we'll talk with the woman who's raising him, and confound it, if *I* call him my son I can't imagine anyone else claiming he is not!"

Her father's words echo through the room. It's true. No one would dare go against her father's declaration, particularly when the required proof is verified. She sips her tea. The warm liquid helps calm her nerves.

"I daresay, child, how you can spin a story in your head! I've no doubt Al... Lord Raby will have no problem. You may find him to be very accepting of Wendell when all is said and done."

He's right. How silly she is.

ALEXANDER RETURNS TO Harlaxton. The Archbishop of Canterbury provided him with a special license because a reading of the banns is not possible since the wedding is happening so quickly. Preparations for the wedding are being made. Two steps into the entranceway, Victoria folds her arm into his and leads him into the parlor.

"The wedding breakfast is all arranged. In addition, Mama and I enlisted the help of Madame Beauchamp. She has just returned from the continent and has a most delicate hand in dressmaking. You will find her work exquisite." She plops him on the settee and walks around to the back.

Alexander turns sideways and lengthens his arm along the back. "Shall we see this work?"

"What?" Victoria's eyes pop wide. "You most certainly will *not* see the dress before the wedding!"

"Why then did you bring me in here?"

Victoria ignores his question and continues. "Even if I need to stay away from Aria until the day of her wedding, I know she will forgive me once she learns of the pains I took on her behalf."

"Of course, she will forgive you."

"I must do this for Aria. It's the least I can do after having avoided her for so long. Most reluctantly I might add."

What is wrong with her? Is she even listening?

"She will be pleased once everything comes out I am sure. You must make sure to have the servants deliver the dress. Promise me!"

Alexander sits still. Does she want him to answer?

"Alexander, promise?"

Apparently, she does. "Yes, Yes! I promise. How else can it be accomplished?"

"What? What do you mean? Do you wish it done otherwise?"

"No, no. Of course, not. However, you feel it best." Such complexities.

"Now, we must decide on what you will wear."

"What I will wear? I had thought to decide that for myself."

"No, no. Well, actually it depends on what you might choose. If it matches Aria, then yes. If not, well, no. And we need to find out what your parents will wear. I have already arranged with Lord Stratford what he will wear."

Is she seriously telling us what will be worn by the guests?

"I had thought to wear..."

"How about this?" Victoria pulls out a caricature from a drawer in the desk by the wall.

"What? Where did you get that?"

"I doesn't matter. It's one of papa's. Anyway. I like what he is wearing. Do you think you can find something like that?" Alexander is sure her father would not be thrilled at the idea of Victoria rummaging through his things and finding this picture. It certainly has meaning for which she does not understand.

"Yes. I believe I can find something along that line."

"Good. Then all we have left to discuss on clothes are your parents."

"Yes, well I will leave that up to you. But, please. Put that picture back and pray do not share it with anyone else."

"Is it really so awful?" She really doesn't know.

"Let's just leave it. Shall we?"

"It doesn't matter one way or the other to me. Now we must talk of the flowers." Victoria reaches for another book and opens it to reveal pages of dried flowers.

No more. "Unfortunately, I must stop here."

"But, Alexander. I must go over with you the floral arrangement."

Alexander raises his hand. "Victoria, my dear. I am very grateful for your help. I trust your judgment and that of your mama's. You know Ariana's favorites in her garden. Please, do as you see fit. Consult with your mother if you're not sure."

"But, I want it to be perfect."

"And, so it shall be. I must leave now to St. George's to finalize the date and time of the wedding." Alexander stands up to leave.

"Now?"

"Yes, now." Alexander leaves Victoria to her preparations. He needs to leave within the hour.

St. George's. It's going to take another two days to finalize. Maybe he can send his steward. No, better he do it himself. Away from the preparations. Ariana should be helping. It is her wedding. She should be able to have things done the way she wants them done. Leaving the truth until the day of their wedding? Would she really see the humor in it? Her father still believes she will. It's been ages since he has seen her, touched her, held her close. As soon as he is back from London he'll take her for a ride in his curricle. Better yet, his carriage. Now that the wheel rod has been replaced.

"I KNEW YE WOULD COME!" Ariana greets Alexander as soon as he steps through the doors of Wentworth Hall. How much she misses him rolls waves in her stomach. She can hardly contain the excitement.

"How could ye have stayed away so long?" She flings herself full body into him just as he gives Hawthorn his coat and hat. He wraps his arms around her and leans back to look at her face to face.

"I promise it was necessary"

"Necessary? What could possibly have been so important to have kept ye away for four days?" She plays with the folds on his cravat.

"How about a trip to London to obtain the special license?"

"Four days?"

"I'm sorry. I didn't want to be away so long." He plays with a strand of her hair. It tickles her cheek. "I've come to take you for a ride in the carriage."

"Yes, I need to get away and out of the house. Let's go."

"Don't you want to let someone know?"

"No. Ye have your groom?"

"Yes, but..."

"Well then we're fine."

"What about your father?"

Ariana grabs his hand and pulls him out the door and down the steps. "I cannae bear another minute inside. I feel stuck and papa's tucked away in his study anyway."

The privacy of his carriage with him warmly installed by her side soothes her nerves. Alexander wraps his arms around her waist and immediately gives attention to her left earlobe. It tickles and delights. She places her hands on his chest and stops him. She wishes she didn't need to do so.

"I have so much I need to tell ye." Alexander stops his attentions, but remains inches from her face. "Oh? What has happened?" His eyes are half open. She wants to kiss him. What will he do if she does? She teases him and leans in, then pulls back and looks at him. Playful and handsome. He feathers soft kisses on her lips and the sway of the carriage hushes her anxiety. She needs to tell him something. What was it? She allows his tongue to part her lips and mingle with hers. Each new encounter creates sensations she cannot explain. It doesn't matter. His touch is urgent and gentle. And, she is soon to be his wife. She takes his hand in hers and intertwines their fingers then places them on her side. A deep groan in his throat escapes. She grasps his lapels and finds herself suddenly lifted and straddling his lap. She looks deep into his holly blues then she is the one who kisses him hard on his mouth. Ariana is lost. His hands strum her back sending chills down her spine. The carriage slows and she doesn't even know it. Alexander stops. He carefully places her back on the seat beside him.

"We need to get out, love." She adjusts her gown.

"I'm happy to stay right here. Ye did say carriage ride?" Alexander's eyes sparkle and a slight lift at the corner of his mouth lets her know he agrees. But the carriage door opens and the steps are dropped so they may exit.

"It's best we take a bit of a walk, I think."

Alexander arranged for an afternoon of entertainment. How does one pretend nothing occurred after that? Pull him to the ground, that's what. Her cheeks warm with heat. Drat. Alexander stops and tows her close to him. Does he know what she's feeling inside? He takes her hands in his and kisses them. "A few more days, my love, and all will be revealed." Being near to him makes her lose all sense.

"Revealed!" Ariana bursts out. Alexander bobs up, blinks, and looks down at her. "I had something I wanted to talk to ye about and— well— ye know we got distracted."

"Oh, yes. I know just how distracted." Why must he keep doing that? He's practically begging her to kiss him again.

"Yes, what is it you want to talk about?" Alexander escorts her toward a park bench under a dogwood tree where they can sit. Maybe she can concentrate enough to put two thoughts together. He aligns his arm along the back of the bench and flicks her shoulder at the edge. Maybe not.

Ariana scoots closer to him on the bench and he molds his hand firm to her shoulder now. "How do I put this?"

"Is what you have to say difficult for you?" The kindness of his words draws her. It should not be this hard.

"Ye know, we had Wendell and his troupe for dinner the other night."

"Yes." He kisses her temple.

"Which ye still need to make up for missing, I might add."

Alexander nods. "Yes, my love, and how am I doing?" She closes her eyes while he kisses her cheek. "I am very sorry to have missed it." Words will not come. This man touches her heart in places she did not know exist. "Go on." He touches her hands resting on her lap. "I'm listening." She looks over at him. His calm features reassure her. Surely, nothing will change once he knows.

"It turns out, Wendell is my brother." She studies his reaction. Good, he's not angry.

"Your brother?" He leans his head close to hers. "How did this come about? Are you sure?" She looks back up at him, inches from his lips. She can't help staring at them. A gentle smile replaces tight lips. She looks down at their hands still resting together on her lap.

"As sure as can be. Papa has no doubts. He'll do all the required verifications, of course. Although I dunno all the details, it seems my mama died in childbirth and a Sir Lewis Rockingham— do ye know him?"

"Yes, I believe I do. A banker, yes?"

"Yes. And, he's our cousin. It seems he is behind it all." Alexander's attention is locked on her as she speaks.

"Behind it all? How can you be sure?"

"Well, I've no doubt papa will speak to ye about it and he can give ye more details."

"How exciting! You have a brother! *We* are to have a brother!"

"So, ye're not upset?"

"Upset?" He reaches behind her to pluck a bloom from the dogwood. "Why on earth would you think I should be upset?" He places the white and purple blossom in her hands.

"I dunno, but I thought ye might not like the idea. It may alter the arrangements, ye see." He begins to wrap a finger around a stray hair at the back of her neck, kisses her temple again, and then shifts his arm from behind her to take both her hands in his. He removes her glove.

"I think it wonderful you and your father have found him!" He kisses the top of her bare hand. "I think it to be very good news indeed!" He kisses the inside of her wrist. He needs to stop before someone sees them on this tucked away bench.

"I'm so glad. I was so worried ye wouldn't like the idea of being related to a circus performer."

"But he is your brother and surely he will be cared for now, no?"

"Yes. That is or was the plan. But I really dunno what will happen because Wendell has returned with the troupe for now."

"Hmm."

Will it matter to him now? Now, that Wendell will not be staying on at Wentworth Hall?

"Ariana, look at me." She's afraid to look but does. "I love *you*. I would not care if you were related to the entire troupe. It would not change a thing. I would still marry you." Relief surges through her.

"I do love you so." She rests her head on his shoulder. "How we did not find each other before now, I will never know." She links her arm with his.

"Let's be glad we did." They sit quiet and enjoy the afternoon breeze.

"And, donna forget I'm going to help ye with your cloud predictions."

"Yes, my love." He pats her hand and squeezes. "Do you want to start now?"

"Now?"

"Yes. Look, there!" He points to where white bulgy clouds sit on the horizon. "See those clouds?" He pulls her to her feet and places her glove in her hand. "Let's chase them."

CHAPTER THIRTY

London, England – Spring, 1798

It's here. Her wedding day. And she is happy. Arriving at their London townhouse two days ago is a blur. Today, the morning sun fills her room. Everything would be perfect if Vicky were here to share it with her. The days when she said she would never marry are a distant memory now. Things are as they were always meant to be. Arranged or not, she is marrying a man she loves. But not seeing him again for two days puts kinks in her stomach.

She sips hot tea in her room and Becky comes in to dress her hair. Ariana blows on the hot liquid so she can drink it fast, but it still burns her throat. Why must she rush anyway? She deserves a little coze in her room to settle her nerves, does she not? Nerves. That must be what this feeling in the hollow of her stomach is. Becky moves about the room singing. What is she singing anyway? The hollow is swelling into a cave. Soon she will not be able to speak. Becky's sounds echo in her ears. Ariana stands and stares. Becky stands ready at the dressing table with a brush in hand. Dark emptiness continues to toil inside.

Becky brushes, pulls, and molds her tresses up to a most elegant style twisting loose around her head. Lengths of pearls are weaved throughout and lavender buds are placed strategically with them to match her wedding bouquet. She turns her head to one side and then the other. Her bouquet. Her favorite part of the ensemble. It will be of lavender, white roses and both purple and red fuchsias tied with lavender and green silk ribbons.

Lavender. Memories of her mother spill into her head. Ariana brushes her cheeks with powder and rouge to add a little color to compliment her eyes. She swallows a knot threatening to form in her throat. Her mother.

Becky laid out her wedding dress earlier and is now holding it to help her step into. The finest silk gown she has ever owned, beautifully adorned with the daintiest lace. The fit is perfect. She stands for a moment admiring herself in the mirror. She turns to view from the right and around to see from behind. Very elegant. She runs her hands down the front and rests her palms flat on her stomach. The hollow is still there. An emptiness. She cannot help but recognize her strong resemblance to her mother. Ariana is lost. How is this possible? The day has come she wants to share it with her mother. Thoughts slam her consciousness. Vicky and their friendship. Her mother not being here. Tears overcome her. Sit sits on her bed and sobs. Becky drops the clothes in her hands and sits down next to her. She pats her shoulder first then puts an arm full around her.

"There, there, m'lady. All young brides feel anxious about their weddin.' It will all turn out for the best. You'll see. Your husband will teach ya everythin you need to know, don't ya know." Ariana stops and looks at her maid.

"Oh, Becky! Ye donna understand! I cannae do this! I want... Oh, I dunno what I want. I'm so sad about everything. How can I be happy when my best friend hates me, I have a brother whose existence papa kept from me all these years..." Ariana falls to the side of her bed stifling her face in her pillow. Becky pats her back. "Now, now. Careful, you'll be messin' up yer hair now." Ariana cries into the pillow again. Becky stands up and leaves the room. Now what? Ariana can't stop the tears from falling. What a mess.

She lifts her head to look at the pillow splotched with red from the rouge.

A knock on the door reveals her dear friend Vicky. "Vicky!" Ariana wails and reaches out to her. "Can ye ever forgive me?"

Victoria sits down next to her friend and holds her tight until the sobbing subsides. "Aria, there is nothing to forgive. Look at you! You are as absolutely ravishing as I knew you would be. Well, you will be once we tidy up those puffy eyes and clear up that red nose of yours. This is a most joyous occasion! You should not be crying on your wedding day unless they are tears of joy." Victoria pulls her handkerchief from her reticule, wipes the tears from her friend's eyes, and fixes a rogue ringlet that had fallen out of place, all the while encouraging her. "You are marrying a man who is clearly in love with you and whom you most definitely are in love with. Be happy my dear!"

Ariana embraces her dearest friend for her kind words and the tears begin all over again. "But, I'm marrying the man you were to marry. How can ye be so kind?"

Victoria clasps her friend's hand tightly. "My dear, you are my closest friend. You are like a sister to me. I could never bear you ill will. All will be fine. I assure you of this. You will see. I wish you both great joy and happiness. Now, let's get you tidied up shall we? Your future awaits!"

Ariana rises from the bed and follows her friend to the dressing table. Becky is called in to once again adjust the stays, touch up her cosmetics, and freshen her hair. Another knock at the door reveals Lord Stratford. "My dear, may I see you for a moment before we leave?"

"Of course, papa, come in."

Lord Stratford stands silent as if in a trance. Tears begin to well in his eyes.

"Papa, please, donna *you* start now that I have finally pulled myself together for I am sure to start crying again and then Becky will have to fix me once more." Ariana holds her hands out to him. "Come, let's make this a joyous occasion for it is so!"

"Yes, yes, my dear. You simply take my breath away. You are so like her. It is as if I am seeing her again. If she could only be here to see what a magnificent lady you have become."

"Papa, ye know I will always be here for ye. I will never be far away."

"Yes, I know." He walks toward her and holds out a silver box. "Here. I came to give you this."

"What is it?" Ariana takes the box in her hands. It has the Rutledge coat of arms. Her mother's clan.

"I thought you might like to have it. It was your mama's. She had it made not long after we were married. I know she would want you to have it."

Ariana rubs her hands across the top. "It's beautiful."

"It's what's in it that she commissioned to be made."

"Oh. The box is beautiful too."

"Yes, well. That, too, is part of who you are."

Ariana opens it. The most stunning gemstones set in gold filigree are revealed. Teardrop-shaped flower petals made of emeralds with a dot of diamond-shaped amethysts in their center glisten in the light. Blue opals designed in the shape of a butterfly dangle from the flower. Her father places the necklace around her neck.

"You know how your mother loved her garden."

"Yes, I used to help her. It is one of my fondest memories."

"She loved her lavender patch with its vibrant colors of purple and green. She particularly enjoyed the holly blue butterflies that attended her garden."

"The holly blue?"

"Yes, you see, here?" He points to the blue gemstones. "The blue opals are designed to represent the holly blues that frequented her lavender patch. She used to say when she wore this she felt as if she were a flower in her garden."

Tears begin to form in the corner of Lord Stratford's eyes. He clears his throat. "I, of course, knew her to be beautiful and lovely in every way, and I hope, my dear, that wearing this, you will feel closer to her even though she cannot be here with you."

Ariana wraps her arms around father. The hollow in her stomach fills with a comforting glow of warm radiance. Fear is replaced with peace and confidence. She will cherish this gift always. It carries symbolic meaning, this holly blue butterfly. The color of his eyes. Her one love's eyes. Memories of lavender shared between mother and daughter. The emeralds, the color of their eyes. Mother and her children. Ariana feels as though she will burst with elation.

Lord Stratford composes himself. "I believe we have come to the time to begin our journey to the church, my dear."

"Yes, I think I'm ready now." Ariana kisses him one last time on his cheek before they make their way to the carriage. The fabric of the gown folds into the seat so there is barely room for another person. The tossing to and fro of the carriage threatens to bring down her hair, but Victoria pinches it back in place.

They arrive at Hanover Square and Ariana cannot help but notice the beautiful floral arrangements and great attention to detail. She recognizes the carriages of a few of her friends, but it's like a dream where she is only an observer. Victoria kisses her on the cheek and proceeds inside.

Lord Stratford turns to his daughter, "My dear, I cannot bear it if you are unhappy. In light of recent events, I must tell you if you choose to walk away now, I will support your decision. I cannot bear it if you will be forever joined to a man you cannot stand to be with." Ariana smiles at her father.

"Oh, Papa! That is not the least of my pain. I do love him and I know he loves me, but I cannot bear the thought of the hurt I may be causing to those I hold dear."

"Ariana, my dear, this is your day. Do not be worried over others. All will be well, I assure you. However, do not be shocked at what awaits you. Hold your temper, should it threaten to erupt, and I know you will be greatly diverted... and pleased." The smile on his face is true and bright. He is happy for her. This is her father and she trusts him. If he believes all will be well, then it will. What does he mean? Is this some attempt at fatherly wisdom for a daughter about to be married? Nothing will ruin the gift he has just given her.

Lord Stratford takes hold of her hand and holds firm. "Shall we?" They are helped out of the carriage and enter the church. The floral arrangements are exquisite, arranged with the colors and flowers to match her own bouquet. They are strategically placed throughout to accent the grandeur of St. George's. The beaming faces of her friends and family as they stand when she enters serves to lessen her unease. The music begins. Her grip tightens around her father's arm and he pats it. She feels his reassurance. A new face is stationed next to Victoria and she wonders who he might be. Is he the reason her father is so assured? Good. Wendell is here also, sitting in the front row, with his brilliant Stratford smile and exceptional green eyes. He looks very handsome in his waistcoat and trousers. At the end of the aisle, her most treasured man of all.

ALEXANDER STANDS AT the altar. The anxiety builds while he waits. It's rather hot this time of year. The music begins and she is here, magnificent in her gown of champagne silk. The full length train flows behind. The cut and color is most becoming to her form. She slowly moves in his direction. He can barely breathe it is so hot in the church. Ariana is almost to him. The nearer she gets, she is more clear, more beautiful, but there's a sadness. Nerves maybe? He will take care to calm those nerves at the earliest opportunity.

There. She is standing right beside him now. Her father conveys his only daughter's hand into his. He nods his acceptance. Her beauty is overpowering. He forgets she does not yet know him as Alexander until the vicar declares the words, "Do you, Alexander Barrington, take this woman to be your wedded wife?"

"I do," he replies.

"Do you, Ariana Maria Wentworth, take this man to be your wedded husband?"

Ariana stands silent. Did she hear the question? Her face reveals no clue. What is she thinking? The vicar repeats directly to her, "Ariana Maria Wentworth, do you take this man to be your wedded husband?" Nothing.

The silence begins to be broken by whispers from those in attendance. Ariana searches the crowd. What is she doing? Is she going to leave? She stops when she finds her father. He nods to her. She glances up at Alexander. He mouths the words, "Do you?"

Ariana turns to the vicar. Her mind is a spinning web of confusion. What is happening now? Alexander? This man with his anxious smile and warm blue eyes is Alexander, the viscount? The irony of it. He reveals his true identity on the day of their wedding. Hadn't she vowed to do something similar to him? The words of her father reverberate in her head. "Do not be shocked at what awaits you." She glances into the eyes of the man waiting to hear her response. Everyone is waiting to hear her response. Alexander takes her hand in his and bends close so that only she can hear. "Ariana, I will explain everything. I promise. I love you."

The moment stretches while they stand hand in hand. Ariana knows she has no choice because she loves him too. The vicar coughs.

"I do." Alexander sighs relief. A low roar buzzes from those in attendance. Ariana moves her hand to Alexander's heart to touch the book reminding her of the storms they will chase together.

EPILOGUE

Wentworth Hall – Spring, 1798

Alexander and Ariana sit on the bench in her favorite part of her mother's garden. The lavender patch. It's hard to believe a year has passed. They have made their home Wentworth Hall. Alexander holds his wife in his arms, softly whispering stories of their adventures with the clouds and the storms they chased all while he caresses the swell of his wife's stomach.

"Donna forget to tell *her* how ye deceived *her* mother."

"Deceived *his* mother? What about how *his* mother refused to even meet *his* father until the day of their marriage?"

"And let's not forget the sheltering of the first storm."

"First storm?"

"Donna tell me ye forgot. I'm sure, as *her* father, ye'll appreciate the need for a well-trained aviary. Max has added quite a few words to his vocabulary, for your information."

"Is that so? Hmm. I thought we agreed to never own to the event in public?"

"Did we? Yes, I think we did. Ye cannae think that to be necessary now." Ariana snorts.

"Of course it is still necessary! For a father must be a good example to his *son,* don't you know. We can't have *him* cornering helpless females in an aviary can we?"

"Helpless females? Helpless, am I now? I can assure ye, *she* willnae be a helpless female."

"Well, maybe for the present." Alexander bends down and whispers close to speak directly to the baby.

Ariana lets out a squeal of delight. The baby squirms in her belly. "Well, I guess papa was right."

"Right about what, my love?" Alexander still strokes circular designs atop her abdomen.

"On the day of our wedding he told me if I could hold my temper, should it threaten to erupt, I would be greatly diverted and pleased."

"Your father said that? Have you been greatly diverted and pleased?" Alexander stops outlining his patterns only for a minute to give his wife his mischievous grin.

Ariana laughs. "Verra much so. Every day, my love. Who would believe being married to a storm chaser would be so full of adventure!"

"Storm chaser? Since when did you bestow such a title?"

"Since last we chased the clouds."

"Is that so? Storm chaser. I rather think I like being called a storm chaser. Do you think I shall be known for all eternity as the first storm chaser that ever lived, once my predictions prove true?"

"That I cannae say, love, but ye will always be *my* storm chaser."

Alexander raises up and leans over to kiss her lightly. Ariana jumps. "It's time."

"Mmm. It's time," he repeats. His voice is husky as he nuzzles his face in her hair. Lavender. She washed it in lavender this morning.

"My love, I mean it's time." She looks down at the movement in her midsection.

"Oh! It's time!" He jumps up, yells for the servants to get the midwife, and whisks his wife away.

Little do they know of the storms yet to come.

THE END.

If you enjoyed reading **Storm Chasers of Wentworth Hall**, please consider giving it a review.

READ MORE BOOKS FROM **IreAnne Chambers**:

Majestic Estates Series:
Storm Chasers of Wentworth Hall.
Folly at Sausmarez Manor
Mystery at Harlaxton House
Wolfe of Toddington Peaks

Regency's British Empire Series:
Aphrodite Mine
Isle of My Man
Pirate be Mine

Aliens of Extraordinary Ability Series:
Bollywood Bargain

Seasons Bliss Series:
Countess who Kissed a Count
One Man and a Babe

Timeless Twists
Nightingale Songs

Find all books by IreAnne at:

www.IreAnneChambers.com

Join the The Cozy News for New Releases.

ABOUT THE AUTHOR

IreAnne Chambers' books contain the spirit and tone of the traditional Regency with the promise of mystery, adventure, and mishap weaved in to create happy-ever-afters with plenty of fun and surprises along the way.

IreAnne looked to her Scottish and Irish heritage and discovered the name Eireann (Erin). Eire means Ireland in Gaelic and IreAnne was born.

IreAnne also enjoys writing poetry and song lyrics, but her love for the Regency romances of Jane Austen, filled with dashing heroes and feisty heroines, spurs her desire to write Fun, Cozy, Historicals, and Then Some...

As novelist and Nobel Prize winner Toni Morrison said, "If there's a book you really want to read, but it hasn't been written yet, then you must write it." IreAnne does just that.

Follow **IreAnne** here:

BookBub

Amazon

Goodreads

Instagram

Facebook

Pinterest

Twitter

Don't miss out!

Visit the website below and you can sign up to receive emails whenever IreAnne Chambers publishes a new book. There's no charge and no obligation.

https://books2read.com/r/B-A-FKKH-LSAY

BOOKS 2 READ

Connecting independent readers to independent writers.

www.ingramcontent.com/pod-product-compliance
Lightning Source LLC
Chambersburg PA
CBHW030649020726
47493CB00006B/1937
9780996414630